Highlander the Conqueror

Donna Fletcher

Donna Fletcher

No part of this publication may be used or reproduced in any manner whatsoever, including but not limited to being stored in a retrieval system or transmitted in any form or by any means, electronic, mechanical, photocopying, recording, AI, or otherwise without permission of the author.

This is a book of fiction. Names, characters, places, and incidents are either the product of the author's imagination or are used fictitiously, and any resemblance to actual persons, living or dead, business establishments, events or locales is entirely coincidental.

Highlander the Conqueror

All rights reserved.

Copyright May 2024 by Donna Fletcher

Cover art
The Killion Group

Visit Donna's Website
www.donnafletcher.com
http://www.facebook.com/donna.fletcher.author

Chapter One

A familiar noise roused Sky from her light slumber. As she slowly emerged from a fitful sleep, a sense of puzzlement enveloped her. Had she truly heard something, or had she imagined it? Or had it been nothing more than a remnant of a dream she failed to recall? The cloth hood secured over her head, so it could not be removed, coupled with the oppressive darkness of the cell, prevented her from discerning whether it was day or night. She had lost all grasp of time, uncertain of how many days had elapsed since her arrival or the duration since her sisters, Leora and Elsie, had managed to escape.

Struggling against the heaviness of her limbs, Sky attempted to stand. The shackles on her wrists and the chains connecting them to a cold, unyielding metal ring embedded in the stone wall seemed to gain weight with each passing day. The memories of her sister Leora's warning echoed in her mind. *Pace often so that your legs are fit enough to run out of here when either I or Elsie return to rescue you.*

She had lost hope without her sisters there to encourage her and had not continued to do as Leora advised so she could keep her legs strong. She attempted to stand but her feet protested, tingling from numbness. She had sat too long. She moved her feet back and forth to force feeling back into them. Then she braced her hand against the stone wall and struggled to get to her feet, but her legs would have none of it. She collapsed back on the floor with each try. How long had it been since she had initiated a deliberate pace within the cramped confines of her cell? Each intentional step she had taken had become a small act of rebellion, a defiance against the physical and mental constraints imposed upon her. The cell's size had been a mystery, revealed to her only by the exploratory reach of her hands, as the hood had been thrust over her head upon her arrival at Dundren Abbey. She discovered that, even in her shackled state, a stretch of her hand could graze the four enclosing walls.

Occasionally, a sliver of light penetrated the otherwise impenetrable darkness, streaming through a narrow opening in the stone wall. The thin beam offered a fleeting connection to the outside world, ushering in a breath of fresh, chilled air. The spring nights stubbornly clung to the vestiges of winter, a reminder of the unpredictable Highland weather that could defy seasonal expectations.

Would she ever see the beauty of the forest again and visit with the animals? That she even questioned such a thing felt like a surrender to her dire circumstances. She needed to remain strong and believe that rescue would come soon. Her thoughts shifted to her sisters. She missed them. Elsie, the oldest, had escaped first with promises to return as soon as she could to free Leora and her. After what seemed like endless time had gone by but probably had barely been a few days, Leora grew worried that something had happened to Elsie that prevented her from returning with help. Leora's deep concern had her planning her own escape, though she was upset she could not take Sky with her. The shackles and chains made that impossible. Sky had encouraged her to go even though the thought of being alone, her sisters not there offering comfort and support, frightened her terribly.

She had no qualms that either sister would abandon her. Since she could recall, they always protected her, defended her, and prevented anyone from harming her due to her affliction. Lately, she worried that their escapes had failed and something terrible had happened to them.

Her head shot up when she thought she heard shouts. The monks were either arguing again or another poor soul had been left at Dundren Abbey in hopes that the monks could cure the person's madness. If a person did not suffer from madness when brought here, they did so after being here for a brief time. She could not imagine spending years here locked away, never to feel the frosty winter air nip at her face, feel the spring rain kiss her cheeks, or revel in the intoxicating scent of the forest any time of the year.

It had been a shock to her and her sisters upon arriving here to find out they were to be prisoners locked away in cells. Her da would have never sent his daughters here if he knew of the horrors suffered. So why had he sent them there? Her only thought that made sense was that he did not know what he was sending them into.

She had prayed often for her sisters' safety and that one of them or both would soon return and free her. She had been growing more frightened with every passing day that something may have happened to them. She missed her family, her da, her home, and she missed her mum more every day since her passing five years ago. Her family did not see her and judge her because of her affliction as others did. With family, she was safe. She did not feel safe here. She felt terrified.

Her heart ached terribly, and she tried to conjure the scent of the forest, a place that always brought peace to her heart and mind. With spring soon to take hold, the forest would have a subtle yet persistent scent that chased away the decay of winter and welcomed the onset of new birth. And the morning dew would kiss the leaves and grass with freshness. She breathed heavily as if she could truly smell the welcoming scent.

Then there were the forest animals. She had discovered when she was a young bairn that she had a remarkable bond with animals and birds, an affinity of sorts with nature's creatures. The squirrels and rabbits would come feed from her hand. The red tail deer would join her and nibble at the berries at the same bush as she did. Birds would perch on her shoulder and twitter as if talking with her. She made endless friends with cats and dogs and there was not a horse that was not calm around her. The animals did not judge her as people did, and she loved spending time with them.

She hated being away from all that was familiar and safe to her.

A single tear rolled down her cheek. She desperately wanted to go home, the memories tearing at her heart.

Angry shouts startled her out of her musings and fear mixed with a smattering of hope ran through her.

Hope that her sisters had come for her with men from their clan demanding her release or fearful the abbey could be under attack. But from whom?

"Move your arse, monk!"

Upon hearing the harsh command, Sky scurried along on her bottom to tuck herself into a shadowy corner as if the darkness could shield her. Stumbling footfalls followed the shout. Was the monk being pushed or were the rushing footfalls hurrying to obey the demand?

"You have no right to take her."

Sky recognized Brother Emanual's voice. Though no one referred to him as Abbott, Sky had heard enough to know that he presently filled the Abbott position. He was a man of sizeable girth, not one who would stumble easily if pushed or if rushed. That meant the man commanding him had to be of a sizeable girth himself and he was here for a woman. She and Edith, an older woman, were the only two women here.

What Sky heard next sent a shivering fright through her.

"She is bewitched. You are not safe around her. She must be kept locked away."

Fright could be heard in the monk's sudden gasp and the sound of crumbling stone told her that he had been smashed against the stone wall outside her cell.

"Do as I command, or I will rip your tongue out of your mouth."

Fear roiled her stomach and she tucked herself tighter into the dark corner, fearful of what awaited her at the hands of the man threatening the monk.

The door crashed open, and she was not surprised to hear stumbling footfalls. She surmised Brother Emanual had been shoved into the cell. When a flash of light bright enough to penetrate the black hood covering her head followed in behind the monk, she hurried her eyes closed against the flicking brightness of what could only be a flaming torch. Her eyes had been in the dark too long. She feared the damage to her sight if she suddenly gazed upon a bright light.

"Sky!" the powerful voice inquired.

She jumped at the command in the man's voice expecting her to show herself. Fright kept her braced tight against the stone wall as if her prison could suddenly offer her protection, and she kept silent.

"Answer me, woman!" the man called out impatiently.

He would see her soon enough huddled in the dark corner, but fear froze her.

"I will not harm you," he said.

He had tempered his voice, but it still overpowered the cell. She feared whether to trust him or not. How could she be sure he was not lying to her? But what choice did she have? She had nowhere to truly hide, and perhaps he was there to free her.

"Sky."

She gasped. He had to have spotted her, his strong voice sounding as if he was on top of her.

"You must trust me. I mean you no harm."

"Who are you?" She cringed when she felt him crouch down beside her, his arm briefly brushing against hers.

"Someone who was sent to help you and keep you safe. Can you stand?"

"I can try," she said quickly, fearful he might touch her.

Her chains rattled as she braced her hands against the wall for support and she struggled to get to her feet.

A low grumble sounded, reminding her of the warning growl of the wolves in the forest before they viciously attacked. Fear sent shivers through her and what little progress she made was lost, her feet collapsing from under her. A strong arm suddenly hooked around her waist and forced her up onto her feet to hold her steady.

"You will pay, monk, for keeping her chained to the wall like an animal and a hood secured over her head," the man threatened with lethal harshness.

Brother Emanual tried to explain. "She is a danger—"

"Release her!"

Sky cringed at the growl in his command. Who was he and what did he want with her? Had her da sent him to collect her and return her home? Or had her sisters hired him to rescue her? Or had he come on his own, but why?

"You are wrong to do this," the monk said.

She tensed when the man grabbed her shackled hands and raised them up.

"I will not tell you again. Do it now!" he ordered.

The click of a lock sent her heart thumping, and tears threatened her eyes as the shackles that she had endured since arriving here weeks ago dropped off her wrists to clang as they hit the floor. She went to touch the sore skin on her wrists that had been stinging her for weeks, but a firm hand stopped her.

"Do not touch them. They are rubbed raw and need tending," the man warned, and is hand fell off hers.

Her greatest relief came when the hood was unlocked and yanked off her head. She felt like she could truly breath once again. Her lashes fluttered, eager to open her eyes though slowly and intending only a slight peek. She was anxious to get a look at her rescuer, hoping she would recognize him and alleviate her fear, but his abrupt command stopped her.

"Keep your eyes closed. They will need to adjust to the light slowly."

That was fine with her since she feared he might change his mind and leave her there once he looked her in the eye.

His warm breath drifted down across her cheek as his arm remained strong around her waist and he eased her to rest against him. With her head brushing his shoulder, she surmised he was taller than most men. He was more than ample size, his chest solid with muscles and his presence alone felt like he consumed the space around them.

"Trust me," he whispered and in the next instant she was swept up into his arms.

She gasped and rushed to brace her hand on his chest for support. *Iron.* He was so muscular that his chest felt like iron even through his garments.

"Please put me down," she pleaded, embarrassed and concerned to be in a man's arms, "or the odor of this horrid cell will stain you as it does me."

"Through no fault of yours," he said and carried her out of the cell.

"I beg you, my lord, do not do this," Brother Emanual said, scurrying behind him.

Sky was surprised upon hearing the man referred to as, my lord. Why would a noble bother to free her?

"Free the other prisoners," the man commanded, harshness returning to his voice.

"They are not prisoners. They have a sickness in their heads and have been brought here for us to help them," Brother Emanual attempted to explain.

The man swung around so fast to face the monk that Sky grew dizzy and had no choice but to rest her head on his shoulder. It further confirmed what she suspected. He was thick with muscle and that he carried her with no difficulty proved it even more. She was not petite like her sister Elsie nor as tall as her sister Leora. She was somewhere in between their heights. And she was not skinny with slight curves like Elsie or shapely like Leora, she was slim with soft curves as her mum used to say.

"Free them! NOW!"

His commanding shout had her raising her head off his chest as a shiver rushed through her.

His cheek brushed hers as he whispered, confirming once again, "I mean you no harm."

The faint warmth of his breath and the strength of his tone sent another shiver through her, and she was not surprised to hear the familiar sound of a key turning in a lock. Brother Emanual was wasting no time in obeying the man's command.

"Who are you?" she asked.

"All you need to know right now is that you are safe with me. On that you have my word."

Safe. She had not felt safe since arriving here, and as far as the man's word… many men gave their word when it suited them and honored it when it suited them or so Leora had warned her. She had had little contact with men and only knew what her sisters had to say about them, which was not always complimentary. So, until she could judge for herself how honorable this man was, trusting him would be difficult.

Cool air gently kissed her face once outside, and she yearned to open her eyes.

She was hesitant to speak, but she desperately wanted to know. "Is it day or night?"

"Day, and the sun is bright, so keep your eyes closed," the man said.

She wished she could bask in the warmth of the sun and cast her eyes on the sunlight after spending so long in the dark. But the man was right about keeping her eyes closed for now, and so she did.

"Ross, make certain everyone is out of the abbey," the man ordered.

"Aye, my lord."

He walked a bit of a distance, keeping her tucked tightly in his arms. "You will wait under this tree until I return for you."

As soon as Sky leaned back against the tree trunk, she sighed softly. She might not be home but being near woods, a place that brought her much comfort, felt as close to home as she had felt in weeks.

"Warriors guard you," he said before he walked away.

Sky's fear rumbled through her stomach. Who were these warriors, and why did she need guarding? Not mercenaries she assumed since their leader was referred to as my lord. Unless—she shivered. Elsie had agreed to wed a warrior, Cavell, who had recently left the Gallowglass, an elite group of noble mercenary warriors infamous for their fighting skills and fierceness, choosing death rather than surrender to the enemy. Elsie and Leora had traveled with her to the monastery, where they had been told Cavell would be waiting for her, but that was not what happened. And she wondered who was responsible for the lie.

Had Elsie found Cavell, and had he sent a friend with his troop of warriors to rescue her? If so, she would be on her way home soon. It would also mean that the man had been informed about her affliction and there would be no need for worry.

"Time for penance, monk!" the man shouted.

"Nay! Nay! Stop! Please stop. I beg you," Brother Emanual pleaded.

Sky smelled it... smoke. She gasped softly. Was he burning the abbey?

"Let it burn like the fires of hell," the man shouted. "And you're lucky I don't burn you along with it."

"Where will we go?" Brother Emanual sobbed.

Anger spewed from the man's mouth. "To hell where you belong."

"You have taken possession of her for only a short time and look at the evil she has you doing," Brother Emanual warned.

"I have done far more horrible and worse things, monk, than to torch an abbey."

Sky shuddered and rubbed her arms, the coldness in the man's voice leaving her with a chill. Whatever worse things he had done had left him with no guilt, no remorse. Did that mean he had no heart, no soul?

"You cannot mean to leave us here without shelter and food," Brother Emanual begged.

Desperation marked the monk's plea as his voice began to draw closer to Sky. Was the man returning to her and was the monk hurrying to follow him? Her imagination conjured the scene in her mind's eye of the monk's hands steepled in prayer as he followed the man with anxious footfalls while begging for mercy.

The man's voice sounded closer to her as well when he responded to the monk. "I do what I please and I protect what is *mine.*"

Mine?

How did the stranger believe she, in any way, belonged to him? Her fear grew. Who was he and what did he want with her?

"Please! Please, I beg you, Lord Slayer, do not leave us here helpless."

Lord Slayer.

A chilling fear gripped Sky right down into her bones. Everyone in these parts of the Highlands knew, respected, and feared the name. Lord Slayer was the leader of one of the most vicious, elite mercenary groups that comprised the Gallowglass. He was known for his fearlessness and endless victories and for leaving the battlefield strewn with the bodies of his enemies.

The monk's pleading turned to anger. "Sky's father sent her here for us to help her."

"Sky's father believed he was sending her to safety," Slayer chided angrily. "He did not know that Abbott Kendrick had died and that you turned Dundren Abbey into a place of horror. He would never have left any of his daughters here if he knew that."

Lord Slayer was right. Her da would have never sent his daughters into such a horrible situation, and Sky was relieved to finally learn the truth. But how did Lord Slayer know? Had he spoken with her da or her sisters? Were her sisters safe?

"She is your brother's wife, and you have no right—"

Wife?

Sky's eyes almost popped open in shock. That was not possible. The monk was lying. Her da understood her fear of marriage and he had agreed it was for the best that she not wed. Her affliction left her too vulnerable and there was no telling how a husband would treat her.

"My brother, Warrand, is dead. Sky is mine to protect."

Dead? In a few words, she had gone from a wife to a widow. The revelation disturbed her, as did the death of a husband she never knew she was wed to. She prayed it held no truth, but regardless of whether it did or not, the only thing Sky wanted was to go home to find her sisters safe and once again be wrapped in the security and love of her family.

"Sky belongs to Clan Ravinsher now and she is mine to protect. She goes with me and remains with me," Lord Slayer said as if his declaration confirmed it.

Remain with him? That could not be. The thought frightened her. She wanted to go home where she belonged. She did not want to live with a clan who did not know her. She did not want to imagine the horrors she might face there.

She gasped when Slayer scooped her up into his arms once again.

"You will ride with me on my stallion, Skell," he said.

"My lord," Brother Emanual called out.

"I am done with you, monk," Slayer said. "Say another word to me and you will lose your tongue."

She was hoisted up and onto a horse and he mounted quickly to settle behind her. His arm went around her waist to secure her tightly against him, much like the manacles that had been secured to her wrists, leaving no doubt she would remain with him.

He lowered his head, his lips resting near her ear to whisper, "I am not a kind man, but I will not harm you."

That, Sky thought, remained to be seen.

Chapter Two

They had traveled a distance before the pungent scent of smoke lingered only slightly in the air and during that time Lord Slayer had not said a word and neither had Sky. She had endless questions for him, but fear of what she might hear kept her tongue prisoner.

As if he sensed her discontent, he said, "You have nothing to fear from me."

She was not sure about that.

"As long as you obey my word."

Obey my word.

The monks were forever saying the same to her. Obey their word. But it did not matter if she did or not, they still believed she was evil. She had spoken up little for herself through the years, always having her sisters to rely on to defend her. But not now. She was alone and would learn nothing of her situation if she did not speak up for herself. A frightening thought but a necessary one. "You say I have nothing to fear from you, but I do not know you, though I do know *of* you."

"Of me or of the Gallowglass?" Slayer asked, glancing over her dirt-smudged face and light-colored hair that needed a good washing to be able to see its true color. Her odor was not that bad. He had dealt with far worse smells. Besides, the fresh spring air would help to dissipate it.

"A bit of both," she admitted, too fearful to speak anything more than the truth to him.

He was abrupt in his response. "You need not be concerned. No harm will come to you."

Her stomach roiled and she had to force herself to say. "And yet you sound annoyed."

"I am not annoyed with you, and I owe you no explanation."

His anger at seeing her chained like an animal and made to suffer with a hood over her head had yet to subside completely. Burning the abbey did not seem like a fitting enough punishment for what had been done to her. It had taken extreme control for him not to strangle the monk. But that was no concern of hers. She only needed to know she was well-protected.

Sky tried to keep her stomach calm, but his annoyance set her on edge, leaving her anxious. He was a powerful man who explained himself to no one, and though that intimidated her, and grew her even more anxious, she feared she would never find her way home if she held her tongue. The thought of never returning home, never seeing her da and sisters helped to loosen her tongue.

"You said that I am your brother's wife and now his widow. I am truly sorry for your loss, but I know nothing about an arranged marriage to your brother."

"Your father and my father arranged the marriage."

Sky needed to hear that from her da, but she could not very well call the mighty Gallowglass warrior a liar. She chose to present a more rational reason for him to take her home to her family.

"You are kind to offer me a home even though I never knew your brother, but I would prefer to go home to my family," she said, her heart thumping madly, worried that he would deny her.

"You have a new home now and will remain at Clan Ravinsher."

It was a proclamation issued with authority, leaving her no choice in the matter, and it sent a chill through her.

Her affliction had caused her to shy away from confrontation for fear of the endless trouble it could cause. Couple that with her sisters never failing to defend her, and it left her with a lack of courage to defend herself.

She thought a minute and asked, "At least a visit so I can find out if my sisters are home and safe?"

"Elsie is home with her husband, Cavell. Leora has yet to be found," he said as if that should suffice.

Her heart thumped more madly at the news. Eslie had agreed to wed Cavell for the sake of their clan, and Sky hoped—prayed—the marriage would be a good one. She prayed even harder for Leora, fearful that something dreadful had happened to her.

"Elsie will search for me. I must get a message to—"

"By now she knows, but I will see that a message is sent to Cavell."

"And Leora?"

"I sent my most skilled Gallowglass tracker to find her."

That was a relief, though no doubt Elsie was doing what she could to find her, and Elsie would also do all she could to bring Sky home. She would not rest until she did. The thought gave her hope. Worry surfaced soon enough when she realized it would probably take time before she returned home. What would happen when Slayer learned of her affliction? Or did he already know?

Her da would have never arranged a marriage for her without revealing her affliction to a future husband. Though not a secret, it was not often spoken about, clansmen fearing to mention it, worried it would bring harm upon them. So, it was not widely known.

Leora would have come right out and asked him directly if he knew. Elsie as well, though more mannerly. Sky found the prospect daunting, so she decided to talk around it to see if it would surface during the conversation.

"Do you know why your brother chose to marry me?"

"Why does anyone agree to an arranged marriage? Convenience. Benefit to the clan. An alliance." He hesitated before saying, "Duty."

"I cannot see what benefit I would bring to Clan Ravinsher."

"Evidently, my father and your father thought differently."

His father, of course. "Perhaps your father can shed some light on my query."

"He's dead as well, though he was poisoned, whereas Warrand was attacked after leaving your clan and killed."

"Good, Lord," Sky said, and recited a silent prayer for both men.

"I will avenge their deaths and those responsible will not meet their deaths easily."

Sky did not know what to say. Her concern for her own dilemma seemed trivial to what Slayer was going through. At least her sisters were still alive.

"We will camp at dusk. It will be a good time for you to open your eyes and allow them to adjust to the fading light and a low campfire."

Fear surged through her. Even in the fading light he would see why everyone thought her evil, possessed, a witch, and countless other names she had been called. Her clan had accepted her because her mum and da had given them no choice. Though the clan truly never accepted her since they had paid her little heed. It never mattered to her, since she had her sisters and the animals who loved her, or at least that was what she told herself. She had no idea what Slayer, his troop of men, and his clan would do when they looked upon her and that frightened her.

With nothing more to say, though truly not knowing what to say, Sky remained silent. She was not wise in the way of men, mostly averting their glances when they spotted her, others shaking their heads at her as if she had done something wrong.

When she was just a young lass, a lad approached her one day when she was drawing with a stick in the dirt. He smiled and they talked and for a brief time she had been thrilled to have made a friend. But when his mum had caught sight of him, she had yanked him away from Sky and admonished him for speaking with her. The lad had avoided her after that.

Through the years people grew accustomed to her and some would nod a greeting, but no one ever sought her as a friend. Hence, she relied on her sisters for friendship. Again, she realized how alone she truly was and that she only had herself to rely on. There was no one, absolutely no one she could turn to for help. That thought continued to frighten her, and the ache to go home squeezed at her heart.

The steady rhythm of the ride soothed her and gently rocked her senses into a state of calm. Each stride of Lord Slayer's mount seemed to synchronize with the beating of her heart, creating a comforting cadence that enveloped her. The warmth of his body pressed against hers, a tangible shield against any chill, while the firm strength of his arms wrapped around her provided a sense of security she had not known in ages.

Finally free of the oppressive confines of the abbey, she allowed herself to relax, if only for a fleeting moment. Weariness, like a heavy blanket, settled over her, pulling at her. She fought to keep her head erect, to stay vigilant, but exhaustion overpowered her. With a soft sigh, her head fell to rest on Lord Slayer's shoulder, finding an unexpected pillow to comfort her.

As she drifted off into a light sleep, her mind remained on high alert, a skill honed through her wanderings in the forest and her time imprisoned in the abbey. Every rustle of leaves, every distant sound was noted, her instincts attuned to the slightest sign of danger.

"We follow as planned?"

"Aye, Ross. It would be best for now."

Sky recognized Lord Slayer's voice through her hazy slumber. It was distinct and held authority that one was not likely to disobey. His powerful voice alone would capture one's attention. But what of his features? Did he have fine features or plain features? Or common features like most folks? What color were his eyes? His hair? She knew it was long since her face rested against several thick strands that laid on his chest. It was softer than she expected, and she was not sure if the scent of smoke came from his hair or had lingered in her nostrils. She did, however, catch a hint of pine in the hair strands and wondered over its color. Was it dark like the earth in the forest or lighter, perhaps touched by the light of the sun?

Her thoughts drifted along with her uneasy slumber and a sudden chill raced a shiver through her for a moment, leaving her to think she was still imprisoned in the cell at the abbey. Her tremble barely ended when she felt a blanket slip over her and get tucked around her. The tender gesture and added warmth were enough to further relax her and she allowed herself to linger in a light slumber.

"The camp awaits just ahead."

Sky recalled the voice. It was Ross and his words worried her. Soon she would open her eyes. What then? She pulled the blanket tighter against her as she heard Ross ride away.

"Are you cold?"

That he thought to ask could mean he was not completely unkind. "A slight chill, nothing more. And thank you for the blanket. It was most kind of you."

"I am not kind. I gave my word that I would keep you safe. You were chilled and required a blanket. I gave you what you needed," he said matter-of-factly.

It was difficult carrying on a conversation with only a voice, no face to put to it. So much could be learned from a simple look and what was reflected in a person's eyes. But then one paid more heed to the words when there was only a voice to speak to.

I gave my word that I would keep you safe.

To whom had Slayer given his word?

"We camp by a creek," Slayer said. "You can wash your face to help ease your eyes open."

It was an order, not a suggestion, but then he expected obedience as he had warned her.

The scent of campfire smoke struck her nostrils, letting her know that they were not far from their destination. It would not be long now. He would see for himself, and she wondered and worried what would happen when he looked into her eyes.

Sky's stomach roiled when he brought the stallion to a stop, removed the blanket from around her, and dismounted. His hands settled at the sides of her waist, and he gently eased her off the horse and released her once she had firm footing.

"I am going to take you to the creek," he said, closing his hand around her arm. "It is nearly dusk so you can open your eyes once we are there and let them adjust to the twilight before sitting in front of a low-burning fire."

Once again, she was reminded of his strength, the way his fingers dug into her arm just enough to keep her from tripping or falling as he guided her steps. She wished she could run, but her legs were not strong and how safe would she be on her own? And with his many warriors, she was bound to get caught. Before Leora had escaped the abbey, she had told Sky to rely on her courage and stay strong until she or Elsie came for her. She did not know what courage Leora was talking about, but if she did have any, she certainly could use it now.

"Stand here while I spread the blanket for you to sit on," Slayer said when they came to a stop.

Sky's heart began to pound in her chest and no amount of trying to calm herself helped.

His hand returned to her arm, and he helped her to sit. "The creek is in front of you. I will return shortly."

She listened as he walked away. With the creek in front of her that meant the camp was behind her, leaving her a modicum of privacy. She did not waste the time she had alone. With a soft flutter, she opened her eyes slowly.

Everything was a blur, but she had expected that. She focused her eyes on the edges of the brown blanket beneath her and her sight slowly began to clear. She allowed her eyes to linger on the blanket until she believed her sight strong enough to shift her focus to the creek. The water flowed gently and was too tempting to ignore. She leaned over and scooped up a handful of water and drank. She had forgotten how refreshingly delicious drinking from a stream could be and she scooped up two more handfuls.

The chilly water invigorated her and though it first stung her raw wrists, it did not take long to soothe them. She eagerly set to scrubbing her face and cleaning what felt like grit from her eyes. She wished she could scrub her whole body but that was not possible. She scrubbed and scrubbed as if she could scrub away the horror of the last few weeks, until she finally took a deep breath and stopped.

She raised her head, and a soft gasp left her lips as she gazed upon the sky. She had forgotten how beautiful the sunset could be. A deep orange and blue mingled in a dance across the sky as it heralded the night.

"A cloth to dry your face."

His sudden appearance startled her, but she kept her head turned away from where he stood by her side, not looking up at him. She stretched her hand out to take the cloth.

"Look at me, Sky," he said, ignoring her waiting hand.

The timbre of his voice made it clear she was not to refuse him.

What choice did she have? She could not continue to hide it from him. She had to face him eventually, even as terrifying as that was. She disliked the shocked reaction from people who met her for the first time and how they quickly turned away from her. The hurtful memories had her turning to him with her eyes closed.

She heard him crouch down in front of her and was shocked when his fingers grabbed her chin to turn her face toward him.

"I detest repeating myself. When I tell you to do something I expect you to do so without hesitation. It is time to open your eyes, Sky," he ordered.

His remark struck something strange inside her. Was he right? Was it finally time to open her eyes in a deeper sense? Had she kept them closed too long to all that went on around her? Could that be why she was in this predicament, because she always shied away from situations or hid herself away, and relied on others to speak for her?

His tongue snapped at her. "I grow impatient. Open them, Sky."

She was trapped. She had no choice. She opened her eyes slowly.

Chapter Three

Slayer felt it like a punch to his gut. With the grime gone from her face, her beauty stunned the eye, and it surprised him that what caught his eye first was not her affliction. Her beauty far outweighed anything else about her.

Sky stared at him and seeing his stoic expression, she said, "You knew."

"Aye, I did. My father made me aware that you were born with one blue eye and one green eye. Though he assured me that you were a good, obedient woman and was possessed of no evil. I trust my father's word, and I trust my brother even more. Warrand would have never agreed to the marriage if he had any doubts about your nature."

He could not take his eyes off hers. The two different colors were strangely beautiful and undeniably distracting. Both colors were bold or perhaps it was the contrast that made them bold. An intense blue like the sky on a hot summer's day and a vibrant green that could rival the rolling green hills after a spring rain. He found himself utterly captivated by them and he could not tear his glance away, no matter how hard he tried.

Sky did the same, her eyes focused on his face. She never expected him to possess such defined features, angles and curves molding perfectly into the handsomest face she had ever seen. His intense eyes were a greenish grey and intimidated with one glance and his slim lips were drawn tight. His hair was a darker shade of blond. At least she thought it was since it was difficult to be sure in the dwindling light, but she had been right about its length. It fell over his shoulders and onto his chest. It wasn't so much his fine features that caught the eye as it was the look on his face. He exuded power and fearlessness, warning all he was not a man to cross.

The thought brought her to her senses, and she could not help but keep the sorrow out of her voice when she said, "Your brother was rare and most kind in his opinion of me since most presume me evil, a cohort of the devil, a witch."

"As I said, I trust my brother's opinion. You will be safe and treated well at Clan Ravinsher."

Sky had no doubt he believed that, but she was not as sure about it as he was, and it only made her want to return home to the safety of her family even more. A shiver of worry raced through her.

"Night brings a chill with it. Come sit by the fire and get warm." Slayer stood and leaned down to hook his arm around Sky's waist and with a swift lift she was on her feet to stand beside him.

She was right about his height, her head only reaching his shoulder. She had never seen a man of his size before. His height alone commanded awe and respect.

He snatched up the blanket and draped it over his arm, then he rested his hand on her lower back as he directed her to the camp.

Twilight was quickly fading, the vibrant colors appearing as if they were sinking into the earth to sleep until tomorrow evening when they would wake and dazzle the sky once again. And she was grateful she was able to enjoy the beautiful sight once more.

She remained close to Slayer as they approached the campsite, where his men were busy talking and laughing among themselves. But how soon would that all stop when they laid eyes upon her? She lowered her head as she usually did around strangers.

"Keep your head up," he ordered.

His strong command had her obeying without thinking about it.

"You have nothing to be ashamed of and nothing to hide. Do not let me see you lower your head again."

She nodded, though worried it was an order she might not be able to obey since it was a habit formed throughout the years. The delicious scent of roasting meat caught her attention, tempting her nostrils and gurgling her stomach as they entered the camp.

"You are hungry," he said upon hearing her stomach protest. "You will sit by the fire and stay warm until the meat is ready to eat."

Sky was beginning to understand that Slayer expected compliance to his every word. It was his way, but then how else could he command a large army of warriors if he did not lead with strength and confidence? However, she would prefer not to sit too close to the fire even if a chill filled the night air. The darkness would help conceal her eyes, whereas the fire's light would reveal them.

Slayer placed the blanket on the ground close to a low burning campfire compared to the other two, whose hardy flames roasted the meat on spits.

He assisted her to sit and with a snap of his finger at one of his warriors, a cloak was soon brought to him, and he draped it over her shoulders.

"Keep your head up," he warned before walking away to speak with one of the warriors.

She wondered what would happen if she disobeyed him. Unfortunately, being in an unfamiliar environment she thought it unwise to find out, not that she had the courage to do so, but at least she had bravely given it thought. So, she kept her head up and though the fire burnt low, it burnt enough to highlight her face and make the color of her eyes more prominent.

The stares started first as if they did not quite believe what they were seeing, then they swiftly looked away as if fearing they would be touched by evil if they continued to look upon her. Then the whispers began and those warriors nearest to her began to move away.

Her hunger vanished as fast as a snuffed-out flame, and she desperately wished her sisters were with her, especially Leora. The warriors' attention would be focused on Leora's beauty, or her punishing words defending Sky, and she would be left in peace.

She gazed carefully at the flickering flames, worried that the light might disturb her eyes and was relieved when it presented no problem. She stretched her cold hands out to the fire's warmth, eager to chase the chill that had settled in them.

"ENOUGH WITH THE WHISPERS!"

Sky jumped at Slayer's forceful shout.

"She is not evil. You have nothing to fear from her."

The whispers ceased instantly and talking resumed among the men a short time afterwards, but Sky was no fool. Slayer may have quieted them for now, but he did not change the fear they had of her.

Even though she had slept a good portion of their journey, she found herself tired from the exhausting day. With her stomach far too upset to eat anything, she wanted nothing more than to close her eyes and sleep. Then she would wake in the morning to find it had all been a horrible nightmare and that she was home in her room, cuddled in her bed beneath her soft, sweet-smelling blankets.

She sighed at her foolish yet hopeful thought and watched as one of the warriors sliced into the cooked meat on the spit, cutting several pieces to place on a cloth that he wrapped and gave to Slayer. While she knew hunting animals was essential to survival in the Highlands, she avoided it when possible, having befriended so many forest animals since she'd been young. But that was the way of survival and life in the Highlands.

Slayer approached her and lowered himself to sit down next to her. He unwrapped the cloth the warrior had handed him and took a piece for himself, then offered her some.

"Eat," he said.

A demand always seemed to edge his voice and she heard it now. She shook her head and kept her focus on the fire. "I am not hungry."

"You need to eat."

"I cannot stomach food right now."

"Never let anyone rob you of your strength. Eat."

She was too tired, nor did she have the courage to argue with him. She took a piece of the offered meat and nibbled on it to appease him.

He kept his eyes locked on hers as he placed the cloth holding the meat in her lap and snatched another piece. His eyes continued to remain on hers as he ate.

She wondered what he truly thought of her mismatched eyes. He wore a constant stoic expression, except when he commanded. That one warned not to question him. Otherwise, it was difficult to know what he was thinking or feeling.

She took the opportunity, since he had seen her eyes, to find out if he might want to return her to her family. "My family is accustomed to my affliction. They would be only too happy to have me home again."

He shrugged. "So, you have two different colored eyes. What difference does that make?"

"You heard the whispers, and you commanded your warriors to stop—"

"And they did," he said, before she could finish and cast a glance over his men, some turning their heads away.

"You cannot stop their thoughts, their worries, their fears of me."

"My warriors do not fear."

"Everyone fears the strange, the different, the unexplainable and blames it on evil, on the devil," she said, having experienced it all too often.

"You let their whispers worry you and you worry for your safety."

That he understood her misgivings surprised her. "The only place I am safe is at my home."

He captured her eyes with his again, not letting her look away. "Nay, you are safe with me."

His eyes felt as if they burrowed into her, as though he searched deep down inside her to see all her fears, doubts, and hopes. And his voice was full of such confidence that it made it difficult not to believe him. There was only one problem.

"I do not know you, so how then can I trust you?" she asked.

He responded without hesitation as though the answer was simple. "You will grow to know me. Besides, I honor my word. You can always trust me."

"It takes time to trust."

"We have plenty of that, so it need not concern you," he said as if it was settled.

She tried to keep her worry out of her voice, but she heard the tremble herself. "You make it sound as though Clan Ravinsher will be my home forever."

He nodded and as if the matter had already been decided, said, "Aye, forever." He grabbed another piece of meat before he stood. "Be wise and eat more before you sleep."

Sky watched him walk away and saw how his men looked at him in awe, as if he had just faced evil and conquered it.

***

Slayer woke before dawn and sat staring at Sky from across the camp as she slept. He was not sure what to make of her, but then he didn't think she was sure of what to make of herself. Her family obviously protected her. She never learned to stand on her own and find her own strength and courage. Never learned to accept who she was with pride rather than fear.

Her strangely colored eyes did not bother him. They somehow provided her with a mysterious beauty as if she contained a treasure of sorts that begged to be discovered. He shook his head at the absurd thought. He had no time for such nonsense, no time for women.

"The clan will not easily accept her," Ross said, joining him in front of the dwindling fire.

"They have no choice," Slayer said, his focus remaining on her.

"Have you told her yet?"

Slayer turned to Ross. "She will learn soon enough."

"What if she protests?"

"It will do her no good. What is done is done and nothing will change it."

"Are you sure about these plans?" Ross asked.

"You sound your skeptical self."

"As long as you are not skeptical, we are all right," Ross said with a chuckle.

Smiles had been something that eluded Slayer for some years now. When he was young, he laughed often and more times than he could count with his brother Warrand and Ross, but once he started training and joined the Gallowglass everything changed.

"Then we have no worries," Slayer confirmed with confidence.

"Good to hear," Ross said. "I hope the men you sent to make inquiries concerning your da and Warrand return soon with news that will help us find the culprits. So that someday you will smile again and maybe even laugh."

"That would take a miracle," Slayer said.

Sadly, Ross knew his friend hadn't meant it to be humorous.

"I cannot make sense of their murders," Slayer said, shaking his head. "Why would anyone want them both dead? If I can find the answer to that question, I believe it would be easier to find the person responsible for their deaths."

"We will find them, and they will pay for the evil they have done," Ross said.

Slayer was glad for Ross' longtime friendship, though he was more like a brother than a friend. He, Warrand, and Ross had spent endless time together when they were young, so he took Warrand's death as badly as Slayer had. And he wanted to avenge Warrand's death as badly as Slayer did.

Ross was the only close family he had left. His mother had died a few years ago, and no grandparents were left. He had joined the Gallowglass with him and had fought endlessly by his side, and by his side was where he would stay and serve the new lord of Clan Ravinsher.

Slayer turned, seeing Sky stir awake and stretch her arms lazily about her head.

"Her problem is going to be a problem, Slayer," Ross warned.

"At first, but I will see that it does not take long for her to be accepted."

"Accepted or forced?"

"Whatever it takes," Slayer said. "Now wake the men. The sooner we leave the better."

Chapter Four

Sky watched the activity with interest and concern. The troop was being divided in two groups, one smaller in number and the other larger, and she wondered why. As she expected, the warriors avoided looking at her and she did her best to avoid looking at them. Hoping it would alleviate senseless blame if one or more of them were harmed or took ill and claimed it was because she glanced upon them.

Ross had taken the folded blanket from her but left her with the cloak, and she was glad he did. There was a chill in the air, the sun not having shown itself this morning, and the ever-present chill she had suffered in the cell continuing to linger in her bones. She bounced on her feet lightly, her need to see to her morning duty growing stronger.

Slayer had yet to speak with her, busy with his warriors, and there was no reason to bother him. All she needed was a few minutes alone in the woods. This was one time she was glad no one paid her any mind. She turned and slipped into the woods.

It did not take her long to see to her morning needs and was on her way back to camp when she spotted two frisky red squirrels at play. They chased each other up and down around a tree trunk. She stopped and smiled at the familiar scene, having witnessed it time and time again in the woods and enjoyed it every time. Sky had never felt more grateful for standing here right now after having been locked away in a dark, damp cell. The confinement had been horrible, and she never wanted to be forcibly imprisoned and robbed of the beauty of the forest ever again.

How she wished she could linger and visit with the animals, or simply sit and inhale the numerous lovely scents the forest had to offer. But she had been gone long enough and she did not want to do anything that might cause Slayer to forbid her from going into the forest alone. The forest was where she found solace, a peaceful heart and mind, complete contentment. She could not lose that, especially now that she was deprived of seeing her family.

"SKY!"

Slayer's powerful shout echoed through the woods sending the two squirrels fleeing in fright and having Sky ready to flee as well.

She took two calming breaths before calling out, "I am here!" Then she retraced her steps back to the camp, though it was not necessary since instinct served her well in the woods.

She heard rushing footfalls and a tingle of fear raced through her. He would be angry, and she had seen for herself the consequences of his anger at the abbey. She continued walking. This time in the direction of the rushing footfalls.

Sky almost stumbled when she halted abruptly after catching sight of Slayer's face and worry knotted her stomach. Anger contorted it and, for a moment, she thought a demon possessed him. It was only when he got closer, and she surprisingly caught a spark of concern in his eyes that her worry eased. At least she thought it was a concern that she saw there since it was gone so fast, she could not be sure.

His hand closed around her arm as soon as he got close enough. "Never. Not ever, do you go off by yourself again."

"You were busy—"

"Then you wait."

"I waited as long as I could. I did not think—"

"About that you are right. You did not think. You were foolish," he admonished, and keeping a firm grip on her arm, headed back to camp.

Sky wanted to defend herself, but she was too fearful.

"I gave you no permission to leave camp," he snapped, and quickened their pace.

"I did not think I needed permission," she said, the prospect of seeking his permission for various things a daunting thought.

"You need permission from me for everything," he decreed.

Such a command truly sounded unreasonable, and she had to ask, "Why?"

"Because I say so," he commanded, his heart pounding in his chest and his anger yet to calm completely, and worse was the spark of fright that had ignited in him when he discovered her missing from camp. Fright was not something he suffered from, so why then had he felt it?

"Nay," she said softly, sensing something was amiss. Why would he threaten her with punishment for a simple wander in the woods? It made no sense. "There is more than you are telling me."

The oddity of the colors of her two different colored eyes seemed more pronounced here in the forest and they captured him for a moment and would not let go until he forced himself to look away.

He did not respond and Sky wondered if it was because they had reached the camp or that he did not want to acknowledge her concern.

Sky was surprised to see that only ten warriors remained at the camp. The camp had been laid bare and the campfires doused. The warriors and horses appeared anxious to leave and with a nod from Slayer, they all mounted their horses.

He swung her up on his horse when they reached his stallion and he mounted with ease behind her. Two warriors took the lead, Slayer following behind them.

They traveled a distance in silence. It was unsettling, and Sky considered saying something, anything that would ease the tension she felt sitting tucked against him. His body was as taut as the string on a bow that she expected to snap at any moment. Which was what had her holding her tongue, fearing she would be the target if he did. By now, however, she had expected to feel his body at ease and that he would have at least said a few words to her even if he admonished her again.

Not able to sit in worry any longer, she tilted her head back to look into his eyes. "You are not an easy man to come to know."

"You know what you need to know about me."

She frowned. "I know very little about you."

"That is more than most. Now be silent. We need to keep alert."

"Are we in danger?" she whispered anxiously, not having considered the possibility. "Is that what you are keeping from me?"

She caught a flash of conflict in his eyes and sensed he debated about answering her, leaving her to believe the news would upset her.

She rested her hand on his arm, giving it a light squeeze. "Please tell me."

Her voice was whispery soft, her touch tender, and the worry in her eyes disturbing, though more disturbing was the danger she had placed herself in earlier. He could keep it from her no longer. "You cannot go home. You and your sisters' lives are in danger."

It took a moment for Sky to digest and believe the shocking news, then questions spilled out of her. "Danger? Why would our lives be in danger? Are my sisters aware of this? Are they well-protected?"

"It is a puzzle that needs solving. Cavell and Elsie are aware of it, but with Leora unable to be found, I doubt she knows of it. All that is presently known is that someone wants one of you dead and since it isn't known which one of you it is, all three of you have been targeted by any mercenary group willing to accomplish the mission."

Concern for her sisters' safety took priority over everything and forced her to speak. "Why didn't you tell me this sooner?"

"Until there was more to share with you there was no reason for me to worry you needlessly."

"Yet you tell me now. Why?" She shook her head, realizing the answer. "It is the reason you don't want me going into the woods alone."

"Aye. I need you aware and alert to your surroundings and for you to realize the severity of the situation."

"Does the danger my sisters and I face have any connection to your brother and father's deaths?" she asked, needing as many pieces as she could get to help solve the odd puzzle.

"I do not know, though I do not see why they would be connected."

"It is a thought to consider since your brother died after visiting my da concerning the marriage arrangement."

"But if it had anything to do with the arranged marriage, it would have been more likely that the attack on my brother would have taken place before arriving at your clan."

"Unless the documents had yet to be signed," Sky suggested and with worry for her sisters mounting she asked, "Do you think this man you sent to find Leora has a good chance of finding her?"

"No man is a better tracker than Noble. He will find her," Slayer assured her.

"I pray you are right, and Leora is found safe and unharmed. I still cannot fathom why anyone would want us dead. We are of no importance to anyone."

"Evidently, someone believes differently."

Sky's brow scrunched. "If danger stalks me, why did you divide the troop and have the smaller group of warriors go with us?"

"The sizeable troop will be the one followed, thinking I surround you with more warriors. It will give us time to reach a different destination then they do," he said.

He had not planned to discuss any of this with her, at least not yet. But with her little escapade into the woods, it left him no choice. She had to be made aware of the dire situation if he was to keep her safe.

However, what he had not expected was the rush of concern and even more so the spark of fright that had gripped him when he discovered Sky missing. He had steeled himself, voided his feelings so that nothing would stand in the way of victory. Where had the stab of concern for this woman, most people deemed evil, come from and how had he not been able to stop it?

"We take a different path to your home?" Sky asked.

"We are not going directly home."

"Where do you take me?" she asked anxiously, fearing he might place her in another abbey.

Slayer spotted the fear in her eyes, and it was easy to understand what caused it. He was quick to assuage her worry. "You go to a safe place and the only place I know for sure you are safe… is beside me."

***

Sky had a restless night of sleep on the cold ground and was not looking forward to another day of endless travel. She also worried over the distance growing between her and her family. No matter what Slayer said about her remaining at Clan Ravinsher, she intended to find a way home sooner or later, though sooner was preferable. The growing distance would only make it that more difficult.

Sky stood with her hands braced on her hips as she arched her back to work the ache out of it. She looked around for Slayer and fear ripped through her when she saw his face filled with rage as he rushed toward her. Instinct told her to run not from him but toward him and she did not hesitate. When she got close, his hand shot out, gripped her arm, and flung her to the ground, vaulting over her. She hit the ground so hard that it dazed her, and she lay there gathering her wits about her. It was not long before she was being swept up off the ground.

"Bloody hell," Slayer said and brushed her hand away when she went to reach for her nose. "Don't touch it."

She did not need to be told her nose was bleeding profusely, she felt the blood pouring from it and tasted it on her lips. She needed something to stem the flow of blood and was surprised when Slayer tore his sleeve off from the top of his shoulder, scrunched it, and pressed it to her nose.

"Hold it there," he said and took hold of her arm to walk her over to sit by a campfire that was nearly extinguished. He crouched down beside her. "I need to look at your nose. If it is crooked, broken from the fall, it is better I try to straighten it now before any bones can mend."

Sky nodded, having seen it done to men who had the misfortune to break their nose. It was painful though some looked better for it, others worse. And all she needed was a crooked nose to go along with her mismatched eyes for people to deem her evil, since tales persisted about witches having deformed faces.

Slayer turned away from her a moment to call out to his two warriors who held the man who had foolishly attempted to kill Sky in front of them but failed.

"Keep him secured," Slayer ordered, though that wouldn't prove difficult since he was still reeling from the powerful blow he had delivered to the man's jaw.

"He's not going anywhere, my lord," one warrior assured Slayer.

Slayer knew his men would not fail him, but he was impatient, his anger still seething, anxious to see what he could learn from the man. However, Sky came first. He had to tend to her nose, an injury he was responsible for while attempting to keep her safe.

He eased the cloth, nearly soaked through with blood, away from her nose, pleased to see the bleeding was no more than a dribble. It did not take long for him to see that her nose had suffered no break, an image of her beauty having been burned into his mind since first meeting her. Though it did surprise him how relieved he felt. It disturbed him to think that it might have been necessary to cause her such pain and that troubled him as well. He always did what was necessary without any concern for anyone. It was the only way he could lead. If he allowed himself to feel, decisions would be that more difficult to make.

"It isn't broken," he said, and without giving thought to it, he tore off his other sleeve, folded it, eased it against her nose, then took the soaked cloth from her and tossed it on the campfire. The cloth sparked the embers to life, and they quickly fed on it.

Sky sighed. "That is good to hear."

"Sit here and rest until I return for you," he said as he stood.

Sky watched him fist his hands as he walked, the muscles in his bare arms growing taut, and she did not want to think about what he intended to do to the man who, no doubt, had all intention of taking her life.

"I have met many fools in my life, but I believe you are the most foolish one I have ever met," Slayer said, coming to a stop in front of the sizeable man whom two warriors held tight. His jaw was swollen and already bruising but Slayer couldn't care less what the man suffered. "Do you really think you could rush into my camp, kill the woman, and escape to collect the coins?"

The man shrugged. "Coins don't matter to me, only her death matters."

"You care nothing for the coins?" Slayer asked, troubled by his remark.

"The only thing I care about is to see her dead," the man said and spit on the ground as he laid eyes on Sky.

His words infuriated Slayer and he wanted to kill him there and then, but he needed answers first. "Why? Why do you want her dead?"

"I will tell you nothing, so kill me and be done with it. It is a fate I deserve for failing my mission and dying without honor." The man snarled. "She deserves to die."

Slayer landed a blow on the man's jaw that would have knocked him off his feet if his warriors hadn't been holding him.

The man laughed, blood dripping from his mouth. "Do what you will to me, I will not give you a shred of information. I am as loyal to him as your men are to you and I would suffer the torments of hell before betraying him. So do what you will."

That he almost challenged Slayer to torture him gave Slayer reason to pause. He could be trying to gain time for more men to join him. He could not take the chance, not knowing how many men might follow him.

"Your reputation is well-known and well-respected. I would have enjoyed fighting you. At least then I could die with honor."

Another delay tactic. He had to move fast. "I would give you such a chance, but you intended to kill the woman I protect and for that you can die without honor."

Slayer moved so fast that the man's eyes bulged with shock when he grabbed his hair on the top of his head, yanked his head back, and slit his throat.

The two warriors released the man after Slayer wiped the blood from his dagger on the man's shoulder. They let him drop to the ground as his life spilled out of him.

"Take his weapons and make haste. We leave here now," Slayer ordered, then pointed at two other warriors. "Go find out if anyone follows him and find out how he reached the camp without being noticed."

While his men saw to the task, Sky watched as Slayer approached her. He slid his dagger back into the sheath at his waist while the muscles in his arms remained taut. The death of the man had not diminished his anger.

"Are you in pain?" he asked, crouching down in front of her.

"I don't feel anything right now," she said, thinking it odd, then realizing she did feel something. She felt numb and that frightened her. She had witnessed a horrible sight and all she felt was numb. Was she as unkind as Slayer himself claimed to be, not feeling any sorrow for what she had just seen? Or was she simply too shocked to feel anything?

"I fear that numbness you are feeling might not last once we are on our way. You will tell me if you are in any pain as we travel," Slayer said.

"How long before we reach our destination?" she asked, praying it was soon.

"Two days at the least."

She cringed inwardly, fearful of causing her nose to bleed more. She did not want him to be aware of her worries, so she kept her voice light. "I will do fine."

She did not do fine. After riding for a while, not only did her nose hurt, but her head did as well. She was left with no choice but to rest her head on his shoulder, the pain of holding it erect too much for her. She tried not to tense when a wave of pain washed over her, knowing he would feel it. But it was senseless, and she gave into it. Besides, it would not matter to him.

Slayer steeled himself against the pain he knew she suffered, or at least he thought he did. His anger sparked every time he felt her tense in pain. He thought to stop and let her rest, but a short reprieve would do her little good. It was better they kept a good pace so once they stopped, she could rest for the night. He would, however, stop earlier than planned, so she would have longer to rest.

When Sky woke from a fitful sleep, she tilted her head back to look at him. "I need to stop for a bit."

"We stop just ahead to camp for the night," he said and saw the relief on her face. He also saw that the hit to her nose had caused some bruising to form under her eyes and again, his anger sparked.

It sparked again a short time later when he saw how exhausted she appeared as he reached up, his hands taking hold at her waist to lift her off the horse.

Alarmed at the strange way he looked at her, she could not help but ask, "Do I look that bad?"

The fact that she was able to detect the slightest display of expression on his face stunned him, though more so that he allowed it to show. He had to be mindful not to let that happen again. It was far easier and wiser to never let anyone get a hint of what he felt, or it could prove disastrous.

"Your eyes are bruising some, not badly but enough to last a few days," he said after lowering her to stand beside him.

She sighed. "I must look a fright."

"I doubt there is anything that can rob you of your beauty."

His unexpected remark left her speechless and with a strange, yet pleasant flutter in her stomach. Her da had been the only man to ever tell her she was beautiful. Most men made disparaging remarks about her or avoided acknowledging her at all.

What the bloody hell was wrong with him? He never spoke such flowery words to a woman.

"We camped by a creek. Go clean the blood from your face," he ordered gruffly, annoyed with himself, and grabbed his stallion's reins and walked away to settle the horse for the night.

The flutter in her stomach faded and was replaced by a twinge to her heart. He probably regretted his words, but why say them in the first place?

With a few sorrowful expressions and many shocked ones that she received from the warriors as she walked past the campfire, she assumed she looked even worse than she thought. There was little she could do about her appearance except wash the dried blood off. Time would heal the rest.

With a soft moan, she lowered herself to the ground at the edge of the narrow creek. Her body ached from the hard fall she had taken and riding all day on a horse had not helped. She still had the second sleeve Slayer had given her and she soaked it in the creek. A shiver raced through her from the biting sting of the chilled water, and she hurried to rub what blood she could from the cloth and rinse it so she could use it to wash the dried blood off her face.

She gasped and her shoulders cringed when she placed the wet, cold cloth on her face and another shiver ran through her.

The cloth was suddenly snatched out of her hand as Slayer dropped down beside her. His hand slipped under her chin to turn her head toward him, then he proceeded to gently wipe the dried blood away.

"You should have told me how exhausted you are instead of moaning and gasping," he admonished.

"You heard me?" she asked with a small gasp. "I did not mean for anyone to hear or know of my discomfit."

"Well, I did," he said, though did not bother to clarify that it was not because he had heard her but that he had seen it in her uneasy movements. "Now be still and let me clean your face."

Sky's eyes drifted closed as he gently scrubbed her face, rinsing the cloth a time or two before he continued. His tender ministrations relaxed her tense and aching muscles, and she wished she could linger in his gentle touch.

Slayer never tended to a woman before Sky. He could not recall a reason why he would or perhaps he never paid heed to it before now. Though most likely he was seeing to her care because it was his duty to keep her safe. Whatever the reason, he did not seem to mind. An odd thought for him since women were not a priority to him. Their purpose was minimal and yet that was not the way with Sky. She had been utmost in his mind since meeting her and her protection grew more important to him by the day.

He ran the cloth lightly over her lips even though they were clean as was the rest of her face. She required no more tending and yet he could not take his focus off her lips. There wasn't anything different about them, except they seemed rosier than most and he wondered if rosy lips would taste any different to kiss.

Kiss?

What was he thinking? Why had he let his thoughts wander? That would not do. He controlled his thoughts. They did not control him.

Her eyes fluttered open when she no longer felt the cloth on her face. She was sorry it ended since his touch had comforted her. "I am most grateful for your help."

He stood and reached down to take both her hands and help her to her feet. "Food will be ready soon. You can eat then rest. Tomorrow will be a long day since I wish to reach our destination before nightfall."

Sky easily got to her feet with his help. The strength in his hands alone was remarkable, but the way the muscles in his arms shifted and tightened demonstrated an even greater strength. He could easily protect and just as easily cause harm, just like the various animals in the woods she befriended. So, she would be wise to come to know him and befriend him since that would be far better than fearing him.

Chapter Five

Sky stood staring.

It had taken an entire day and into the late afternoon of the following day to arrive at their destination. Slayer had ordered two stops yesterday so she could rest, which delayed their arrival as planned. But they were finally here, and she could not be more relieved or surprised.

She continued to stare, not believing what she saw as Slayer spoke to a few of his warriors. Amidst a lush forest, nestled among towering pine trees and surrounded by a carpet of moss and wild ferns, sat a charming cottage. Its thatched roof, weathered by years of rain and sun, sloped gently downward almost touching the ground. The walls were wattle and daub made with interwoven sticks covered with mud or clay. A green vine weaved its way through the wattle and daub along one side and over the top of the lone window.

A narrow footpath wound its way to a thick wood door that needed a lovely spring wreath to greet visitors, though a large, iron latch warned all to knock. Fairy flowers bloomed profusely. Their rich blue violet color was in stark contrast to the white anemone that also grew in abundance around the cottage. A bench worn by time and use but still sturdy sat beneath a large oak and another bench sat under the cottage window.

The scent of woodsmoke had her glancing again at the roof to spot smoke curling lazily from the hole in the roof fashioned for that purpose.

It was the perfect place for refuge and peace, and she could live there happily for the rest of her days. Whoever it belonged to was blessed to have such a lovely home.

"You may go inside, Sky," Slayer said, having watched her smile grow as she stared at the cottage.

"I don't wish to intrude on anyone," she said.

"You won't. It is home for the next few days, possibly weeks," Slayer said.

The news overjoyed her. She would be quite comfortable here on her own. She would make friends with the forest animals and hunt for berries and silverweed, something she enjoyed doing and missed. It was so deep in the woods that no one would find her, though Slayer would no doubt leave warriors to watch over her. She finally felt free, and she was overjoyed.

Sky hurried inside eager to make herself at home and what a lovely home it was. It was a considerable size, larger than most cottages, yet cozy and inviting. The fire pit sat in the middle of the room and a bed that could fit two people, depending on size, was tucked in a corner and dressed in fresh bedding. A chest sat at the foot of the bed with an extra wool blanket folded on top of it. A sturdy wooden table sat to the side of the fire pit with two benches tucked beneath it. Shelves lined one wall that held jugs and covered crocks. Sitting on a bench beneath the shelving were buckets and baskets, most empty but one held bramble leaves and another cowslip. The bramble leaves would make a delicious fruit-flavored tea. Lastly, she was happy to see that fresh rushes covered the earth floor. This cottage was perfect, and she looked forward to her time spent here.

She stepped outside and walked around to the side of the cottage and spotted the remnants of a garden. She would start a new garden just as she was starting anew herself. There was a worn path behind the cottage and standing quietly, she was able to hear the gentle flow of a stream. It could not be more perfect. She would gather a couple of buckets of water and give herself a good scrubbing and wash her garments as soon as she got a chance.

With lazy steps, her focus more on the forest and the treasure it held for her, she circled around to the front of the cottage. That Slayer had not stopped her from wandering told her that he had warriors stationed close by and watching her every move.

She smiled when Slayer headed her way, the last warrior disappearing into the woods. "I am going to enjoy it here."

"Aye, I always do," he said.

"This is your cottage?" she asked surprised and sat on the bench under the window, the lovely day meant to be enjoyed outdoors.

Slayer joined her. "Aye, my grandfather built it for him and his bride. I spent a lot of time here with him. He preferred it to the castle. It is where I spend my time now when I can. I enjoy the solitude."

"You are blessed to have such a peaceful place. I look forward to my time here."

He reached out to take hold of her chin and instinct had her snapping her head back, fright widening her eyes.

"You need to trust me, Sky, when I tell you I mean you no harm," he said and gently took hold of her chin to turn her head slowly from side to side. "It is going to take a while for the bruising to fade."

"Then it is good I will be here alone where no one will see me."

He released her chin and stood. "I go to the stream to catch fish for our meal."

"I will go with you and fill a bucket with water for later use," she said and rushed into the cottage to retrieve a bucket, relieved he had not corrected her about being alone here.

It did not take long to reach the stream and while Slayer whittled the end of a branch into a point to spear the fish, he glanced at Sky. She had settled herself quietly upstream from him, taking in her surroundings. Her endless smile and happiness heightened her beauty and set things stirring in him, something he hadn't expected. Gone was the fear in her eyes, when not on him, replaced by a joy he envied. Even with her bruised eyes, she was attractive or perhaps it was her pleasant smile that appealed to him. Whatever it was he found himself favoring her and never had he ever favored a woman. Women served a purpose, no more than that, and yet he found he favored his time with her. But then time here would serve a purpose as would she.

He had just about finished the spear when he saw that she looked as if she was speaking with someone, yet she was alone. He stood transfixed, watching her smile and chuckle as if in conversation. Then suddenly a squirrel jumped into her lap. The bushy-tailed animal looked up at her and Slayer was stunned to hear a squeaky chatter spill from his mouth as if he was talking with her. He was even more shocked when she patted him on the head, and he curled himself in her lap ready to nap. Never had he seen a squirrel trust a human enough to befriend him.

He walked to the edge of the stream and stopped to glance at Sky once again. She sat with her head tilted back, her face to the sun that had maintained its dominance of the sky longer than usual, while the squirrel continued to nap in her lap. He thought he might have imagined what he saw, though that was doubtful since he was observant, but his second glance confirmed it.

If there was one thing he had learned about animals through the years, it was that they had a good instinct for who they could trust. He had seen horses who refused to let some men ride them, dogs who kept their distance from men and women alike, and cats, who bloody hell, let no one command them. If the squirrel trusted Sky upon meeting her enough to sleep content in her lap, then Sky had to possess the kindest of souls. Such a kind soul was rare and could be more harmful for a person than helpful, for they would trust far too easily. Yet she voiced her concern about trusting him. Perhaps it was only animals she found worthy enough to trust.

He shook his heavy thoughts away and got busy fishing. It was not long before he caught two nice-sized trout.

With them speared on the branch, he called out to Sky. "We return to the cottage."

The squirrel popped his head up and cast him a look, then stretched himself out of his curled position and chatted at Sky before hopping off her and scurrying away.

Sky stood, grabbed her filled bucket, and joined Slayer. He took the bucket from her when she reached him.

They walked in comfortable silence until Slayer asked, "How is it that the squirrel appeared to talk with you?"

She did not think he would understand, most people didn't. She sometimes did not understand it herself. The only thing left to her was to be truthful with him. "I listened and learned. Squirrels use different sounds to communicate. They chatter when they talk among themselves. When excited you will hear a shrilling chirp and when they are happy, they whistle. If you hear them bark, they feel threatened."

He scrunched his brow and got annoyed that he did. "That makes no sense. Animals do not speak."

She almost grinned at the confusion on his face and the annoyance in his voice. They battled each other. But she had learned through the years that what people did not understand often confused and annoyed them.

She kept a soft smile as she said, "Everything speaks if you listen."

"You talk nonsense."

"Do I?" she asked with an inquisitive tilt of her head. "The sun rises, telling us it is morning. Sets, letting us know it is night. The clouds warn of rain, the air of snow. When squirrels grow fat they warn us of a harsh winter—"

"That is common knowledge," he argued.

"Only to those who listen and learn from what they see. I see animals as friends. You see some of them as food and others to command and serve you."

"And rightfully so."

"I think differently, and the animals understand that and do not fear me for they know I will not harm them."

Their conversation intrigued him, though others would think differently and condemn her for voicing such nonsense and even think her ability came from evil.

"Were you born with this strange skill and knowledge?" he asked, curious.

Sky's smile grew as she shook her head. "I was not born with it. I acquired it through my years of observation, and it is not strange knowledge. It is there for anyone to learn if they simply watch and listen."

"Some would consider it evil, the work of the devil."

"If it were the work of the devil, would he not want to see the poor animal suffer and die?"

"That is a reasonable observation to consider."

"Something else to consider… my affliction is the reason for my ability to understand animals more than most. My two sisters were my only friends. No one in the clan allowed their children to come near me. I realized soon enough that none of the other children would play with my sisters if I was around and I did not think that was fair. So, I would go into the woods and explore, and the animals began to make friends with me, not caring about my mismatched eye color. They showed me what others did not... kindness."

He felt the need to remind her. "I am not kind."

"I do not believe that. Kindness is a decision left to the person and the given situation."

"Like a warrior who cannot pause to think of being kind when someone is about to run a sword through him," Slayer reasoned.

Her smile faded and sadness surfaced in her eyes. "Aye, battle knows no kindness."

"But a lass with mismatched eyes, through no fault of hers, is no reason to treat her unkindly."

Her soft smile returned. "The young ones did not care. A young lad talked with me one day when I was alone drawing with a stick in the dirt. He asked what was wrong with my eyes. I told him I was born that way and he shrugged and began to draw in the dirt with me. It was not until his mum pulled him away and told him my eyes were evil and he was not to play with me that his opinion of me changed." She sighed. "I may look different than others but that does not mean I am. I hurt and feel pain just like anyone else, but no one sees that or even bothers to look. They judge me simply because I look different from them and, therefore, will have nothing to do with me."

He could only imagine the pain and ridicule she had suffered for her difference, and it caused him an unsettling pain in his heart. It was not fair. Either was the reason his father had chosen Sky for Warrand to wed. He had not spoken the truth when Sky had asked why a marriage was arranged between her and

Warrand. His father had told him. He wanted to find a wife for Warrand who would not consume him with desire or one he could not possibly lose his heart to. He claimed that wives were more a hindrance than a benefit. He assumed Warrand would have no interest in a woman with two different colored eyes, nor would he find any passion with her. It was a cruel decision for both Sky and Warrand.

He now better understood why she possessed a gentle manner and why she kept to herself, and it hadn't been by choice. Just as he had had no choice but to train endlessly as a warrior and join the Gallowglass as his father had demanded. He'd been raised to protect his brother and the clan. His father had gotten what he wanted from him. It was his only thought, only mission. It raged in him with a fierceness that made some think him insane. Even his father had seemed fearful of him at times. But Slayer had done whatever was necessary to honor his father's word and see that Warrand would safely inherit the title and responsibility of Clan Ravinsher once their father was gone. No one ever expected it would be Slayer who claimed the title, least of all him.

"You are pensive. Lost in your thoughts?" she asked of his silence.

"Aye," was all he said.

"Sometimes a good place to be and other times not so much."

"Very true," Slayer said and realized he had never held an interesting conversation with a woman until now with Sky.

He had had no time for women. They served a need and that was all and there were plenty of women who sought out Gallowglass warriors. They were free with their offerings, so he never lacked a female when in need of one. He found, to his surprise, he very much enjoyed talking with Sky. He also realized that she was far kinder than any person he had ever met, and it did not sit well with him that he was keeping the truth from her as to why he rescued her. He needed to tell her.

"I will clean and cook the fish," he said, concerned she might lose her appetite once he revealed the truth.

"I can clean and cook the fish, if you'd like."

"You know how to do both?" he asked, thinking that her family had sheltered Sky far too much for her to know how to do simple tasks.

"Aye. I asked Cook to teach me, worried that one day I may need such knowledge." She chuckled. "And that day has come. I will be able to feed myself while you are gone."

"I will clean the fish. You can cook it," he said abruptly and walked away from her.

Sky wondered what she said that caused him to get annoyed. But she refused to allow herself to worry over it. The day, so far, had been the best in weeks, and with the squirrel making friends so easily with her today, and Slayer soon to take his leave, she knew she would enjoy her time here. She entered the cottage to prepare a few wild onions to cook with the trout as Dea, the clan cook, had taught her to do.

It was not long before they sat down to eat.

"You did well," Slayer said, not used to offering compliments but the trout had been tastier than he expected.

"Dea, our cook, was kind enough to teach me when no one was around or else no one would have eaten the food if they knew I helped prepare it." Sky could not keep the sadness from her eyes. "I caught her one day dropping the food I made into the scrap bin for the animals. She begged me not to tell my da that she would not do it again and she would continue to teach me as my da had ordered her to do."

Slayer would have punished the woman for what she had done to Sky, and he had to fight to keep the anger out of his voice. "Your da punished her for what she did, didn't he?"

Sky shook her head. "I did not tell him. I understood Dea's fear. If anyone learned that she was feeding them food I made, they would never speak to her again and my da would have had no choice but to remove her from the kitchen. That was not fair to her. I learned a bit more from her, then stopped the lessons. I cooked some when the kitchen was empty and shared my fare with the forest animals. They enjoyed it."

"You are far more understanding and kinder than most. How you can sustain such a kind nature when you have been treated so unkindly puzzles me," Slayer said, perplexed and annoyed at how much she had been made to suffer.

"It puzzles me at times myself, but it is who I am."

"Perhaps you inherited it from your parents or sisters?"

She chuckled. "Not from my sisters. They are far different from me. And I definitely did not inherit it from my da who loses his temper on occasion. As for my mum, she was kind in her own way and stubborn as well. Your brother Warrand, was he like you?"

Slayer crossed his arms over his chest. "Define like me."

"Fine looks, strong stature, commanding nature," she said without hesitation.

"Those are not words anyone would use to describe me."

She amended her description with a smile. "Unkind. Terrifying. Vengeful."

"So, you do know me."

Sky thought she caught a slight smile on his lips, but it was too brief to be sure. "I am learning more about you and judging you for myself. You cannot be completely unkind when you have treated me well."

"There is a reason I have treated you well," Slayer said, knowing he could not delay telling her any longer.

"I assumed it is out of duty. A pledge you made perhaps to your brother or father to protect me, to keep me safe."

He leaned forward, bracing his arms on the table. "Aye, it is out of duty. The duty of a husband to his wife. We are wed, Sky. You are my wife."

Her eyes sprung wide, and she stared at him, the news so shocking that it stole her voice and sent her heart beating wildly. It couldn't be. She could not be the infamous Gallowglass warrior's wife.

A knock sounded at the door before any explanation could be offered and Slayer went to the door.

"News, my lord, you will want to hear," a warrior said.

"I will be right there," Slayer said and shut the door, then turned to Sky. "I need to go, but I will explain when I return. Warriors surround the cottage, so do not even think of running away. You should also know that you will not be staying here alone. I will be staying here with you, and we will be sharing the bed."

Chapter Six

Shock continued to keep Sky frozen where she sat. This truly was a nightmare she was living. How was it that she was the wife of the most feared Gallowglass warrior when Slayer had told her that her da had arranged a marriage between her and Slayer's brother, Warrand? Had Slayer's father manipulated her da into the marriage or had her da agreed to the change once Warrand died?

She shook her head. What did it matter how it came about? She wanted nothing to do with such a union. Foremost, she was fearful of Slayer and rightfully so. His commanding nature and superior strength often left her feeling vulnerable and that was not something she would want in a marriage… to be afraid of one's own husband. If that weren't enough, she would be part of a new clan. No one would accept her and without her sisters she would be more alone and vulnerable than she had ever been.

Feeling helpless and fearful, tears threatened her eyes. She did not know what to do or if there was anything she could do.

Proof.

She should seek proof that what Slayer told her was the truth. But why would he lie? There was no benefit for him in a union with her, just as there would have been no benefit if she had wed Warrand. So, why did Slayer's father arrange a marriage for her with Warrand in the first place? The question poked at her, thinking it was something she needed to know.

Stop feeling sorry for yourself!

Sky jumped and looked around the cottage expecting to see her sister Leora standing there, her voice had been so strong in her mind. Leora was right. It would do her no good to dwell on the problem. One thing was certain though, until the issue could be settled, she and Slayer would not be sharing a bed.

***

Slayer had no intentions of being gone long, and there was no reason for him to be concerned about Sky's safety while he was gone, though he found he was. He had not told her that the cottage sat in the middle of the Gallowglass compound. The Gallowglass came from all over to practice here in the woods and in the fields. Several longhouses housed endless warriors. Smithies and arrow and bow makers were in abundance and a well-guarded structure held prisoners who could prove useful if kept alive. No one dared to come near it and those who had foolishly tried never reached the perimeter, the first line of sentinels never failing to stop them. To reach the cottage, four perimeters would need to be breached and the Gallowglass would never allow that to happen.

The sun had lost its dominance to the clouds and Slayer wouldn't be surprised to see it rain. He kept a quick pace through the woods knowing exactly where the warrior with the news waited. It was the spot where messages were left for him when he stayed at the cottage so he would not be disturbed unless it was an emergency. He temporarily changed those orders being here with Sky. Any news was to be delivered immediately.

He grew anxious to speak to the warrior waiting there when he spotted it was John. He had sent John and Angus to various areas in the Highlands that were ripe with gossip and tales to see if they could learn anything about his father and brother's deaths. Tales often liked to be told when drink was involved. Some were truthful, others nothing more than boastful encounters, while some were born from a seed of truth.

John would not disturb him unless he had important news, and he was eager to hear it, calling out to him as he approached, "What have you found out, John?"

"A boastful tale that may hold some truth," John said.

"Tell me."

"Angus and I were at a market enjoying some ale while talking with the locals in hopes of hearing something relevant. Someone mentioned the Gallowglass and during the conversation someone talked about a man bragging how he supplied the poison that killed your father. I made mention of him being a fool for saying such a thing and the one fellow said that the man was a known liar and no one in those parts believes anything he says. He was right. The man lied. We found him and he was more than willing to talk and with little persuasion. He says he overheard a conversation and decided to turn it into a tale since storytellers never have to buy their own ale."

"Do you trust he tells you the truth since he is a known lair?" Slayer asked.

"Aye, he was too fearful not to since we invited him to join us in our travels to confirm what he told us," John said. "He heard two men talking, mentioning Lord Bannaty by name and that he would be dead soon enough and that no one would ever suspect that he had been poisoned. The person would dispense the poison a little at a time until it finally killed him."

"Which would mean it was someone who frequented the keep or someone already there." Slayer grew anxious to get his hands on the two men. "Tell me that this liar knew these men and you found them."

"He was familiar with one of them and he was not hard to find—" John hesitated briefly. "He was dead when we found him."

"And the other?"

Again, John hesitated. "We cannot find him. He seems to have vanished."

"Or was never there to begin with."

"Angus and I thought the same, so we brought Rory, the liar, home with us figuring he might be more prone to the whole truth while a guest of the Gallowglass."

"I will question him myself tomorrow," Slayer said.

"Aye, my lord. Angus and I will make sure he is ready for you," John said.

Slayer made his way back to the cottage, the overhead clouds growing darker. It would not be long before it rained. It had rained the day he learned of his brother Warrand's death. He and his men were just returning home from helping a nobleman protect his land from a neighboring clan who claimed it belonged to their clan. What should have been nothing more than a skirmish had turned into a bloody battle with heavy losses on both sides, though he had lost no men. Then came the news of his brother's death and he wished he had a battle to ride into, needing to release the overpowering rage that consumed him for failing to protect Warrand as he was meant to do.

He would not fail his brother again. He would find out who was responsible and make them suffer brutally before killing them.

Shaking his head too clear away his burdensome thoughts, he approached the cottage. It was time to talk to Sky about their marriage, though there was little to say. They were wed and nothing would change that.

He opened the door and stepped into an empty cottage.

***

Sky sat by the stream wishing the sun hadn't vanished, though she was glad her squirrel friend had returned and brought a friend with him, though they were busy nipping at the ground for what insects they could find.

The cottage had lost some of its charm after learning she was wed and would be sharing it with her husband. Her disappointment had brought her to the stream, not to think but simply to be. Her sisters could never understand her need for solitude, how she could spend hours alone in the woods and not mind. It was something she had always done, even when young. She had longed to make friends at one time but not anymore. She had all the friends she needed in the forest. She could truly live her days out here and be content.

The squirrels suddenly sat straight up, their eyes alert and their heads held still as they listened. They heard a foreign noise and with a quick look at her, they took off.

Slayer's presence filled the forest before he was even seen. It frightened the animals, caused the birds to take flight and the wind to whisper in warning. She shivered, worried at what the future might hold with such a powerful man.

Sky did not move, she stayed as she was, listening, just as the squirrels had done and finally heard his footfalls. They were strong and quick, and she could almost feel the anger in them.

He came to a stop beside her, and she kept her eyes on his boots, a bit fearful to glance up at him and see anger in his eyes.

"Give me your hand. We will return to the cottage," he said, and held his hand out for her to take hold of it.

She did not argue even though she would have preferred to stay where she was. A conversation with him was inevitable and so was the outcome. He would inform her that they were wed and there was nothing she could do to change that. She was to accept it and be a dutiful wife, something she did not want to hear.

She reached out and took his hand and it closed firmly around hers and, with an easy tug, he pulled her up onto her feet. He kept hold of her hand, to her surprise, as they walked back to the cottage in silence. She wondered if it was on purpose, a warning sign that he had no intention of letting her go. Raindrops began to fall, and he tucked her snug against him as though he could protect her against the rain and hurried their steps to the door.

Once inside, he slipped her cloak off her and hung it on a peg, then he went to the fire pit and added more wood, the fire having dwindled.

The raindrops had left his sleeveless arms wet, rainwater glistening on them, defining their strength. He had pushed his long, blond hair out of his way to rest over one shoulder and his face was, as usual, stoic, leaving her to wonder about his thoughts.

He stood and with a nod to one of the benches at the table, ordered, "Sit."

She sat as he demanded, though more so because she feared she would not be able to remain standing, her legs trembled so badly.

Wondering if she should ask when the answer seemed obvious, but needing to know for sure, she asked, "Will you command me with your every word?"

"Will it be necessary?"

"You're giving me a choice?" she asked leerily.

He remained standing and she wished he would sit, his imposing size alone making her anxious.

"You have a choice, Sky."

"I did not have a choice to become your wife," she argued.

"Nor did I have a choice to become your husband."

"So, this marriage was forced on us both?" she asked, not having given thought that he might be just as displeased with their marriage.

"Duty was forced on us," he said as though it explained it all.

"Please, could you sit," she said, pointing to the bench opposite her at the table, feeling far too vulnerable with the way the breath and width of him consumed the room. "And explain how it is that I became your wife when it was your brother I was to wed."

Slayer was prepared for tears and demands like many women when things did not go their way. But Sky spoke softly with him even though her hands trembled slightly, and fear lit her eyes, turning the two different colors bolder.

He sat. "Warrand died before the marriage arrangement could be completed, my father was already showing signs of illness and, fearing for the future of the clan, he put my name on the marriage document."

"So, my da knew nothing about the change in the marriage agreement?"

"Aye. He knew nothing. His sole purpose in seeing you wed was to make certain you were protected and kept safe. The heart of the marriage document remained the same. You would have what your father so desperately wanted for you with me as your husband. My father made sure I understood the reason for the marriage and that I would honor the agreement. I will protect you, see you kept safe, allow no harm to befall you, of that you have no worries. Since I honor the agreement, I see no reason why your father would object to it."

She could not argue with what obviously made sense, but still... "I would like to speak with my da about this before the marriage is sealed."

"That is not possible. I do not have to remind you that it is presently not safe for you to travel to Clan Murdock, and your father is ill and cannot travel here."

Fear raced through Sky, turning her skin to gooseflesh. "My da is ill? What happened? What troubles him?"

"It is my understanding that your sister Elsie is taking good care of him and there is presently no need for concern. I would advise you to allow him time to rest and grow strong before you deliver any unsettling news."

She feared for her da's well-being but knew Elsie would take good care of him. It also gave her a good reason to wait to seal their vows. "Then until I can confirm that my father does not object to our union, we will wait to consummate our vows."

"Nay, we will not. The marriage document is valid as is the marriage itself. It matters not that it is my brother or me who you wed as long as you are provided with what your father demanded... that you are kept protected and safe. You have seen for yourself that the agreement is being honored. We are husband and wife. Do your wifely duties, bear me bairns, and you will be treated well."

Sky did not know what to say and from what he said, she truly had no say in the matter. The marriage contract had been met as stated and was valid. And if her da had wed her to keep her safe then he would not object to the marriage.

"Think wisely on this, Sky. Wed to me, you would never have to worry about how people treat you again. No one would dare treat you poorly being my wife or dare think of harming you. You will be safe and on that I pledge my word to you."

Could he be right? Could this be a wise choice for her? He was a powerful and respected noble, and a Gallowglass warrior feared and awed by most. No one would dare do her harm and chance his wrath.

"Elsie is wed, and you should know that your father secured a marriage for Leora as well. Both will have their own families. Do you not want a family of your own?" he asked his own question, giving him pause to think about it himself. He had not given much thought to having a family but now that he ruled the clan, it was his responsibility to produce heirs and secure the clan's future. And the thought of having bairns with Sky surprisingly appealed to him.

News that Leora was wed as well did not shock her. If her da had secured marriages for her and Elsie, it would make sense he would do the same for Leora. Sky never expected to have children since she never expected to wed. She had looked forward to her sisters making her an aunt so she could not only indulge the little ones but satisfy her own need for bairns she would never have. Marriage to Slayer would give her a chance to have her own home and bairns. It could be a viable choice, a sensible one, but did she have the courage to make it so?

He could see she was giving it thought as was he. The marriage was secured. There was no changing that and he would see it sealed with the consummation of their vows. Neither of them had a choice. Fate had settled it for them. Besides, something inside him urged him not to lose her, to keep her close, to talk with her and enjoy her gentle voice and her kind nature.

"I suppose our marriage could prove sensible," she said while still considering it.

"Yet something gives you pause. I can see it in your scrunched brow." He reached across the table and gently stroked her brow to chase away the deep lines.

An ease settled over her as though his touch held the magic to dispel her worries. Or was it simply that he noticed and tempted to vanquish them? But then he was a warrior, a conqueror who vanquished his enemies, so how difficult would it be for him to dispel her worries when he was the one truly in command?

"There is something I need to know, and I need you to be honest with me about it," she said.

"Concerning our marriage?"

"Aye."

"There is nothing I hide from you about the marriage agreement," he assured her.

"Except that you have not told me why your father chose me to wed Warrand, then you, when I bring no benefit to the union."

Slayer never expected her to ask that, but he had said he hid nothing from her about their union. So, honor dictated he speak the truth. "You asked for the truth, and I will tell you it. My father was a man who put Clan Ravinsher before anything else. He claimed that wives were more a hindrance than a benefit. He told me that he wanted to find a wife for Warrand who would not consume him with desire or one he could not possibly lose his heart to. He assumed Warrand would have no interest in a woman with two different colored eyes, nor would he find any passion with her."

Sky stared at him, his words sinking in deep, squeezing at her heart. "So, your father believed me undesirable, unlovable, and all Warrand would need to do is tolerate me when it came time to get me with child."

"To him it was a marriage of convenience like most marriages, nothing more," he said, to make it sound less hurtful, but it did nothing to stop the hurt gathering in her eyes. While he kept his feelings stoic, necessary for a Gallowglass commander, he could not stop the anger that sparked in him for causing her pain. He never expected to hear her say what she said next.

"If he expected that of Warrand, then he must have expected the same from you. So, tell me, Slayer, will you only tolerate me?"

Sky had learned for herself that a lack of a quick response demonstrated shock and the inability to answer. She watched as Slayer sat there silently, staring at her. It was all the response she needed. She got up and ran out of the cottage into the rain.

Chapter Seven

Sky ran. She didn't know where she was going and did not care. She just needed to escape the hurt that tore at her heart and soul.

Unlovable.

She had heard that before and had gone with tearful eyes, though she would not allow herself to shed them, to her sisters to tell them what the women had said about her that no man would ever love her. That she was unlovable. Worse they had laughed about how a man would have to slip a sack over her head, so he did not have to look into her evil eyes. Leora demanded to know who the women were, but Sky had refused to tell her, knowing it would only make matters worse. Elsie had told her they were jealous of her beauty and that was why they were so mean. She wanted to believe her sister since it helped lessen the hurt, but the women were right, and Slayer's words had just proved it. No man would ever love her. She was unlovable. Slayer would tolerate her, do his husbandly duties, and care nothing for her.

The rain poured down on her, soaking through her garments, but she didn't care. She just wanted to run, escape, but how did one escape oneself?

Sky gasped when her arm was grabbed, and she was yanked to a stop and spun around to be plastered against her husband's hard, wet chest.

"Don't ever, EVER, run away from me like that again," he yelled to make sure he was heard above the pouring rain and his pounding heart, thinking it could be heard it beat so heavily. "You cannot escape this marriage as much as you may want to and never would you escape me. I would find you no matter where you went. Nothing, absolutely nothing would stop me from finding you."

Though she was locked in no cell, this marriage still made her feel very much a prisoner and one from which she would never be able to escape. Her shoulders slumped and her head drooped in defeat.

He scooped her up into his arms and carried her back to the cottage, the heavy rain soaking them every step of the way. Once inside, he stood her on her feet in front of the hearth.

"You need to get out of those wet garments," he said and went to the chest at the foot of the bed and grabbed the blanket folded on top and returned to her. "Take off your garments and wrap yourself in this." He placed the blanket on the table and stepped away from her and began to strip off his own garments.

Sky stood staring at him, too shocked and fearful to move while he undressed without hesitation.

"Get them off, Sky, or I will do it for you," he ordered.

She forced her chin up and she wished she could force her fear away, but that was not possible. Instead, she did her best to temper it. "Please, Slayer, do not make me do this now. I have only learned I am your wife. Please give me a chance to digest this news and come to terms with it before we consummate our marriage."

She had braved her own fear to speak up to him and for that he admired her, and her plea made sense. This was all shocking news to her, news she had yet to come to accept.

"You make a reasonable request so I will not deny it but when it comes time, I will have your word that you will not deny me but willingly consummate the marriage."

"You will give me time?" she asked, her fear subsiding now that she had been granted a delay.

"I will give you a few days, no more."

"A few days should be sufficient," she said, though she had no idea if it would be. But at least it gave her time to better understand her situation and to learn more about her husband and perhaps befriend him as she had thought it wise to do. Maybe then things would not seem as dreadful as they presently felt.

"We will revisit this in a few days. Now get out of those wet garments," he ordered and stepped away and turned his back on her.

She was grateful he gave her a bit of privacy. He was right about the wet garments. They would do her no good, though the thought of having only a blanket to wear left her feeling vulnerable.

She hurried and rinsed the rainwater from her hair before she began to undress and get the blanket wrapped around her so that she would not be left standing there naked when he turned around.

A sudden chill sent a shiver through her, and she hurried to finish tucking the blanket around her a few moments before he turned to face her. He walked toward her with ease and with no regard for his nakedness as though it was a common thing for him to walk naked in front of a woman. The brief view of his wide, muscled back and taut backside had been compelling enough to see, but the front of him assaulted the senses and sent a pleasurable sensation racing through her. He was an exceptional figure of a man and far too easy to gaze upon.

He stopped in front of her. Her two different colored eyes intrigued him but what intrigued him even more was how easy it was for him to see in her eyes what she was feeling. And he did not like the fright and vulnerability he saw there, though he understood it. He had spoken the truth to her and told her that his father had chosen her as a wife for Warrand because he believed his son would not love her and now, she believed the same of him. That love would never exist between them. That he would tolerate her.

Sky forced herself not to flinch when he raised his hand toward her and with his finger gently wiped the rivulet of rainwater that she felt dripping from her hair down along her cheek.

"I am a man of honor, Sky, on that you can count. I cannot promise you that I will ever grow to love you, for I am not sure I can love or even know how to love a wife. What I can promise you is that I will honor our marriage vows, be faithful to you, do my duties as a husband and treat you well. I can offer no more than that, but it is more than most arranged marriages offer."

That he was truthful with her touched her heart and had her admitting, "I sometimes fear you."

"You are not alone in that. Many fear me, but you have nothing to fear from me. I will never harm you. Will I never be angry with you? I imagine not. We will probably anger each other at times but you will come to know I command and grow accustomed to obeying my word. And again, I will never harm you."

He had told her that often enough and with how he had protected her so far, she was beginning to trust his word, though she voiced another concern. "I barely know you."

"We will grow to know each other. In the meantime, we will be friends."

He commanded more than offered friendship, but that mattered little. He was offering her something no one ever had... to be her friend.

She responded quickly. "I would like that."

"Then it is settled," he said, and as if needing to seal the agreement, he kissed her lips gently, then turned away from her and went to the chest at the bottom of the bed.

Sky touched her lips faintly as she watched him rummage through the chest. His kiss had surprised her and what surprised her even more was that it had been pleasant. She saw that he pulled out a plaid and quickly wrapped it around himself. When done, he pulled another garment out of the chest and walked over to her.

"A shirt for you to wear until your garments dry."

She took it from him and went to thank him, but different words fell from her lips. "That was my first kiss, and it was nice." She felt the heat rise in her cheeks. She was a fool for saying that?

He had not expected to hear that from her, and he definitely did not expect to be pleased to hear it and annoyed at the same time. Though his response offered a sound reason for it. "Aye, your first kiss from me and the last kiss you will ever know will be from me since your lips will touch no others but mine."

His edict confirmed it. They were wed and would remain wed until their dying day. Slayer was her fate whether she wanted him to be or not. So, how did she accept such a fate?

She slipped the shirt over her head, hurrying her arms through the long sleeves and when the shirt fell past her knees, she wiggled out of the blanket and let it fall to the ground. She snatched it up and folded it to place on the bed, then moved the small bench in front of the fire pit and sat. She combed her hair with her fingers, easing the wet strands loose so they would dry, giving her heart time to stop pounding and her mind from reeling. She could not believe all that had happened in the last few days, and she did not want to continue to think about it. She focused on her hair to ease her mind. At least the rainwater had chased away some of the dirt that had accumulated there while she was locked in the cell. She would give her hair a good scrubbing in the stream tomorrow along with her garments, eager to wear clean garments again. And she hoped the squirrel would visit with her and bring more friends with him.

Friends. Slayer offered friendship. She made friends easily with the animals and came to know them well. She could do the same with Slayer… be his friend and come to know him well. Maybe, just maybe, she would not fear him anymore.

That fear burst into a burning flame when he joined her in bed later.

"You may as well get used to me beside you since we will share a bed each night from this night on," he said and discarded his plaid and got in bed with her.

The bed was a decent size for two people of normal size, but Slayer was not normal size. He was larger than most men, so the fit was snug. Sky tried to keep tucked close to the wall, but his weight, from use, had caused the stuffed mattress to sink some in the middle, and she found herself slipping toward him when she moved.

After a few times of brushing up against him, Slayer grabbed hold of her and rested her against his side. "I gave you my word. I will not touch you yet. You can rest against me without worry or fear. That way you can remain still and allow both of us to get some sleep."

"I have only ever slept alone," she said softly as if trying to explain her restlessness.

"And now, you will sleep alone no more," he said, and his arm tightened around her, reminding her that was where she would stay... beside him. "Now go to sleep."

His tone held annoyance and she laid still and stiff in his arms, too worried to move. Needing to calm that worry, she asked, "You are my friend, Slayer, right?"

"Aye, Sky, I am your friend and always will be. Now sleep. You are safe with me."

For some reason, his words reassured her, and her body relaxed against him, and it was not long before she fell asleep.

Not so, Slayer. He laid awake thinking... about Sky. She was not what he expected, though it was more that he had not expected to find her appealing, not only in appearance, but her nature as well. And it disturbed him that he actually had looked forward to simply sleeping with her, holding her as he did, confirming that she belonged to him and always would.

He would think she had worked a spell on him if he believed her evil as some did. But he had seen true evil through the years and Sky did not come close to being evil. He did not think evil could even survive around her since she had such a kind soul. Not once had she gotten angry at him, fought with him, yelled at him, complained to him, or cried over her misfortune. Her words to him were soft and her smiles gentle. Even with the bruises under her eyes she was still beautiful, and she had suffered her hurt nose in silence, not offering one complaint about it.

It was his mission in their marriage to keep her safe and he had failed her that day even though his warriors had prevented the man from killing her. That culprit never should have gotten close to her. He still had not discovered how the man had gotten past his warriors, a worry that had caused him to double the sentinels around the cottage. Even though it sat in the middle of the Gallowglass practice area, it was not likely anyone would get this far. However, he would take no chance.

With how busy his mind was tonight, he would be lucky to get any sleep at all, though that also might be because his wife had draped her arm over his chest and had rested her slim leg over his leg. She had gotten comfortable against him in her sleep, and he found he enjoyed the feel of her body against his. An odd thing for sure, since like her, he had always slept alone. But no more. She would be there resting against him every night and he felt a smile touch his lips as his eyes closed.

***

Slayer woke with a stretch, feeling good even though he probably had not gotten much sleep. Realizing he didn't feel his wife beside him, he jolted up and looked around. Sky was nowhere to be seen. How had she gotten out of bed without him feeling her movements or even sensing them?

He hurried out of bed, snatched a clean shirt from the chest, and got his plaid wrapped around him with haste. He raked his fingers through his long hair just before he opened the door and stepped out of the cottage.

He stopped after only taking a few steps to find Sky smiling and talking to Skell, his stallion, as she fed him wild onions. And bloody hell if the horse didn't nod at her as if he understood her. His eyes also caught sight of her garments and his from yesterday when they had been caught in the rain. They were hanging from tree branches and appeared freshly washed, as did she. Her hair shined a lovely, reddish blonde and fell in careless waves around her face and over her shoulders. He had not noticed the red in her hair before now, which meant she had washed it as well as their garments, which also meant…

"You went to the stream without me," he accused with a raised voice as he walked toward her. She turned the most beautiful smile on him, and it almost stopped him in his tracks.

"I had company," she said, feeding the last of the wild onions she had gathered to Skell.

"Who?" he demanded when he stopped in front of her and caught the scent of fresh pine on her.

"The squirrel who visited with me yesterday and his friend as well as a doe who shared a berry bush with me. I would have woken you, but you slept so soundly and peacefully that I thought it best to let you be. Besides, I was sure you had sentinels posted so there was nothing for me to fear." She tilted her head back and smiled at the sun that shone brightly. "Besides, I usually wake just before dawn. I love the chance of catching a gorgeous sunrise and I was lucky enough to watch one this morning."

Slayer realized how late he must have slept with all she had gotten done and with how high the sun was in the sky. It was rare that he slept so late, usually being up at dawn. It was even rarer that he felt so rested but pushed the thought from his mind.

"Wake me the next time," he ordered, casting a glance around for the spear he had fashioned yesterday for fishing. "I will fish for breakfast for us."

"I have eaten my fill of blaeberries. It was plenty for me."

She was more self-sufficient than he had thought. She did not wait for someone to take care of her. She saw to taking care of herself, a trait he had not expected her to possess.

"I kept extra berries for you if you would like some, though I suspect that will not be enough food to fill you." She walked a short distance away to grab a small basket that sat atop a large rock and returned and held it out to him.

Slayer took a handful, blaeberries being a favorite of his.

"I spotted a patch of juniper berries. They will flavor a meat stew quite nicely if you hunt today."

"My warriors will hunt for us, and food supplies should arrive today."

"Why do we stay here, Slayer?" she asked as he reached for another handful of berries. "It cannot be for my safety alone since you have told me enough times that I am safe when I am with you. So why are we truly here?"

He nodded at the bench under the large oak tree and, placing his hand low on her back, urged her toward it. He waited until they were seated to answer her. "Ross is the only one who knows that we are husband and wife, and it will remain that way even when we return to Clan Ravinsher. No one must know, not even your sisters, at least not yet. I thought the news best delivered when we were alone, and you were given time to accept the marriage."

"But why keep it a secret?"

"Until I can find out why my brother and father were murdered—"

She gasped. "You think your father and brother were murdered by someone who wishes to lay claim to

Clan Ravinsher—" She gasped again. "If that is so, then your life is in danger as well."

"Yours as well since you can produce an heir to the clan," he said, amazed that she had thought of him being in danger before even considering that her life was in danger for two distinct reasons.

"Do you have any suspicions of who it might be?" She shook her head and did not give him a chance to answer. "It doesn't make sense. Only a fool would kill the brother and father of a renowned Gallowglass warrior. It would bring the Gallowglass down on him." She gasped again and grabbed hold of Slayer's arm. "Unless the culprit is part of the Gallowglass."

"That brings us to another reason for us being here," he said, appreciating his wife's sharp mind since he had thought the same. "This cottage sits in the middle of the Gallowglass training ground."

She squeezed his arm. "Are we surrounded by Gallowglass warriors? Are they all loyal to you?"

"The ones in the surrounding area are, but they come from all over the Highlands, and those I cannot vouch for, though I would be surprised if a Gallowglass betrayed one of their own. Honor is something the Gallowglass lives by."

Sky turned quiet, not saying a word, and her hand fell off his arm.

"I know what you are thinking, Sky," he said, annoyed that he favored her touch. It was not like him to feel that way about a woman's touch, and yet he found Sky's innocent, casual touches oddly comforting.

"You are observant so I would say you probably do know my thought."

Slayer proved it with his response. "You think my warriors would wonder why I brought you here and so they do not discover the truth, you believe I told them the reason was to drive the evil out of you."

"It would serve a double purpose since you could bring me home to your clan a cleansed soul."

Again, he admired her quick mind, but it also cautioned him to be careful, for she could find out things that might be better kept from her. Or was he worried she would discover things before he did?

"You could benefit from such an assumption," he said. "People would not fear you and would begin to befriend you."

"You do not truly believe that, do you?" she asked as if she could not believe she had to ask, and she shook her head. "I fear there will come a day that you regret our marriage."

"Never!"

He responded with such force that Sky drew her head back quickly.

"Never will that day come. I will never regret having you as my wife. I may be a fierce, brutal warrior, but I am an honorable man and will do right by you."

"Aye. I am sure you will since duty calls for nothing less from you," she said and did not understand why that saddened her.

"I must go to the Gallowglass compound. There is someone there who may have information on who poisoned my father," Slayer said and stood.

Sky stood as well and rested her hand on his chest. "Will you share with me what you learn? I would very much like to help you solve the mystery of their murders as well as solving my sisters and my dilemma."

"Perhaps," was all he would offer her.

"Please do consider it," she said as her hand fell away from his chest.

"Do not go wandering in the forest while I am gone. Stay close to the cottage, though you may go to the stream. The men guard that area well." He went to his horse and began to saddle him. "I do not know how long I will be gone."

"I will keep busy with cleaning out the garden so the new sprouts can grow."

At least the task would keep her occupied, though he did not want to tell her that she wouldn't be there to harvest the plants. They would be long gone from here before then.

"We will talk more when I return," he said and mounted his stallion.

"I look forward to it," she said and realized the truth of her own words and hoped it was a good beginning to their growing friendship.

He felt the same, but he did not tell her. He rode off not glancing back at her but wanting to and that annoyed him.

Chapter Eight

Slayer sat at one of the tables in the longhouse staring at Rory, a short, wiry man who had no trouble providing answers to his many questions. He talked without being threatened, beaten, or prodded. The problem was Slayer didn't know if it was truth or tales that the man spoke. He glanced at Angus and John, who stood behind Rory, and one shrugged and the other shook his head.

Angus had told Slayer upon his arrival that they barely laid a hand on Rory, and that he talked and talked, not only answering their questions but providing them with information they never asked. The problem continued to be whether the information Rory was telling them was the truth or nothing more than a tall tale.

"He was an old man, old, lots of gray hair and endless wrinkles," Rory said, repeating the description of the man he heard talking about poisoning Lord Bannaty for the third time, and he shook his head. "But he was spry, able to get around good. I tell you the truth, my lord. I would not lie to you."

"Yet you add something to what you tell me each time you repeat it," Slayer said and saw that Angus and John nodded, agreeing with him.

"Because I recall something and I want to make certain I tell you it all correctly," Rory insisted, eyeing the jug of ale on the table. "I probably would recall more if I was not so parched, my lord."

"Or would your information become that more elaborate after having some ale?" Slayer asked, then downed the remaining ale in his tankard and refilled it from the jug on the table.

Rory licked his lips. "Nay, my lord, I tell you the truth. I swear to you that I tell you the truth."

"So, this man who you heard talk about poisoning my father is old with wrinkles yet spry," Slayer said, trying to find some consistency in the man's words that might prove to be lies since he found through years of questioning prisoners that lies were often elaborated on whereas the truth was told more simply.

"Aye, old he is, very old, but gets around good, though slow so no one pays him much heed," Rory said. "He was gleeful about his part in the poisoning and boasted how easy it had been to accomplish the deed without ever meeting Lord Bannaty or stepping foot past the castle wall."

Slayer sat forward on the bench and glared at Rory. "Mind how you answer me next, Rory, for if I find you lied, I will cut out your tongue so you can never lie again."

Rory locked his lips tightly and nodded vigorously.

"Are you saying this old man admitted to being the one who poisoned my father, yet he had never met him?" Slayer asked, finding that difficult to believe.

Rory spoke fast. "I cannot say that for sure since he never admitted that it was him who did the deed. I can only say what I heard and how he seemed to boast about it."

If Rory spoke the truth, then it was at least a lead Slayer could follow, which was more than he presently had, but if it was a lie, he would be wasting his time.

"This other man found dead," Slayer said, "how do you know him?"

"Jeb was a loner. He didn't pay much attention to anyone."

"Tell me why a stranger would confide in Jeb about poisoning my father."

Rory shrugged. "I don't know. Maybe a need to boast before he ran off."

"And this man said nothing about why he poisoned my father?"

Rory scratched his head. "I think he said that your father deserved it."

"You *think* he said that?" Slayer snapped, annoyed at what he was beginning to think were endless lies.

Rory took an anxious step back and bumped into Angus and John, who pushed him back to where he'd been standing.

Rory clasped his hands together, twisting them nervously as he spoke. "It was hard to catch all of what the two men said since they whispered at times. So, I caught only a few words clearly."

Frustration with the man had Slayer pounding the table with his fist. "Did you hear anything clearly or did you make assumptions on the whispered words you heard?"

"I may have added one or two words," Rory admitted.

"Bloody hell!" Slayer roared. "You will tell me again all you heard and this time only what you heard not what you assumed you heard, or I will take my fists to you myself."

***

"A waste of a good morning," Angus said when midday arrived, and Rory was finally returned to his cell. "You cannot tell if any truth spills from that man's mouth."

"Well, at least we know blood does," John said and rubbed his red knuckles. "Though the earlier punches did little good. He continued to tell the same tale, elaborating even more on it every time he told it." He shook his head. "Torture would be wasted on him since his tale would probably grow along with the torture."

"Something doesn't seem right. He will remain a prisoner and continue to be questioned until somewhere in all of his senseless rambling we can discover a germ of truth," Slayer said.

"We will see to it, my lord," Angus said with a firm nod.

The door to the longhouse opened and a warrior hurried in a bit out of breath and rushed to the table where Slayer sat.

"I have important news, my lord."

"Sit, Ogden," Slayer ordered and nodded at an empty tankard. "Quench your thirst before you tell me." He then looked at Angus and John and nodded to the door and the two men left.

Ogden downed the entire tankard of ale without stopping, then dragged his sleeve across his mouth before saying, "Thank you, my lord. I needed that."

"Have more while you tell me the news." Slayer pointed at the jug of ale for the man to help himself.

Slayer had sent warriors far and wide to speak to his many contacts and learn whatever they could, not only about his father and brother's deaths but also about the Murdock sisters. So, he was eager to hear what news Ogden had for him and pleased that his warriors were finally returning with news.

Ogden spoke as he filled the tankard. "This news comes from those you know in the Lowlands. It seems that years ago, there was a group of Lowland women who helped women in trouble, women who gave birth to unwanted bairns for one reason or another. These women found homes for the bairns in the Highlands so they would be safe and no one could find them. It turns out that someone is searching for a female taken at birth and given away who belongs to a prominent, aristocratic family from the Lowlands. It is not known who searches for her or why."

"Two different reasons could be made for why someone searches for the now grown woman, the most prominent being that she is the sole heir of a sizeable fortune. Or she is an obstacle to someone inheriting a fortune," Slayer surmised, concerned by the news.

"Your friend did mention a dispute amongst a prominent family," Ogden said.

"I sense there is more you have to tell me, Ogden."

Ogden nodded and took another swallow of ale as if needing to fortify himself before he spoke. "Chieftain Norris and his wife took in three of those unwanted bairns and raised them as their own."

Slayer took in the shocking news, thinking of what it meant and the possible ramifications. "That would mean the Murdock sisters are not sisters after all."

"Aye, my lord," Ogden said, agreeing.

"You are to keep this to yourself, Ogden," Slayer ordered.

"I have not said a word about it, my lord, nor will I."

"I will let you know if I need anything more from you," Slayer said and left the longhouse.

He mounted Skell ready to return to Sky, his thoughts consumed with the startling news and if he should share it with anyone just yet, even Sky. She would have to know sooner or later. But was it better to wait or to tell her?

This news would change so much for her. To find out that her parents are not her true parents, and her sisters are not her true sisters could devastate her. But the news could also offer a plausible reason as to why someone wanted one of the Murdock sisters dead. It was a lead that could possibly help solve the baffling mystery.

Decisions normally came easily and quickly to him, so why he continued to debate whether to tell her the news or to wait as he rode annoyed him.

***

Sky stood with pride looking over the garden. She had pulled endless weeds that had been stifling the growth of the fresh sprouts and had carefully hoed and raked the entire garden until she got it into pristine shape. It looked wonderful and would produce a good harvest, not that she would have the pleasure of harvesting it. She doubted they would spend the summer here, though she wished otherwise.

The thought saddened her, and she rested the long-handled hoe and rake against the side of the cottage, her task done. Her hands showed the signs of a day well spent in the garden, dirty and blistered, and in need of a good cleaning and gentle care. She could do both at the stream and visiting with her squirrel friends would help her smile to return.

She wasn't far from the stream when she spotted the doe she had shared the berry bush with earlier now busy munching on a shrub. She hadn't mentioned to Slayer that the doe carried a fawn and would give birth soon. She intended to keep watch on the doe to see that all went well for her and her newborn fawn or fawns, some does often birth more than one fawn.

Once at the stream, she plunged her hands into the chilly water and cringed, the blisters stinging, though not her wrists. They were healing nicely. As she carefully cleaned the dirt off her hands, her thoughts of the pregnant doe had her thinking that she could very well get pregnant soon herself. If Slayer's seed took root quickly, she could get with child before summer and deliver a bairn in the winter. The thought amazed and frightened her. She had not given much thought to having a bairn, thinking she would never wed. And no mothers in her clan had ever let her hold their bairns, so she had no experience with newborns. And without her sisters' help...

"How will I know what to do?" Sky whispered to herself, upset, and removed her hands from the water to dry them gently with the hem of Slayer's shirt she wore.

She caught the rustle of leaves and turned to see the squirrels nearby, but they did not approach her. They were scurrying up a tree away from her. That meant someone was close by. A sentinel or had Slayer returned?

"Sky!"

She smiled recognizing Slayer's powerful shout.

"I am by the stream," she called back.

"What happened to your hands?" Slayer demanded when he reached her and looked down to see them laying palms up in her lap, raw blisters on both.

She glanced up at him and grinned. "Remnants of my garden task."

She spoke with such pride in her blistered hands that he almost smiled but caught himself when recalling the news that he had yet to decide whether to share with her.

"Those blisters could use some honey," he said and without asking if she was finished at the stream, he stepped around her, slipped his hands under her arms, and lifted her to her feet.

When first meeting Slayer, she had been eager to look upon his face and when she was finally able to, his stoic expression left no room to know what he thought or felt. It was only recently that she began to catch the slight differences on his face and began to understand them.

Presently, his eyes held concern and hesitancy while his body was taut as if concealing something. He had something on his mind that she surmised he was reluctant to tell her.

That grew her anxious and she said, "You have something to tell me."

"I have some news," he said, not surprised by her remark since she knew he went to talk with a man who might have information. But it was not information she would ever expect. "We will talk once in the cottage."

The walk was a short one, but she grew more anxious with each step, endless worries racing through her mind at what he may have learned.

"Sit and I will get the crock of honey," he said once inside the cottage.

"Something is wrong. Please tell me, Slayer," she said, having worked herself into a fitful worry. "Has something happened to my da? My sisters?" She caught the slight rise of his brow when she mentioned her sisters. "Is it Leora? Did something happen to her?"

"I have received no word about Leora yet and Elsie is fine as is your da," he said and set the small crock of honey on the table, then pulled the bench around to sit closer to her at the table.

"Then what is it? Your hesitance to tell me is causing me alarm."

Sky's worry made the decision for Slayer since lies would serve no good purpose here. She deserved to hear the truth.

"This is not easy news, Sky, but you have a right to know," he said and began to explain. "News arrived from the Lowlands. Years ago, there was a group of

Lowland women who offered help to women in trouble, women who gave birth to unwanted bairns for one reason or another. Homes were found for the bairns with families in the Highlands so they would be safe, and no one could find them. But the past has caught up to the deed and now someone is searching for a female bairn taken at birth and given away. It is believed that she belongs to a prominent aristocratic family from the Lowlands. Who searches for her and why is not yet known. Two varied reasons could be made for why the now-grown woman is of interest to someone. The most prominent reason would be fear of what she could inherit, a fortune perhaps, if she were discovered. Or the need to find her so someone can inherit a fortune."

"What does this have to do with me?" Sky asked.

If she gave it thought, Slayer had no doubt she would have the answer for herself, though the disbelief or pain of such news might have her turning a blind eye to it.

He didn't wait, he spoke the words that would bring everything she thought she knew about herself crashing down around her. "Your da and your mum took in three of those unwanted bairns and raised them as their own daughters."

Sky's eyes turned wide, and she slowly shook her head at the shocking news. "It is not true. It cannot be true." She continued to argue against it. "It cannot be possible. It cannot be. My mum and da would never have kept something like that from me and my sisters. And Elsie and Leora are my sisters and my mum and da are my parents. Someone made a mistake." Sky sat staring but seeing nothing, her mind scrambling to try and make sense of what she'd been told.

Slayer remained silent, letting her be, letting her think through the alarming news. And feeling an unusual need to comfort her, when he never offered comfort to anyone, he took her hand and gently applied honey to her raw blisters.

His touch was tender and oddly enough comforting to Sky and the shock began to slowly dissipate, leaving her to absorb the ramifications of what it all meant.

"This means I truly do not have a family. My parents are not my parents, and my sisters are not my sisters." She shook her head. "Nay, my sisters will always be my sisters whether we share the same blood or not, and my parents as well. But this leaves me wondering who I truly am."

Tears began to surface in her eyes. Women's tears had once irritated Slayer, until he learned to ignore them, give them no credence, care nothing about them. Women either used tears to manipulate and get what they wanted or shed them out of weakness. Yet he thought neither of those when he saw the tears in Sky's eyes. Her tears upset him and caused an ache in his chest, and he wanted to spare her the pain, take it from her, and stop her suffering.

She rested her hand on his arm as one tear slipped out and rolled down along her cheek. "I know I did not lose my parents or my sisters, but why does it feel as if I suffer their loss?"

He had no answer for her just as he had no answer as to why he hurt so much for her. Why did he want so desperately to stop her suffering? It overwhelmed him and forced him to respond without thought. He stood, scooped her up into his arms and walked to the bed with her to sit and cradle her in his lap, holding her tight against him as if somehow his body could take the pain from her.

Sky pressed her face against Slayer's chest and let a few tears fall softly. She lingered there, feeling safe and comfortable and cared for, though Slayer would deny it. He was doing what he believed was his duty to her as a husband. But he would be wrong. She felt it in the way he kept her tucked close against him, in the way his arms restrained her not with force but with tender firmness, in the way he let her shed her tears on his shirt, and the way he rested his cheek on top of her head. He was there for her, trying to keep her pain at bay and letting her know she was not alone.

For a man who claimed he was unkind, not knowing if he could love, he knew how to comfort, and that revelation changed things for Sky. It meant that one day it was possible that he could at least come to care for her.

She lingered there letting the initial shock wear away and the pain of such news subside before she tilted her head back slowly to look up at him. "What else can you tell me about this?"

He wiped at her tear-stained cheeks with his thumb and though tears shined in her eyes, he was glad no more fell. He detested seeing her cry.

"I have so-called friends far and wide, learning long ago it was wise to know people in many places. They are mostly people who owe me favors, many of them large favors for what I have done for them. I have several of those so-called friends in the Lowlands. It helps to know what is going on there and it keeps me abreast of any matters that might affect the Highlands. One such person discovered this news."

"How can you trust what he says when you trust no one?" Sky asked, looking for anything that could prove the startling news was false.

"I do not trust him, but I know he would not report falsely to me for fear of what I would do to him if he did. He would only send me news that he confirmed beyond a doubt."

Her stomach roiled as she asked, "So, you believe that Elsie and Leora are not my sisters?"

"Not your blood sisters, but as you said yourself, sisters, nonetheless. You were raised together and as such have a bond that only sisters could have. It matters not if your blood does not run through each other's veins, it only matters that you care and love each other as sisters do. Ross and I are not brothers, but that does not stop me from thinking of him as my brother. We have shared things through the years that only brothers can, including my father and brother's deaths. He will always be a brother to me as your sisters will always be your sisters. I know this is difficult for you, but you will realize it for yourself soon enough." He raised his hand, his finger reaching for the corner of her right eye where a tear lingered, as if not sure if it should fall, and he brushed it away. "Besides, you are not alone. You will always have me. We will be together for the rest of our days until death parts us, wife."

He kissed her, not out of passion but out of need to comfort her.

It was a gentle kiss that Sky favored, and it was a kiss that to her sealed his words as a promise, that he would always be there for her.

When the kiss ended, she smiled softly and said, "You are kind."

"I am not," he insisted.

"I cannot deny what is in front of me."

"You do not see clearly," he admonished lightly.

Her heart skipped a beat, sure she had caught a slight turn of his lips, the start and quick ending of a smile that was near to being born, a playful one. "The animals have taught me to see more clearly than most."

He purposely frowned. "If it is the animals who you see clearly, then you must think me an animal?"

She gasped. "Never would I think that."

"But you said—"

She pressed her fingers to his lips. "You twist my words."

He brushed her fingers away. "I heard them. They were clear."

Again, she thought she caught a smile so light that she could be mistaken, but she did not believe herself wrong. She wanted to believe he was being playful with her, trying to ease her pain.

"Perhaps you are right, husband, for if you are an animal, it will be much easier to tame you."

She saw it again, slight as it was, only this time his smile warned rather than teased.

"Some animals are too wild and vicious to tame, and I am one of them."

The sudden coldness in his voice and emptiness in his eyes should be enough for her to pay heed to his warning, but she didn't.

She rested her hand on his cheek, its warmth seeping into her. "Maybe, or maybe you never felt the touch of a hand gentle enough to trust."

Chapter Nine

Slayer watched Sky as he stacked firewood near the cottage. She was busy fashioning a wreath from slim branches she had collected. She appeared content but he could tell by how her brow scrunched now and again that her thoughts were busy.

They had spent much time talking last night not only about the news concerning her and her sisters but also about what Rory had told him. She asked pertinent questions and offered suggestions that proved wise. While he had never considered discussing important matters with a wife, he found talking with Sky valuable and enjoyable. He was beginning to think that their marriage could prove beneficial in many ways.

One was that he would no longer need to look for a willing woman when the need struck him. Sky would be right there beside him in bed. That he found her appealing was an added benefit.

Maybe you never felt the touch of a hand gentle enough to trust.

Her words from yesterday had kept repeating in his mind since he woke and at the oddest times throughout the day. He had not given much credence to them since he was in no need of a gentle touch. He was a hardened warrior and needed to remain that way. And yet he had found her causal touch had brought him a strange comfort at times. He particularly liked the feel of her snuggled against him in bed and lately he found himself unable to stop himself from growing aroused when his mind drifted to Sky. Something that was happening far too often. He surmised it was because his need for a woman was growing and he would appease it soon with Sky, and the thought stirred his manhood. He did not want to wait much longer to consummate their vows since if he went too long without satisfying his need, he could be demanding when coupling. Experienced women found his demands enjoyable. He doubted an innocent like Sky would feel the same.

The sudden sound of birds taking flight had Slayer hurrying over to Sky. He yanked her up from where she sat under a tree and shoved her behind him to walk them toward the cottage.

"Your attention remains sharp," a voice called out.

"As always," Slayer shouted, "but you, my friend, are tardy."

Ross stepped out of the woods with a smile. "But I bring good tidings and," —he held up a jug— "ale."

Slayer did not know what tidings Ross had to share with him and after yesterday's disturbing news, he did not want Sky suffering any more or hearing something that did not concern her.

"I have a taste for more berries. I will go pick some while you speak with Ross," Sky said.

It was as though Sky read his mind and settled it for him, making things easier for him.

"Do not go far or be too long," Slayer ordered and leaned down, his face close to hers. "And save some berries for me."

Her face burst in a bright smile and her two different colored eyes filled with delight and, bloody hell, if her joy was not contagious rushing a smile to his lips that he barely stopped before it sprang free.

"I will," she whispered conspiratorially and with his cheek so close, she could not help but kiss it.

Her innocent kiss stunned him, and he stood there as she grabbed a basket off the blanket beneath the tree and rushed into the woods. What stunned him even more was that it pleased him, filled him with pleasure, and sent a spark to his loins.

"I had my doubts about you bringing her here, but I see it was a wise decision. It did not take her long to accept you as her husband," Ross said when Slayer turned and walked toward him.

"She is getting there," Slayer said and joined Ross on the bench under the cottage window and gladly took the tankard of ale he handed him.

"With the way she looks at you, I would argue that she is already there." Ross shook his head. "Though I wonder how you accomplished that since you were never one to court a woman."

"She is my wife. Why would I need to court her?"

Ross chuckled. "It is a good thing you didn't need to since she probably wouldn't have agreed to marry you. Though with her affliction she no doubt worries you will change your mind and does what is necessary not to lose you."

Instinct to defend her had him snapping at Ross. "Her affliction has no bearing on our marriage."

"You defend her readily." Ross pointed out.

"Why wouldn't I? It is my duty as her husband," Slayer argued.

"Or do her strange eye colors hold you captive?"

Slayer scowled at him. "Have you lost your mind?"

Ross shook his head again. "Nay, I wanted to make sure that you haven't lost yours."

"My mind is as sound as it has always been."

"What about your heart?" Ross asked.

"What about my heart?"

"Uh oh."

"What is that supposed to mean?" Slayer demanded.

"Whenever I would mention your heart, you would always respond with… what heart? Now you acknowledge that you have one. I think your wife may have awakened it."

"Enough with the nonsense," Slayer cautioned, annoyed at his friend's suggestion. "What news do you have for me?"

"Melvin has taken residence at Clan Murdock. He should have news for us soon."

Melvin was one of Slayer's best and most reliable warriors. There was not a battle or mission he feared and that was the reason he had sent him to spy on Cavell.

"Good, he can keep me abreast of what Cavell finds out about this mission to see the Murdock sisters dead. And see that some warriors and supplies are sent to Clan Murdock. Cavell could use the help with the dwindling clan."

Ross turned quiet, focusing on drinking his ale.

"Spit it out, Ross," Slayer finally said, knowing Ross grew quiet when he was reluctant to tell him something that might anger him.

Ross hurried to preface it with, "I tell you what I hear and what I see for myself."

"Understood. Now tell me," Slayer urged.

"Sky's affliction has been made known to the clan and whispering tongues are busy spreading fear. Many claim she is a cohort of the devil. She will not receive a warm welcome when you arrive home with her."

"Then they will face my wrath, so make sure that news spreads just as fast."

"I will try, but there is a good chance the clan will never accept her," Ross cautioned. "Your own warriors avoided looking at her when her strange eye color was spotted. By now the truth of that incident has been embellished into a tale told before a hearth in whispers. You must know having her as your wife will not be easy."

"Battle is never easy, and this is just another battle to win."

"Be careful, my friend. Your men have been at your side in every battle that has seen victory. In this battle, I fear you may only have me to stand with you."

Screams brought both men to their feet and tossing their tankards aside before running into the woods.

***

"Nay! Nay! Don't kill him!" Sky screamed, waving her hands at a group of warriors as she ran to place herself in front of a massive stag that snorted and pounded the ground with his hoof.

"Get away from him."

"He will kill you."

"Are you insane!"

"He'll make a fine feast."

"You will not kill him!" Sky commanded with a strength that surprised her.

"What are you doing, woman?" Slayer shouted when he caught sight of Sky shielding a stag from his men, whose arrows were ready to take down the majestic beast.

The stage snorted and held his head high as if warning them off with his impressive set of antlers that could easily spear a person. He let loose with a rougher snort that echoed throughout the surrounding forest, a primal warning that reverberated, deterring anyone from getting too close. The stag's entire demeanor conveyed a readiness to charge at the slightest provocation and in front of him, dwarfed by the creature, stood his wife bravely yet foolishly defending him.

"What are you doing?" Slayer demanded. "Move away from him."

"Nay!" she shouted. "Something troubles him. He searches for help." She turned to face the stag.

Slayer, stunned that she disobeyed him, wanted to rush at her and pull her out of harm's way, but knew the stag could grow alarmed and lash out at Sky.

All that was presently left to him was to shout, "Stay away!"

Sky took slow steps toward the stag and when their eyes met a silent understanding seemed to pass between them.

"Keep your arrows ready," Slayer commanded.

Sky's hand shot up in protest, not taking her eyes off the stage. "Nay! Do not hurt him. He needs help." She spoke gently to the stag. "I can help you. Show me what troubles you."

The stag responded with a bob of his head, snorted, turned, and bolted into the woods. Sky, undeterred, followed him, her movements swift and agile.

Slayer shook his head and released several oaths as he ran after her. She had not given a moment's thought to her own safety. Her only thought was for the stag. He did not bother to call for Ross and his men to follow him. They would do so without being told.

Sky's speed and agility surprised him. She kept a good pace ahead of him and did not stop until the stag did, not far from the stream. The stag protested when Slayer drew near, pounding the earth with one hoof and snorting.

"Stay back. Your annoyance threatens him," Sky called out in warning. "He protects his mate. She requires help."

Slayer could understand the stag's protest since he was as riled as the magnificent beast in his worry over Sky and the dangerous situation she had placed herself in. He raised his hand to bring his warriors, who were close behind him to an abrupt halt. He could not see what Sky was doing but he did hear the cries of an animal in distress, the stag's mate, and the reason for his upset.

"Easy love, I am here to help you," Sky said gently, realizing it was the doe from the other day and she reminded the animal of that. "Remember me? We shared berries off the same bush. I am a friend. You can trust me. I will not harm you." She continued talking in a soothing tone and with great care crouched down beside the doe. She was in the throes of delivering her fawn but there appeared to be a problem.

Slayer was ready to call out to his wife, not seeing her or hearing any movement but a hand clamped down on his shoulder stopping him.

"I would wait. That stag looks ready to charge," Ross warned.

Sky's head finally popped up above the bushes and she rushed a look at Slayer. "His mate is having difficulty delivering their fawn. I am going to help her. I have done it before, worry not and I trust you to not harm the stag."

She disappeared before Slayer could respond and he did something he never expected he would do. Because it was the wisest thing for him to do or because she placed her trust in him to do so, he could not be sure. But whatever the reason, he ordered his warriors not to harm the stag in a tone that warned of dire punishment if someone thought to disobey him, not that that was likely.

"This will only add to the gossiping tongues," Ross warned.

Slayer ignored him, though knew he was right. This was not going to help Sky to be accepted by his clan.

Sky kept her mind on the task at hand. She had been lucky to have witnessed several does giving birth and had helped two who had had difficulty, the fawns having twisted during delivery and gotten stuck. That was the problem now.

She kept a soft voice as she stroked the doe's head. "With a little help your fawn will be born soon."

The stag calmed as well, though didn't take his eyes off the men, and pounded his hoof now and again to warn them he was ready to charge if necessary.

"A few careful tugs and it will be all over," Sky said, knowing careful was what she needed to be, or things could go terribly wrong.

When the doe cried out, the stag got upset, snorting and pounding his hoof.

Slayer was ready to charge the beast, but his wife's strong, encouraging words stopped him.

"Worry not, she does good, and the fawn will birth soon."

It got quiet after that, and it was as if the forest held its breath in anticipation and surprisingly Slayer and his warriors did as well.

Sky's head suddenly could be seen above the bushes, and she smiled at the stag. "A fine fawn that will grow into a mighty stag like his da."

The men unexpectedly cheered, and the mighty stag pounded the ground with his hoof and nodded his head proudly.

"You all must leave now and give the doe time to tend her newborn," she said.

The warriors turned to Slayer, awaiting his command.

"Go and the stag and his family are to be left in peace," Slayer reminded and when he looked back at Sky, she was gone.

"She is headed to the stream," Ross said.

"Remain at the longhouse tonight. There is something I need to discuss with you tomorrow," Slayer said and did not wait for a reply.

He hurried after his wife.

"Are you completely mad, woman?" Slayer scolded loudly when he reached the stream to see his wife washing her hands and arms in the stream.

She turned her head and smiled at him. "There is no reason to yell. I can hear you well enough."

"Evidently not since you failed to obey me," he reminded, dropping down beside her.

"The stag needed help," she said as though it was explanation enough.

"Don't ever do something so foolish again," he warned.

"I cannot promise that," she said, not giving her quick response a second thought. "The animals are my friends, and I will help them when in need."

People would think her foolish, perhaps even insane, if they heard that, or worse that she was evil. After all, if she could understand those animals, what diabolical creatures could she understand and make do her bidding?

It annoyed him that she did not even give thought to the possibilities of her unusual actions.

"Friends or not, you will not put yourself in harm's way for them," he ordered.

She spoke softly without a trace of anger in her voice. "Friendship is important to me. So, please understand that I would put myself in harm's way for any friend and that includes you."

Her remark fired something fierce in Slayer and he grabbed her arm, yanking her to her feet as he stood. "NEVER, will you put yourself in harm's way for me."

"But you would for me, wouldn't you?" she asked and knew what his reply would be.

"It is my duty."

"It is not a duty to me. I would do so because you are my friend and I care for you."

Slayer had suffered endless punches in his life, but the impact had been nothing compared to what he felt now. It hit him so hard he almost expected his legs to give way, and never had he suffered a punch that had almost knocked him off his feet. But never had a woman ever told him that she cared for him and never had he expected it to matter.

"My lord, are you all right?" Sky asked, resting her hand on his chest and worry filling her eyes.

He did not like it when she referred to him as my lord, even if it was the proper thing for her to do. He enjoyed hearing her say his name, gently, caringly.

Caringly.

He spoke without thinking. "I am not a caring man."

She chuckled softly and, as insane as it sounded, he thought he heard the birds chuckle with her.

"I believe you are a more caring man than you know."

He grabbed her other arm and yanked her against him. "Do not make the mistake others did and think I have a heart. I do not. And you forget you are my wife and meant to obey me."

That he held her a bit roughly did not trouble her nor did the fierceness in his eyes disturb her or that he reminded her to be an obedient wife. It was that he genuinely believed he had no heart that hurt her own heart the most.

"Everyone has a heart, Slayer, but it depends on what you feed your heart that makes a difference. Your heart has known little to no caring," —she smiled broadly— "but no more. I am going to care for you whether you want me to or not."

Joy snuck up to squeeze at his heart, but rage followed quickly behind it. He was a mighty Gallowglass warrior who led a large troop and reigned over a clan. A caring heart would not serve him well nor would a wife who did not obey him.

"I have no heart and care for nothing, and you, dear wife, need to learn a lesson."

Chapter Ten

Sky felt her body clench anxiously as Slayer swung her up into his arms. He easily carried her to the cottage, and she wondered what lesson he was about to teach her.

Slayer lowered her to her feet as soon as they entered the cottage and ordered, "Disrobe."

She eased away from him. "Why?"

"You do not ask why, wife. You do as I say," he ordered.

He could not mean to consummate their marriage now. He had given his word that he would give her a few days, and, besides, it was only late afternoon. Nightfall was hours away. Weren't wifely duties done at night? And how was consummating their marriage a lesson in obedience?

"You gave me your word that you would give me a few days before we consummated our vows," she reminded, to see if that was his intention.

"Aye, I did, and I will keep my word to you."

"Then why do you want me naked?" she asked, gripping the large shirt she wore at the neck.

"That is not for you to ask, but to obey," he said, intending she learned her lesson of obedience well.

Sky shivered. "I have never been naked in front of anyone."

The thought that anyone other than him would view her naked sparked an unexpected anger in him and he snapped at her. "And you never will be... except in front of me. Now obey me and disrobe."

Obey.

Obedient was something she had been from an early age. Though it was fear that made her so. Fear of the consequences of her affliction if she did not obey her parents. But since arriving at the cottage and having been able to enjoy the freedom of the forest once again, and help any animal in need, she had not given thought to seeking permission. But marriage had changed that.

Having no recourse that she could think of Sky slipped her shoes off, then hesitated, turning away from him. She felt vulnerable now in bare feet. Once she slipped the shirt off, how would she feel?

Terrified.

Nay, she could not do that. She could not do what she warned Slayer against. She would not feed her heart terror or fear her husband. If she did, she would forever fear the intimacy of marriage. They were wed and they would remain wed. If she did not take some control of her fear now, it would forever haunt her and their marriage and that was not something she wanted. It was not how she wanted to live her life.

With a silent prayer on her lips for courage, she slipped the shirt off and turned to face him.

His back was to her. He was completely naked. She turned her eyes away, thinking it was wrong to look upon him even though she had done so recently, but she could not help but sneak another peek. His back was broad with muscles, his waist slim, his backside taut and his legs long and muscular. There was power in his every simple movement. She could only imagine the power he exuded when in the throes of battle. And she wondered what kind of power he would have over her when they coupled.

Slayer turned and walked slowly toward her amazed by her beauty. Her soft curves enticed, his hands aching to follow every bend and line of her lovely body. Her breasts were high and firm and would overflow in his hand. Her nipples were puckered and a rosy color just like her lips, and he intended to taste both. To him, she was perfection, but... he did not like that she shivered. Did she tremble because she was cold or because she was frightened of him?

It mattered not. He had decided to teach her a lesson and he would see it done.

When he reached her, he scooped her up in his arms and carried her to the bed, placing her down on it, then joining her.

He stretched out on his side beside her, his hand reaching up to cup her cheek while he brushed her rosy lips with his thumb. "I am going to explore your body and you are going to submit to my touch as is your duty as my wife and as it is your duty to obey me."

Her eyes turned wide. She was not expecting that. She did not even know if it was proper for him to touch places on her body that she rarely touched herself.

I will never harm you. You are safe with me.

She was glad she recalled his often repeated and reassuring words and since he had kept his word since meeting him, there was no reason to think that he would not keep it now.

She said the one thing she felt would help ease her worry. "I trust you, Slayer."

Bloody hell, but the woman could land a good punch and this one hit directly in the heart. That annoyed him even more since his plan was not only to teach her about obedience but also to prove he had no heart. But who was he truly trying to prove it to, Sky or himself?

His hand itched to touch her and that was unusual since he had never been so eager to touch a woman as he was to touch his wife. He intended to keep control of his desire since this was not about consummating their vows but when his hand drifted slowly along her slender neck, his manhood had other ideas and took control.

He stilled his hand when it reached her silky-soft shoulder, having never felt such soft skin and enjoying the feel of it. But he was eager to reach her breasts and when he did, he cupped one gently in his hand and ran his thumb faintly over her puckered nipple.

Sky did not expect his languid touch to feel so good or for it to spark something inside her, and she gasped.

Keep focused, he reminded himself, hearing her surprising response to his touch but it was proving difficult. He enjoyed touching his wife more than he expected or intended to. Soon his hand left her breast to explore more of her while he settled his lips on her nipple.

Sky gasped again when his tongue rolled over her nipple then tugged gently at it with his teeth. She could not contain the moan that slipped from her lips, nor could she stop her body from squirming beneath him, her body awakening and responding to his touch. He'd been truthful with her when he said she would come to know his touch, but he had failed to tell her how much she would enjoy it.

She was soon lost in a haze of passion she had never known existed but found she quite favored. And the more his hands explored her, kissed her, the more she wanted him to.

"Slayer," she cried out shocked when his hand slipped between her legs and was more shocked when his finger slid into her. Her body responded, arching, welcoming him. His touch felt as if it woke some primal sensation in her that once awakened would never sleep again, never be ignored, would always demand attention.

His lips captured hers, strong and demanding, urging her to respond, though it was not necessary. She was eager to return his kiss, eager to experience more, feel more, share more.

Sadness gripped her and could be heard in her moan when his lips suddenly left hers, but it was not long before she moaned with pleasure once again, as he explored her body with intimate kisses and in places that blushed her cheeks red.

His touch soon turned demanding, and her body did as well. She became a prisoner of the passion that surged through her, and she did not mind being held captive by it. Captive of her husband's intimate touches that were pleasurable beyond words.

Instinct or pleasure had her pleading, "Please, Slayer. Please."

She lay stunned when his touch came to an abrupt halt. She rushed her eyes open and hurried to connect with his. Seeing that he had gone still and stared at her with a look in his eyes she did not recognize, she waited anxiously for what would come next, not knowing what to say or do.

She sighed with relief when his touch returned, and soon after his thumb brushed across a spot that had her crying out with intense passion and grabbing hold of his arms as if she needed to anchor herself.

Slayer rested his cheek against hers to whisper in her ear, "Let go, Sky, I will catch you. I will always catch you."

His whispered reassurance that he would be there for her was all she needed to let go and fall into what seemed like a never-ending spiral of exquisite pleasure, where in the end, she would find herself safely in Slayer's arms. And she did.

Only as soon as she opened her eyes, Slayer left the bed, grabbed his shirt, slipped it on, and left the cottage.

She stared dumbfounded at the closed door, her breathing having yet to calm down and the sensation that consumed her body still sparking in her. Had she done something wrong? She did not know what to think or do, but then her mind was far too hazy, sparks of passion still spiking in her and not allowing her to think clearly.

She lay there trying to calm her body and clear her mind. *Think, Sky, think*, she silently urged herself.

Lesson. He meant to teach her a lesson, to be obedient. She smiled. After all the years of being dutiful, this was one duty she would have no trouble obeying. So, why had he left her so abruptly? Had he not found the pleasure that she had? Or had she disappointed him? She did not like to think that, but not knowing what to think and having no experience with it, left it ripe with good or bad possibilities.

She could make no sense of it. It was no wonder she fared better with the animals in the woods. They were far less complex than humans.

A shiver reminded her that she was naked, and she hurried to slip on her shift, preferring not to be naked when her husband returned. Though not at all sure what she would say to him.

***

Slayer went to the stream, yanked off his shirt and emerged himself in the chilly water. He expected to control his need like he always did when he was with a woman. He had never expected his passion to take control of him. He had had to fight to keep himself from plunging himself into Sky and satisfying a need, a passion that overwhelmed him. His intention had been to introduce her to pleasure, bring her to the brink of climax, and end it there. Explain that they would wait a few days to consummate their vows as he had promised. A lesson that his word was law, and she would obey it. But he could not do it. Seeing the passion smoldering in her eyes, he could not leave her on that edge. He had to let her fall into pleasure and catch her.

He had failed in what he had intended to do and all because he could not stand to hurt Sky that way. To leave her wanting, aching, unsatisfied. And what did that prove? That somehow Sky had touched his heart. That somehow, he had come to care for her, deeply care for her, and that shocked him.

Slayer sat by the stream trying to make sense of it all, but his thoughts only went round and round in circles. He did not realize how long he had sat there until he realized dusk was settling over the land. He returned to the cottage not knowing what he would say to Sky. And he was relieved when he found her in bed asleep. Tomorrow would be soon enough for them to talk and by then, perhaps, he would come to his senses and return to his heartless ways.

***

"Wake up, Slayer. Wake up! I need your help. I need it now!"

"Warrand! Where are you, Warrand?"

"Hurry, Slayer! Hurry!"

"I'm on my way, Warrand. I will be there soon."

"Too late. Too late. Wolves. Pay heed to the wolves."

Slayer jolted up in bed, breathing heavily and jumped when he felt a hand rest on his shoulder.

"Are you all right?" Sky asked, her heart beating madly from being jolted awake and concerned for what had startled her husband awake.

"Aye, go back to sleep," he commanded and slipped out of bed.

He went to the fire pit and added more logs to the dwindling flames, then stood there and stared at them.

He dreamt of Warrand every now and then. It was always the same dream. He would never reach him in time to save his life, but this dream was different. In this dream, Warrand warned him to pay attention to the wolves. What had wolves to do with his brother's death?

Slayer shook his head. He should have been there for his brother. He should have saved his life and given his own life if necessary. It had been his duty to keep his brother safe and he had failed him. He could not fail in avenging his brother's death. He had to find whoever did this and make them suffer before he took their lives.

Sky watched her husband standing naked by the fire, his back to her and his head bowed. Something had disturbed his sleep, a nightmare, she presumed since he woke with such a start, and it appeared it still disturbed him.

She hadn't known when he had returned to the cottage since she had grown tired waiting for him and had fallen asleep. The nightmare had left him upset. He reminded her of a wounded animal in the forest all alone with no one to help him. She had helped many animals in need, her heart would not let her do otherwise. And her heart hurt terribly seeing her husband facing his upset alone.

She got out of bed, her linen shift falling just above her ankles, and quietly made her way to him. She was not sure what she would do once she reached him but then instinct took over. A hug often helped animals and humans alike. She did not hesitate when she reached him. She slipped her arms around his waist and pressed herself against his back and laid her head there as well.

Slayer was so lost in his thoughts that he had not heard her approach and he almost jumped when her arms locked around him, but he didn't. He maintained his detachment until she pressed herself tight against his back and hugged him with the fiercest, most meaningful hug he had ever felt. She was offering comfort, and her kind and caring gesture broke through his defenses.

He turned, his arms circling her waist to ease her from behind his back and tuck her against him, then he rested his brow against hers.

"I am here for you, husband," she whispered softly.

I need you. Slayer was startled by his thought and even more startled that it was true. He needed her. He needed to lose himself in her gentle kindness, tender touch, loving heart.

When he raised his brow off hers, she saw something in his eyes that she never expected to see... indecision. She was glad to see it there since it told her that he had feelings, which meant he was not heartless. It also meant that he presently battled with himself over his response to her.

"Whenever you need me, I will be there for you," she said, accepting and committing to her vows and to her husband.

That she willingly, selflessly pledged she would be there for him whenever he needed her solidified her acceptance of their marriage. It tore at something in his heart, or had it awakened something in him? Something he long ago buried. Whatever it was did not matter. The only thing that mattered was Sky.

He hurried her shift off her, scooped her up into his arms, and carried her to the bed. He stretched out beside her and took hold of her chin. "Once this is done, nothing can undo it. You will be mine forever."

"And will you be mine forever?" she asked, her question surprising her.

"Aye, I will," Slayer said without giving it a thought. "And we will seal that pledge between us now."

He kissed her, his lips firm on hers, and she welcomed him. She enjoyed Slayer's lips on hers, gentle at times, demanding at other times. She could not imagine enjoying a kiss with anyone other man than Slayer. It was as if fate had matched them perfectly.

Slayer found immense joy in kissing Sky. It was as if her lips were made specially for him and no one else. Just the thought of her kissing another man sent his blood boiling. His lips would be the only one to touch hers. She was made for him and no other and he feared he would never get enough of her.

He wanted to take his time with her, explore as he had done earlier, but his need for her had grown him so hard that he did not think he could wait long. And yet his hands could not stop exploring the curves, valleys, and lines of her lovely body. To him, she was perfection, and he loved the feel of every inch of her.

She responded so easily to his touch that her moans of pleasure grew him even harder. He needed to be inside her, or his seed would spill before he had a chance to slip inside her and seal their vows.

What nearly pushed him over the edge was the look in her eyes when he slipped his arm under her waist and lifted her just enough to fit beneath him perfectly. Never had he seen such trust and caring as he did in her eyes. For a sheer moment, he almost stopped and moved off her, freeing her of a marriage she had known nothing about. But he didn't. He did not want to let her go, not ever. She belonged to him always and he needed to make sure of that.

She felt his hesitancy and felt compelled to say, "If you do not want this—"

Rage fired his passion at the thought of her slipping away from him and he plunged into her and cursed himself when she cried out in pain.

He stilled. "I hurt you."

"Just a bit," she said, biting at her lower lip.

Slayer wanted to pummel himself for hurting her. He had not intended for it to be like this for her first time. But then he had not intended to have feelings for her, feelings he had yet to come to understand.

He kissed her brow, her cheek, her lips. "I did not mean to hurt you."

Sky knew it was the closest to an apology she would ever get from him, and it touched her heart.

She smiled softly. "It would hurt much more if you did not finish."

A smile lightly touched the corners of his mouth. "You want me that much, wife?"

"More than I ever thought I would."

"I want you more," he said, surprising her as well as himself and showed her just how much.

Her moans filled the cottage as he moved within her slowly, rapidly, slowly again, then rapidly and growing ever stronger. She gripped his arms as if she feared he would slip away from her and held onto him as tightly as she could.

She cried out with pleasure and Slayer rested his cheek next to hers and whispered, "Let go and I will join you and be there to catch you."

"Always?" she asked with a gasped breath.

"Always, wife," he assured her.

Sky let go and plunged with her husband into exquisite pleasure, assured that his arms would always be there to catch her.

Chapter Eleven

Slayer woke with a smile. He never ever recalled waking with a smile but after last night with his wife, he could not keep the smile off his face. It vanished fast when he realized he did not feel her beside him in bed.

"Bloody hell!"

He jumped out of bed and hurried into his garments. How was it that he did not feel her leaving the bed yet again? He raked his fingers through his hair as he glanced around once outside. Of course, she was nowhere in sight, but he knew where to find her. He hurried to the stream.

He heard her laughter, a full, hardy laugh, before he reached her, and he found his smile returning. He stopped to peer past the trees and bushes and watched her. She laughed at two squirrels scampering around her in play and she waved at them when they rushed off up a tree.

He was about to step forward when he saw movement in the bushes not far from his wife.

"I have food if you're hungry," he heard her say and he waited to see who she had spoken to.

His eyes went wide when a scrawny fox appeared and took cautious steps toward her.

"I have berries," she said and scooped a handful from the basket beside her and held them out to the fox.

"Come and enjoy. They are tasty." She placed some on the ground.

The fox hurried forward and gobbled up the berries.

"Oh my, you are thin," she said, looking over the animal with concern. "It appears that you injured your leg and that has left you unable to hunt while it heals. Though it does appear it is healing well." She scooped up a bigger handful of berries from the basket. "Here you go. Eat as much as you like. I can pick more."

The animals recognized her trusting and kind soul immediately and he had to admit he had felt it himself, even more so last night when they coupled. There was something about her innocent touch that was different. While her touch easily enflamed his passion it had also soothed something in him that left him feeling more complete, more satisfied than he had ever felt in his life.

Sky stood. "I am eager to see my husband who waits, I believe, impatiently in the bushes, so follow me and I will leave more berries for you where no one will disturb you. I will be right back, Slayer."

He shook his head. How did she know he was there?

"Do not go far," he called out as he made his way to the stream, and she disappeared into the woods, the fox keeping pace with her.

"I won't," she called back.

He kneeled at the water's edge and scooped up a handful of water to scrub away the last vestiges of sleep. He heard her approach as he wiped his face dry with the hem of his plaid and smiled when he felt her hand rest on his shoulder. He quickly snatched her around the waist and brought her down into his lap and kissed her to satisfy the ache of missing her lips since he woke this morning.

She tasted sweet from the berries she had eaten, and he ran his hand up one sleeve to stroke her arm, aching to feel her soft skin. He told himself it would do until he could get her naked again, but he found his desire for her could overwhelm him quickly and he had to be careful and not chase after her like a barbarian who could not control himself.

Sky eagerly returned his kiss and sighed contentedly when it ended. "I never imagined I would enjoy kissing so much."

"Me. Only me," he ordered with a fierce scowl and got annoyed when she scrunched her face in disgust, thinking she did not agree.

"That is a terrible thought." Disgust grew on her face. "I only want your lips on mine. I could not stomach another man kissing me."

A smile hurried to his lips, but a sudden thought stopped it short of surfacing. "I am glad to hear that, but tell me, Sky… are you all right? Did I hurt you last night?"

A soft smile lit her face. "I am good, and you did not hurt me." Her cheeks blushed pink. "I quite enjoy coupling with you."

"Then you don't mind if we do it often?" he asked teasingly.

She chuckled lightly. "It is my duty."

"Nay," he ordered firmly. "I never want you to couple with me out of duty, only out of desire."

"Will you do the same? Couple with me not out of duty but out of desire?"

He did not stop his smile from surfacing. "Believe me, wife, it will definitely be out of desire."

She was shocked that he desired her, and it filled her heart with joy and hope for the future.

"That makes me happy to know," she said.

He did not mean to voice his thoughts, but he did. "I never make people happy, just the opposite."

Sky kissed his cheek, wishing his smile would remain on his face. "Well, you fill me with joy, and your smile makes my joy that more joyful."

"A smile is not something you will see on me often," he cautioned. "Besides," —he poked at her stomach— "you smile enough for the both of us. So, did you save any of those berries for me or did you give them all to the fox."

"I saved you plenty."

"Good," he said, easing her off his lap and onto her feet, then standing. "We will take them back to the cottage to enjoy while we talk."

"Aye. I would like that. You can tell me about your nightmare. My mum always made me tell her about any nightmare I had. She insisted the only way to be rid of them was to talk about them. That if I kept them hidden, they would only grow stronger along with my fears."

He took the basket from her as they walked and munched on the berries. "Did you have many nightmares?"

"I had a recurring one when I was young. Perhaps my mum was right about talking about the nightmare since I haven't had it in many years."

"Tell me about it," he urged, eager to learn all he could about his wife.

Sky had shared the dream with only her mum, yet she felt a need to share it with Slayer. "There is a woman dancing before a blazing fire. She is beautiful and she holds a dagger in her hand. I hear chanting and drumming. Though I fear getting too close to her, I cannot help but continue to walk toward her. When I am not far from her, she stops dancing, glares at me, and turns into a wolf. That is when I wake up screaming." She shivered at the fearful memory.

Slayer snuck his arm around her, seeing how the retelling of the nightmare frightened her. "I will not let any wolf get you."

"I believe it is the reason I have been hesitant to make friends with the wolves I sometimes see in the forest."

"Wolves are vicious creatures. Keep your distance from them and on that you will obey me," Slayer ordered, the thought of her going anywhere near such ferocious beasts alarming. When she did not respond, he stopped walking, forcing her to do the same.

"Aye, husband," she said, to avoid arguing with him. But she truly did not know that if she came across a wolf in need that she would not help him.

"We may as well enjoy the sun while it lasts," Slayer said and walked to the large oak tree and helped her sit beneath it before joining her and placing the basket of berries on her lap for them both to enjoy.

"What about your nightmare from last night?" she asked.

His brow puckered. "Strange that your recurring dream was about a wolf since I was warned to pay heed to wolves in my dream. I have had similar dreams to the one I had last night, Warrand pleading for help, then telling me I was too late. Only last night he warned me to pay attention to the wolves."

"What would wolves have to do with his death?"

He shook his head. "I don't know."

He watched her tilt her head and her brow narrow as she gave it thought. He did not know how any man could look upon her and not see her beauty before even noticing she had two different colored eyes. The more he looked at them, the more her eyes enticed and intrigued, and the more they added to her beauty.

He reached out and gently rubbed the spot between her eyes. "Don't over worry it."

"Does he warn you of danger? Or is it attention to the wolves, a pack who protects their own that he tries to tell you about?"

"I never thought of it that way," Slayer said, suddenly looking at her and his brother and father's deaths differently.

"What way?"

"That someone may have no interest in claiming the clan for himself." He shook his head slowly. "That his only true interest could be in seeing what is left of my family dead."

Sky's eyes went wide. "That could change the questions you ask yourself and those who may know something."

Rory, the liar, came to mind, and he planned on questioning him again.

There was an even huger worry that came along with that possibility. "If that is a possibility, it is even more imperative that we keep our marriage a secret. You are already in harm's way. I will not see it made worse for you."

"You have no word on Leora yet?" she asked, her worry about her sisters continuing to haunt her.

"Nay, but I have no doubt it will not be long before we hear something," he assured her.

They continued to talk and enjoy each other. Even when clouds drifted in overhead, they remained as they were, talking laughing, kissing. It took a few raindrops falling before they hurried into the cottage.

Slayer barely had the door latched behind them when he scooped his wife around the waist to lift her, leaving her feet unable to touch the ground but allowing him to easily kiss her. His lips moved to her ear to nibble along it and whisper, "I have a hungry desire for you, wife."

"And I for you, husband," she whispered back.

"Time to get naked again," he said and nibbled along her neck.

A pink blush tinged her cheeks.

Her blush highlighted her beauty but also concerned him. "You are uncomfortable being naked in front of me? There is nothing I have not already seen."

"I know. It is just that I never thought to be naked in front of you. I thought married couples just shifted their garments around and was done with it."

"Where is the pleasure in that? Though it would do in a pinch." A quick image of tossing her garment up and satisfying them quickly was quite appealing.

"You will be patient with me while I learn?"

"You do well already."

Sky spoke softly and a bit reluctantly. "But I have yet to explore you as you do me."

"Then we will get naked, and you can explore me all you want."

"You would not mind?"

"I insist," he said, his growing manhood also insisting.

While the rain beat down on the cottage, Sky proceeded to explore her husband's naked body. Smiles and laughter were shared until the passion grew so hot that Slayer took command and satisfied them both.

They talked, ate, and coupled the day away, and when night barely touched the land, they fell asleep in each other's arms, far too exhausted for any nightmares to disturb them.

Chapter Twelve

Time was running out for them and it broke Sky's heart to think that their solitary time here would soon be no more. The last few weeks had been blissful, a dream come true. She had come to know Slayer, the man, not the Gallowglass warrior, and she could not stop herself from falling in love with him. She woke most mornings in his arms and was showered with kisses. Some mornings they coupled, other mornings they lay in bed and talked. Days were filled with walks in the woods or spending time by the stream.

When rain forced them inside, they stayed occupied with tender touches, soft kisses, and endless pleasure. This time with him taught her how love could be born from the strangest of circumstances and no matter how hard one might try to deny it, it simply was not possible. It settled into the heart and refused to let go. And a touch that had been nothing more than an innocent touch was now a caress that trembled the heart, and a tender kiss now sparked passion, and when hands were simply held, it was a reminder that neither would ever let go of the other.

But like all dreams you eventually wake up and Sky feared she would wake soon, and her lovely dream would be gone, and the Slayer she had come to know and to love would vanish, replaced by the feared Gallowglass leader.

But how could she love one and not the other when they were one and the same man?

Sky watched Slayer talking with a large warrior from where she pretended to work in the garden, tending to the plants that were flourishing. She had heard him call the warrior Clyde as the two walked a distance away to talk. That her husband hadn't wanted her to hear what they discussed was obvious, so she had gone to the garden to wait.

A lovely red crossbill suddenly landed on her shoulder and began chirping in her ear insistently.

Many believed that she could speak with animals and birds but that was not true. However, she had learned to understand their actions, thus forming a type of communication with them. Something in the forest had upset the crossbill, hence her insistent chirping, and seeing how Slayer fisted his one hand as he spoke with Clyde, something upset him as well.

"Thank you, my friend, for letting me know that trouble brews in the forest," she whispered, and the bird flew off her shoulder.

She cast another glance at her husband, and she could almost see him transform in front of her eyes. His stance had turned commanding, his shoulders were drawn back tight, and his eyes narrowed. She watched, wishing she could hear what they were discussing.

***

"Lowlanders have crossed the border into the Highlands," Clyde said. "We have yet to find out why they are here, but the substantial fee offered for the mission to see the Murdock sisters dead may have something to do with it. The large fee is drawing endless mercenary groups to the area, though some wisely retreat when they learn it is the Gallowglass they will face." Clyde shook his head. "The foolish or desperate pay no heed to it."

"The promise of wealth can turn the wisest man foolish," Slayer said.

"There is something you need to know, my lord," Clyde said with a quick glance at Sky. "I only learned it and I do not know if the news has reached Cavell yet, but he should be made aware of it as well since it means his wife is no longer in danger."

"Explain," Slayer ordered.

"It has been made known that the woman they search for has reddish blonde hair and only two of the Murdock sisters have that color hair. Cavell's wife is safe."

Not so Sky, Slayer thought with a glance at his wife, and he gripped his fist tighter.

He had been enjoying his time here with Sky, alone, with little to bother them. This news reminded him of his duties not only to his wife but to his clan as well. It was time to leave here and return home.

"You are sure about this news?" Slayer asked, though he trusted Clyde's word.

"Not a doubt about it," Clyde said, his glance falling on Sky.

"Has any word reached us from Melvin yet?" Slayer asked. "He has been gone long enough to let me know what he has learned and also what goes on at Clan Murdock with Cavell and his wife, Elsie."

"Not a peep from him. I could go and see if anything prevents him from sending word to us and deliver the news to Cavell," Clyde offered.

"Take a few warriors with you," he ordered.

Clyde laughed. "This is a one-man mission. I need no help or protection."

"Mercenaries roam the area—"

"And what interest would they have in a single warrior? There is nothing to fear and I fear nothing. But I am no fool and will be cautious. Besides, alone I can travel faster which means I return home faster."

Clyde was one of his most skilled and seasoned warriors and had been with him since he took command of a Gallowglass troop and grew it into the most feared and victorious troop to fight against.

With no argument from Slayer, Clyde said, "I will leave in the morning and return before you can miss me." He looked about to say more but held his tongue.

"Say what you will, Clyde."

"You are a wise leader who makes wise decisions. It would be wise of you to leave here soon and take residence in the castle now that so many more mercenaries fill the area."

"My thought as well, Clyde. We leave here in two days."

***

Two days. Sky managed to catch the two words. Her heart turned heavy, and she glanced over the flourishing garden. "I wish I could be here for harvesttime, but I fear that will not be possible."

Another warrior suddenly appeared to speak with her husband and Clyde stepped aside, walking toward the cottage to stand and wait.

She made her way toward him. He was a large man and older than most of Slayer's warriors she had seen. "Can I offer you something? A brew perhaps?"

He stared at her, and she wondered if it was her eyes that seemed to leave him speechless.

He coughed as if clearing his throat. "Nay. But thank you."

She did not know what else to say to him, never having spoken to any of Slayer's warriors. She had been foolish to try and speak with him, learn something he had told Slayer. His warriors would never reveal anything to her.

She smiled. "Stay safe, Clyde."

He looked at oddly at her.

"Do I have your name wrong? I thought I heard Slayer call you Clyde."

"Aye, that is my name and again, thank you."

Slayer called out to him.

Clyde went to walk away but stopped briefly to say, "Lord Slayer will keep you safe, Sky."

She smiled as he walked away, the warrior having acknowledged her by her name as someone who did not fear her would do, and it pleased her.

She turned and felt a catch in her chest as she stared at the cottage. She had left the window and door open to let in an oddly sunny and warm spring day. She was not prone to constant tears, having learned they did little to help a situation, but she felt them now pooling in her eyes. She had found a spark of happiness here with Slayer, something she had never expected to find. Something she did not want to lose. But there was the worry of the danger she and her sisters still faced and concern for Slayer's safety as well with his brother having been killed and his father poisoned. And there was her husband, a feared Gallowglass leader she needed to come to know more about, love even more, and fear even less.

"Sky."

She brushed away the tears before they could fall and turned to face Slayer with a smile.

Slayer went to her, his hand hurrying to grip the back of her neck as concern filled his eyes. "Why do your eyes glisten with tears? Are you in pain? Did you hurt yourself in the garden?"

She gave no thought to making an excuse. She spoke the truth to him. "Nay, I realized that our time here will end soon and I will miss being here alone with you. I have very much enjoyed our time together and I will always cherish the memories we made here."

"Our memories don't end here," Slayer said, her words sounding as if their time together was coming to an end, something he would never allow to happen. "We have the rest of our lives to fill with memories and I look forward to making them with you."

His remark touched her heart since to her it said that he cared for her and that gave her hope that someday he might come to more than just care for her.

"As do I with you," she said.

He kissed her, a more demanding than gentle one, and she felt the tension in it. Something disturbed him.

"What's wrong, Slayer?" she asked when she managed to break the kiss.

"Nothing," he snapped and claimed her lips again so forcefully that her bottom lip caught on one of her teeth and she gasped in pain.

Slayer pulled his lips off hers.

"That hurt," she said, her hand going to her mouth.

"Bloody hell," Slayer mumbled, angry with himself and left the cottage.

Sky tasted blood in her mouth and fear sent a shiver through her. Slayer, the Gallowglass warrior, had returned, and she was not sure how to deal with him. She shook her head. How could she love part of him and fear the other? It was like the animals in the woods. She loved them but she also knew that they could be dangerous when cornered or hungry. Those times she avoided them or approached them differently.

Then she recalled how he had given his word to her that he would never harm her, that she was safe with him. And if anything, her husband was a man of his word. She told herself to always remember his pledge to her and went in search of him.

He hadn't gone far. He stood under a large oak tree, his back braced against it.

His hand shot up to ward her off. "Leave me be! Anger invades me and I will not have it touch you." He shook his head. "I did not mean to hurt you."

"I know," she said and smiled as she walked toward him. "You are troubled. We should talk before we kiss again." She quickly licked her lip to stop the blood she felt in her mouth from reaching her lips.

Slayer pushed himself off the tree and had his hand at her chin so fast that it caused Sky to gasp.

"Is that blood? Did I cause you to bleed?" he demanded, his fingers tugging gently at her lip to have a look. "Bloody hell!"

He shut his eyes briefly trying to contain his anger at seeing the blood in her mouth. He knew the calm he had known with Sky these past few weeks would not last, that the powerful warrior within him would rise and take command again. But he never intended to visit that fierceness upon Sky.

She tried to reassure him. "It's nothing."

"It most certainly is something. I had no right to hurt you."

"You did not mean to."

"That's no excuse and never should you accept it as one."

"And should I have lashed out at you and suffered the blow of your hand on my cheek for doing so?"

"I gave you my word that you were safe with me. You should have trusted it," he argued.

She eased his hand off her chin. "I did and it is why I came in search of you. Now will you tell me what troubles you?" It was easy to see that he was reluctant to tell her. "We have shared and talked about many things these last few weeks. Please don't stop talking and sharing with me."

He did not want to cause her more pain or upset or frighten her, though the warrior in him warned against such a foolish thought. She needed to know. "It has been learned that the woman the mercenaries search for has reddish blonde hair."

Sky instinctively grabbed a strand of her hair. "That means it is either me or Leora they search for."

"Aye, and it has also been learned that a group of Lowlanders has crossed the border into the Highlands, but the reason is unknown as of yet."

"But you think it may have something to do with the search for the woman with the reddish blonde hair."

"I doubt it is a coincidence," he said and wiped away a small spot of blood on her lower lip with his finger. It fired his anger all over again that he had hurt her, though he was not surprised that he could not harden his heart against it.

What surprised him was that he had come to care a great deal for his wife these past few weeks. It wasn't only the pleasure he found in coupling with her, it was the time they spent together talking and laughing over foolish tales of when they were very young. There was also the contented silence they shared at times. There was not a time spent here that he did not enjoy being with his wife and the realization was something he continued to try and understand.

Sky left him to his silence having come to realize there were times he needed silence to think. She watched his eyes shift with his thoughts, from anger to concern, then troubled. She had come to understand the difference and it allowed her to come to know him better.

"Two days," Slayer said. "We leave for Clan Ravinsher in two days."

"I will be sorry to leave here," she said.

"It is better not to get attached to anything." Slayer almost shook his head hearing his father's words coming from his mouth.

"Too late," she said with a gentle smile. "I have already grown attached to this lovely place but more so to you."

She had not intended to say that and yet she had not been able to stop herself.

"Don't," he warned. "I am not the man you think I am."

"But you are," she said defending him.

He took hold of her arm. "Nay. Do not be so foolish and so blind. I go to the compound. I do not know how long I will be gone."

He walked away disappearing into the woods and Sky could not help but feel he was leaving her.

***

Dark gray clouds filled the sky by the time Slayer returned to the cottage later that day. The door to the cottage was closed but the window was open, and he saw that his wife was busy inside. She was probably preparing the evening meal for them. He had come to cherish that time with her and was glad he had since in two days' time it would be no more.

The thought added to his anger that had flared even more since earlier. Rory had proved useless to talk with, changing his story repeatedly yet again and embellishing it outrageously. He had ordered him taken to Clan Ravinsher where he would be held prisoner until he could determine if the man would be of any use to him. But what annoyed him the most was that he had unexpected feelings for his wife. His intention in staying at the cottage was for her to accept their marriage and seal their vows. Developing feelings for his wife had not been part of the plan and did not help the situation.

He slipped his shirt off and grabbed the axe by the pile of logs and began swinging it, breaking logs in two with just one powerful swing. He split log after log relentlessly until he felt his arm muscles burn though he didn't stop. His fierce swings reminded him of battle when he would swing his sword striking warrior after warrior until the bodies piled around him just as the split logs did now.

He counted on that unyielding fierceness and an uncaring soul to see him through every battle, to see him to victory.

He swung around ready to strike when a hand landed on his back, and he yanked the axe back when he saw it was his wife and that she cringed as if waiting for the blow. It was only then he realized it was raining and he was soaked.

"Go back inside," he ordered, the rain running down his face.

"Come with me," she urged, her cloak nearly soaked.

He stepped away from her, fearing if he touched her that he would not be tender with her. "Go! Leave me be."

There was an anger in his eyes that she did not understand and while she told herself to pay heed to it, she was more concerned with the pain she saw there as well. Her husband was hurting, and her heart hurt for him.

"Nay, I will not leave you be," she said and reached out to take his hand.

Slayer did not move fast enough or maybe he didn't move fast enough on purpose. Maybe he wanted to feel her touch. Maybe he wanted the excuse to... he grabbed her around the waist and yanked her hard against him. His lips came down on hers crushing them in a forceful kiss.

He needed her. He had to have her. He had to lose himself in her.

He yanked her up so that her feet did not touch the ground as he walked to the large oak tree. He tore his mouth off hers before reaching the tree and ordered, "Wrap your legs around me."

I will never harm you.

Those words chanted in her head and trusting his promise, she did as he said and as he lifted her, she brought her legs around his waist and locked them there. He braced her against the tree, keeping one arm firmly around her waist as his hand dug at her garments, pushing them out of his way.

His overwhelming need for her fired her own need for him and she reached down and helped him shift their garments so that he could...

She gasped so loud at his powerful entrance that she feared it echoed past the sound of the pouring rain and throughout the forest.

"Hold onto me," he commanded.

She tried to grip his arms, but it was difficult, the rain making them slippery. She hurried her arms around his neck and locked her fingers tight then rested her face next to his.

Her passionate moans echoed in his ear, fueling his own passion and he drove into her with a need he did not think could ever be satisfied, and yet... he felt. That strange feeling of not just pleasure but something more, something he had never felt before, something he wanted to feel forever.

He pressed his wet cheek against hers and groaned, his passion ready to explode and demanded, "Fall with me, Sky."

She was so close to the edge that she fell right off, screaming Slayer's name as she burst with pleasure.

He joined her, his arm keeping tight hold of her around her waist while bracing his free hand against the tree for support and, dropping his head back, he released a roar that sounded like a mighty beast. When his pleasure finally abated, he shuddered, and he was pleased to feel her shudder as well.

Sky's head fell on his shoulder, unable to hold it up, her pleasure having robbed her of all her strength.

Sanity returned to him and feeling how limp she lay in his arms, how heavily the rain poured down upon them, thinking how he had pounded into her, possibly hurting her, he nearly roared again for what he had done.

As if the heavens agreed with him, lightning struck, a dazzling streak of light splitting through the sky, and thunder pounded the earth viciously. A crack sounded above them, and he heard a branch splinter. He slipped out of her and crushed her against the tree trunk, shielding her with his body as a tree branch came crashing down.

Sky cringed hearing the branch splinter. Leaves and branch debris fell along with it as the rain took on a forceful intensity. She couldn't move, Slayer had her pinned so tightly against the tree trunk. His whole body shielded her, and she worried for his own safety.

Slayer did not budge until the fallen tree branch had settled on the ground, then he eased himself off his wife, anxious to see how she fared.

He plucked a leaf and a couple of twigs out of her wet hair before placing his face close to hers so she could hear him over the rolling thunder. "Are you all right?"

She nodded and gripped his arm. "And you?"

"Good," he said. "We need to get inside."

His arm went around her waist and he lifted her over the large fallen branch that blocked their path to the cottage.

Once inside, he ordered, "Get out of those wet garments."

She turned to tell him to do the same as he shut the door and her eyes widened in alarm. "Your back bleeds." She hurried to him.

She reached him before he could stop her.

"It is nothing," he said, brushing off her concern, though touched by it.

"I will see for myself, then we both can shed our wet garments," she said, snatching a clean cloth from the nearby basket, then took hold of his hand and tugged him toward the bench at the table.

Rainwater dripped off them both as Sky cleaned the blood off his back. Relief was heard in her voice when she said, "A minor wound that a dab of honey will help heal."

Slayer stood. "Later. Now, get out of those wet garments."

He finished before her having only his plaid and boots to be rid of, then he helped her get out of her remaining garments and wrapped a blanket around her. He moved the two benches in front of the fire pit and got them each a clean cloth to dry their hair. The heat of the fire helped dry and warm them, and pops and sizzles were heard from the drops that hit the fiery flames as they squeezed the rainwater from their hair before taking the cloth to it.

"We leave tomorrow," he announced suddenly.

Her stomach plunged at the thought of not having another day here with him. "You said two days."

"And now I say we leave tomorrow," he said abruptly and turned to stare at the flames. "You will leave me be when you see me as I was when splitting the logs... filled with anger and rage."

It hurt Sky to even think of doing such a thing and she reached out to rest her hand on his thigh, still damp with rainwater. "I cannot leave you be when I see you hurting."

"You will do as I say," he ordered sternly.

"I cannot go against what my heart tells me. You are my husband, my friend, and I will not leave you to hurt alone."

His tongue was ready to snap at her, order her to obey him, but something stopped him. He couldn't tell if it was the concern in her soft voice or the surprised look in her eyes as if he had asked her to do the impossible.

He leaned his face close to hers. "I will not chance hurting you when I rage with anger."

"You will not hurt me. You gave me your word and I trust your word." She kissed him gently, sealing a promise.

She stirred something in him again, something that continued to make no sense to him, yet he found it comforting and missed it when not in her company. He had always found solitude, a friend, a good companion to have but now, after this time spent with her, he found that he favored being with his wife and that could prove dangerous.

They ate supper mostly in silence as the rain continued to fall and before they got into bed for the night, Slayer told himself to leave her be, that he had demanded enough from her earlier and nearly gotten them both killed. But his wife thought differently as she snuggled against him and her hand began to roam over him, a bit hesitantly as if she was unsure of his response. He quickly let her know he felt the same and they soon were lost in a world all their own, a world that would turn vastly different tomorrow.

Chapter Thirteen

"We will reach home before dusk," Slayer had told her after placing her on her own horse, a mare he called Star, when they had left the cottage earlier today.

Sky had remained silent at the news, her heart aching when she had looked at the cottage for the last time and the garden she would never get to harvest. The further away they had gotten from the cottage the more her apprehension grew, the more she was reminded of what the solitude of the cottage had allowed her to escape and what she would soon have no choice but to face.

Her stomach churned at the prospect of settling into a new home and grew even more upset with the thought of never returning home to Clan Murdock or when she would see her sisters next. She had offered prayers daily for their safety, confident from what Slayer had told her about Cavell that Elsie was safe with him. But she continued to worry about Leora, though she was strong, the strongest out of the three of them. If any of them could survive on their own, Leora could.

Sisters.

She was still finding the news that her parents were not truly her parents or her sisters, blood sisters, difficult to accept. She had avoided thinking about it since it left her feeling troubled. Her sisters and parents would always be just that to her, but she could not help but wonder who she truly was and where she had come from and why had her mother felt the need to give her away. Where was her true home?

Sky glanced at her husband, his eyes intense as he gazed around keeping alert to his surroundings and the troop of warriors that surrounded them. Home was now wherever her husband was, and she so wished that they were back at the lovely cottage in the woods.

He caught her glance and brought his horse beside hers. "Something troubles you?"

"Many things," she admitted.

"All will go well," he assured her. "You will have a good, safe home at Clan Ravinsher."

"People are not very accepting of me," she reminded, though her heart was touched by how easily he had accepted her affliction. From the first, it was as if he had not noticed it at all.

"They will accept you," he said as though he declared it an edict.

Her husband might be confident about that, but she was not.

"We are almost home," he said with a sense of pride and rode off when a warrior shouted out to him.

They entered a narrow path in the forest and Sky watched Slayer turn his horse around and hastily head back toward her. The attack came before he could reach her. Vicious battle roars filled the air as a mixed troop of warriors poured out of the forest.

Sky froze for only a moment, but it was long enough for a man to knock her off her horse. As she scrambled to her feet, she grabbed a sizeable stone ready to throw it at the man, but four ravens had descended upon him stabbing at his head and face with their beaks, keeping him from harming her. She was suddenly grabbed roughly from behind, the foul odor letting her know he was foe not friend, and she swung her hand back smashing the man in the head. He stumbled back and when she turned another raven was already stabbing the man's head with his beak.

She hurried a glance around and saw Slayer slicing through the barrage of mercenaries to reach her, his face contorted in fury, and her only thought was to get to him as quickly as possible. She dodged and bent past men in combat and jumped over fallen bodies and barely missed hands that reached out to grab her. She was only a short distance away, Slayer having gotten closer in his attempt to reach her, when she was grabbed by the arm, swung around to face a large man who quickly lifted her and swung her over his shoulder and ran into the woods.

Sky battered his back with her fists not that it seemed to do any good, but she kept at it. He was quick for a large man, and she feared he would get too far with her for Slayer to reach her before it was too late. But Slayer would find her. He told her he would always find her, though she would do what she could to make it easier for him.

Her hands stopped their pummeling, and a chill ran through her, hearing a blood-curdling roar. It echoed through the woods like a beast on the prowl and she knew it was her husband. It stopped the man abruptly and she felt him shiver before he continued running. It was only a short time later that he again stopped abruptly.

"REALEASE HER NOW!"

Sky wanted to shout with joy upon hearing her husband's powerful voice, but how had he gotten in front of the man?

Suddenly Gallowglass warriors descended on them, leaving no room for the man to escape.

"I mean her no harm," the man called out.

"Then release her," Slayer demanded.

The man eased Sky off his shoulder but held onto her arm once she was on her feet.

"Let her go," Slayer warned with an icy anger.

"She must come with me," the man said.

Slayer walked toward them. "She stays with me."

Sky knew the forest sounds, what belonged and what didn't. What sounds were no reason for alarm and what sounds were cause for worry. And she saw in her husband's eyes that he had caught the sound too. The soft, whirling sound of an arrow. He was on her in a flash, shielding her with his body as he took her to the ground with such force that her arm was ripped from the man's grasp.

Soon after, she heard the large man fall not far from them and right after that her husband shouted, "Find the archer!"

Slayer braced his hand on the ground to hover above her.

She answered the question she knew was on his tongue. "I am unharmed."

He stood and helped her to her feet and feeling her a bit unsteady, he braced her against him, keeping his arm firm around her.

"You should not hold me so intimately," she whispered, reminding him that no one was to suspect that there was anything intimate between them.

He whispered in return. "I have an excuse for my arm to be where I want it to be."

"I am glad for I want your arm there as well," she admitted shaken from the incident.

He glanced around as if he was more interested in what was going on around him than the woman he held tucked against him.

"How did you get in front of us?" she asked, his arm snug around her, chasing her fear away.

"I know these woods far better than anyone and besides, I told you I would always find you and I will," he reminded.

"I am glad I can count on that," she said and with the last of her fear dissipating, her body went limp against him.

His arm tightened around her waist. "You will ride with me."

"I believe that would be wise," she said and remained resting against him as she turned a glance at the dead man. "Who is he?"

"I don't know, but I do believe there are two different fractions searching for the reddish blonde-haired woman. One who wants her alive and one who wants her dead. We need to get to the safety of the castle, and I need to find out if my warriors suffered any casualties and if any mercenaries were taken alive who could provide some answers."

"How was it that more of your warriors arrived?" she asked, casting a glance at the unfamiliar men around them.

"Word was sent ahead for a troop to meet us since signs were spotted of mercenaries being in the area," Slayer said, then called out orders to his warriors.

It was not long after that that they were once again on the path to Clan Ravinsher. Ominous gray clouds began to gather swiftly in the darkening sky, casting an air of anticipation and it was not too long before Sky spotted a village in the distance. As they got closer, she saw that the village sat outside a high stone wall and beyond it loomed a castle.

Slayer gave her waist a squeeze and whispered, "All will go well. But remember no one can know we are husband and wife."

At that moment, though he held her snugly, she felt him slip away from her and the loneliness that had vanished while at the cottage slowly poked at her.

She took a soft breath and focused on what lay ahead. What she saw impressed and frightened her. Two imposing watchtowers were stationed on the outskirts of the bustling village. Beyond the high stone wall, the upper reaches of the castle peeked through the encroaching darkness. The village, alive with activity, buzzed with the sounds of people engaged in talk and the last chores of the day. Yet, the vibrant scene did not deter them from pausing in their tasks to acknowledge Slayer and praise his victory over the mercenaries.

Hands waved in greeting, smiles were abundant, and enthusiastic shouts of "Welcome home" and "Victory to you, my lord!" echoed through the air. All paid their respect to Lord Slayer and the returning warriors as the group continued their approach to the two large wood doors in the stone wall spread wide open in greeting.

However, smiles soon faded and whispers began when those close enough caught sight of Sky. She was sure word had reached the clan about her affliction and the incident with the stag. News never took long to spread and for trouble to begin. Instinct had her wanting to move closer to Slayer until she recalled that would not be proper with her not being his wife.

"You are safe. Do not worry," Slayer said without glancing at her, though he once again gave her side a squeeze to reassure her.

They passed through the open doors into another thriving village and in the distance the castle. Villagers once again called out greetings to Slayer and once again smiles faded when glances fell on Sky. She thought to lower her head and avoid looking at anyone, but her husband's whispered, harsh command stopped her.

"Do not dare hang your head in shame."

She did as he ordered, though her stomach churned anxiously.

It seemed like it took forever to reach the castle, a large, formidable structure, but once they did, Slayer helped her off his horse and one of his warriors took the reins and led Skell away.

Slayer went to take hold of her hand and stopped himself, muttering, "Bloody hell."

It was not going to be easy to keep his hands off her. Habits had been formed over the last few weeks and one of those habits he enjoyed was holding her hand. He wanted to declare there and then that they were husband and wife, but he had her safety to consider, and the recent attack had reminded him of that.

He followed alongside her up the stairs, muttering his annoyance and ready to rush her off to his bedchamber where he could do more than hold her hand.

He didn't mutter this time. He let his annoyance be known. "Bloody hell."

Sky stopped, worried. "What's wrong?"

"Nothing I cannot fix," he said and opened the keep door, thinking how he would arrange it so that he and his wife would be able to share a bedchamber without anyone knowing.

"Euniss!" Slayer called out upon entering the Great Hall.

Sky was amazed at the size of the room. It was large and adorned with colorful banners that hung from the wood rafters and beautifully crafted tapestries graced the stone walls. A huge fireplace occupied almost a whole wall, its firelight, along with the candles burning in several tall, iron candelabras cast sufficient light around the room. There were too many trestle tables and benches to count, and none were occupied. A dais that sat six people was at the far end of the room and draped with a pristine white cloth. Tapestries depicting battles graced the entire wall behind it.

"Euniss!"

Slayer's repeated shout gave Sky a start and she watched as a stout woman, her plump cheeks glowing red, a pleasant smile on her aged face, and a head full of short, gray curls entered the room and hurried toward Slayer.

"We need food and see that a bath is prepared and have clean garments made available for Sky," Slayer ordered. "She is under the clan's protection and will be staying with us indefinitely."

"So, the battle was more a skirmish and victorious as usual, I hear," Euniss said while staring at Sky. "Goodness gracious, your eyes don't match in color. I have never seen the likes of that before now."

"Will you never learn to hold your tongue," Slayer admonished, the few servants in the room halting their tasks to glance at Sky.

Euniss turned a quick look on Slayer. "If I haven't learned by now to hold my tongue, I never will. And why should it matter.? I say aloud what others will think but will not have the courage to say when they look upon her." She glanced back at Sky. "Are you a witch?"

"Euniss!" Slayer snapped angrily.

The woman folded her arms over her ample breasts. "I promised your dear mum, God rest her soul, on her deathbed that I would look after you. That is a sacred vow I intend to keep." She turned a squinting brow on Sky. "Well, are you a witch?"

Sky smiled at the blunt woman, though not without trepidation. "Nay, I know no witchcraft, nor do I know why I was born with two different colored eyes."

"Well, if you're not in cohorts with the devil then the good Lord must have given them to you for a good reason." Euniss shooed her away. "Go sit by the fire. You look worn out and in need of a good soak in the tub. But first you will eat." She shooed at her again and pointed. "Be off with you, over there."

Shock had Sky not moving. No one had ever suggested her mismatched eye color came from good and not evil, though her mum had assured her that with her kind heart evil could never exist in her.

Slayer pressed his hand lightly on her back and got her moving to a table nearest to the fireplace.

"Euniss has her say more often than she should, and I tolerate her because of her word to my mum. She also oversees the keep and does an excellent job. She is a good soul, and you can trust her."

"I appreciate you telling me that," Sky said as he sat down beside her on the bench, pressing his leg against hers beneath the table. She kept a soft smile on her face as she spoke with a whisper to him. "I miss the intimacy of the cottage already."

He missed it as well, yet he never had any intention of it turning out the way it did. It had simply been part of a plan conceived out of duty. But somehow that had changed, and he was not sure how to adjust to it.

He let her know he felt the same by pressing his leg firmer against hers and she graced him with a lovely smile and damn if it didn't tug at his heart.

Bowls of food and jugs filled with ale and cider were placed on the table in front of them. Sky wasn't sure she had an appetite. She had been so anxious about her arrival here that she feared her desire to eat had all but vanished. But the delicious aroma of the food made her think twice and she eagerly reached for a small meat pie.

As soon as Slayer speared a piece of meat with his knife, one of his warriors approached the table. "A few mercenaries survived, my lord, though for how long is questionable. They will be here soon, and there is no word on the archer yet."

Slayer nodded. "Let me know when they arrive. I will question them."

Sky hurried to swallow the little food in her mouth and looked anxiously at her husband as the warrior nodded and hurried off.

Slayer responded without Sky saying a word. "Nay, you cannot come with me."

"It may concern me and my sisters, and perhaps he knows something about Leora's whereabouts. I truly would like to hear what he says," she said, hoping to change his mind, though knew the likelihood of that was bleak. He would not risk her safety.

He turned to her. "You will not want to see what I do to him to get those answers." He raised his finger to silence her. "Not a word. It is done."

She did not want to think about what the men would suffer, but she did want to know what they had to say. "Will you at least share with me what he reveals to you?"

Slayer was ready to deny her when he caught the concern in her eyes. She did not worry about herself. It was her sisters' safety that concerned her.

"I will consider it," he said.

Relieved that he did not completely refuse her, she smiled appreciatively though she would have preferred to lean against him and give his hand a squeeze. Instead, she simply said, "I am grateful, and I will gladly do my share of whatever chore you set for me while I am here."

While I am here.

Those words irritated Slayer even though they were meant for the servants nearby to think she was nothing more than a guest willing to do her share.

Another warrior hurried to the table. "One prisoner has arrived, my lord, and I do not believe he has much time."

Slayer stood and called out, "Euniss! See to Sky!"

"Aye, my lord," Euniss said from across the large room.

Sky was not surprised or upset when he left without saying a word to her. Whispers could already be heard amongst the servants questioning her presence and that he had even sat with her at one of the tables meant for his warriors and guests. This was not going to be easy being among so many strangers and not one of them knowing she was Lord Slayer's wife.

***

Sky kept her eyes closed and had hoped to be left alone after she had informed Euniss that she required no help bathing. Euniss had thought differently and after much debate, the woman had agreed to leave her alone to disrobe though not to wash.

She had barely gotten into the tub when Euniss returned with two servants, but she cared not since the hot bath water she was immersed in up to her neck felt far too good to care about anything. If only she could linger in it for hours, the heat easing the few aches that plagued her, but the bath water would not stay heated for long. She was relieved that her raw wrists had healed well, and her bruised eyes had long since vanished or it would have made her arrival here that much worse. Gossiping tongues were probably already busy creating a tale about her two different colored eyes that would no doubt embellish with time.

She shook her thoughts aways, wanting nothing more than to enjoy the heated water. The wood tub was a substantial size, far larger than she was accustomed to, a fit more preferrable for Slayer. Though it might be confining for him with the width of his impressive shoulders and long legs. His size alone could intimidate. It certainly had intimidated her and still did at times. Other times, it did not disturb her at all. And his pronounced muscles could cause any man to think twice about challenging him and yet she loved the feel of them, loved feeling his strength when he maneuvered her around in bed with a lift of one arm to fit her perfectly beneath him.

She bit back the soft moan rising inside her along with her passion. There had to be something wrong with her that her need for her husband was so great. She recalled hearing women talking and laughing among themselves, not realizing she was near or perhaps not caring. What was it some of them had said about their husbands?

Mine stirs me to madness.
Lucky you, mine doesn't stir me at all.
Mine makes me tingle all over.
A simple touch from mine stirs me.
I got myself the wrong husband.

Slayer could certainly stir her to madness, and he made her tingle all over and, Lord, help her, his touch alone could spark her desire for him. She smiled to herself and silently thanked the heavens that she accidentally found the right husband.

Strong whispers penetrated her thoughts, though she was glad for the interruption, needing to quell her passion. She listened to the whispers, loud enough to hear. The two servants were pleading with Euniss to be dismissed. They feared helping her because of her strange eye color.

"I can see to washing myself," Sky said softly, understanding the servants' misgivings. "Please let the servants go."

Sky said no more since it truly was not her decision to make. She was not the lady of the keep. Though she wondered if she was receiving such attention because she was believed to be the widow of the previous lord, the large room alone alerted her to that possibility since it appeared fit for the lord of the clan. Everything seemed large in the room, from the fireplace to the chairs, to several chests, and a huge bed, four thick posts reaching almost to the ceiling from its four corners. She would have to ask Slayer if she was thought to be Warrand's widow. But for whatever reason, she did not feel comfortable with the attention.

She was accustomed to seeing to her own needs and required no assistance.

She repeated herself softly. "Please, let them go, Euniss."

Silence followed and she realized that please was not something the servants heard from nobles, but she was not a noble. And she could not be something she wasn't.

"Be gone with you," Euniss ordered the two servant lasses.

"You need not stay either, Euniss," Sky said upon hearing the two servants rush out of the room as if the devil was on their heels. "I can see to taking care of myself."

"Nonsense."

Her voice sounded as if she stood beside the tub and Sky's eyes flashed open to see Euniss standing near the rim, folding up her sleeves.

"I will see to washing myself," Sky said quickly. "I need no help, but I am grateful for the offer."

Euniss picked up a slab of soap that had been placed on top of a stack of folded cloths sitting atop a high stool. "I will wash your hair."

Sky thought to argue but when the woman's hands began working the soap into her hair and scalp vigorously, she sighed with pleasure.

"You must be tired after your long journey," Euniss said.

Long journey. The woman was curious as to how long she had been with Slayer. Surely word must have reached here about Sky. She did not believe warriors would hold their tongues. Unless Slayer had issued orders.

Sky kept her response simple. "I look forward to some sleep."

"Sit up some and tilt your head back so I can rinse the soap from your hair."

Sky did as she asked, almost sighing with the pleasure of the still-heated water running over her head and shoulders.

"Will you be staying with us long?" Euniss asked.

"I am not sure," she said, fearful of saying too much or saying something she shouldn't.

"I should warn you."

"Warn me?" Sky asked, concerned as the woman squeezed the water from her hair.

"Lord Slayer is a good man, not always kind, but a good man. The not always good part is thanks to his father who forced him to become the mighty warrior that he is today. Lord Bannaty wanted to assure that no one dared oppose Clan Ravinsher. It left little time for Lord Slayer to know anything other than the constant need to protect his brother and the future of the clan. Now he is the future of the clan and there is no one to protect him."

Aye, there is... me.

A foolish thought since what could she do to protect Slayer?

Love him.

She did not know how that would help, but since her heart believed otherwise, she would trust it. She would protect him and shield him with her love.

***

Slayer was disappointed that the captured men he spoke with had no new information to give them. It was the same news he had discovered himself. Mercenaries, whether small or large groups, were crawling the Highlands with hopes of being successful in killing the reddish blonde-haired Murdock sister and claiming the sizeable fortune offered to complete the mission. The only lead to who wanted them dead had something to do with the Lowlanders who had entered the Highlands.

He was glad for the late-night hour and the quiet of the village. He often walked through the village at night to check on his sentinels, keeping them alert since they never knew when he might show up. It also left him time alone. Undisturbed time, when he let his thoughts run wild before forcing them into order, into making sense and making decisions. Though some remained stubborn, refusing to comply, refusing to make sense, and that frustrated Slayer. But it always proved only a mere delay in the end since he refused to accept defeat. He was a Gallowglass warrior and the Gallowglass never surrendered.

Once in the keep, he made his way to his bedchamber and approached the bed quietly to see Sky sleeping peacefully. Strands of her reddish blonde hair, much like the colors of the flames that flickered in the fireplace, lay across her cheek, the ends curling slightly. He went to move it aside with his finger, but instead he caught it between two of his fingers. Soft and silky. He favored running his finger through her hair to hold her head still when he kissed her. And he could not get enough of her lovely face. It was flawless, not a blemish on it and pale in color, except for the two, faint pink stains on her cheeks which appeared often, another thing about her that he favored.

He let the soft strands fall from his fingers, hearing the door open slowly.

"A bath is prepared in your mum's bedchamber. I prepared that chamber for Sky to sleep, but she must have assumed she was to use this bedchamber where she bathed and slipped into bed and fell asleep. I was sure you would not want me to disturb her. So, I had a bath prepared there for you."

Slayer approached Euniss, standing just inside the room, and ordered, "Out."

Without speaking a word to her, he walked to the bedchamber that had once belonged to his mother. He hurried out of his garments and into the tub, eager to get done and return to his wife and wrap himself around her in sleep.

He noticed that Euniss was alone with him, no other servants lingered about with more hot water or waiting for further instructions. She had done that on purpose. She had questions for him.

"You can go, Euniss," he ordered.

"You are not going to get rid of me that fast," she said and walked to the tub and took a stubborn stance there, folding her arms across her chest. "What is going on? You are far too familiar with her."

"I do not see how that should concern you."

"And I do not see how it does not concern you. Do you wish to ruin her reputation, or have you already?"

Leave it to Euniss to notice and be blunt about it. She knew him too well and that was something that might just solve his dilemma.

Slayer looked directly at her. "Sky is my wife."

Euniss gasped and slapped her hand to her chest.

"My mum trusted you, therefore, I trust you. This is knowledge that cannot yet be made known. Ross knows and now you. No one, not even Sky's sisters, knows of this. Until I can make certain that Sky will be safe being my wife, no one will know we are wed. But I will also not be kept from my wife's bed. So, you will be the only one who tends to these upper chambers. Sky is a kind soul, Euniss, and I will not have her treated badly."

"That might prove difficult, sir."

"Then let your tongue spread the word that there will be severe consequences to anyone who treats her poorly," Slayer said with a snarl of anger.

Euniss realized she had said enough. He would tolerate no more from her and with a quick, "Aye, sir," she took her leave.

Slayer wasted no time in washing. He normally would linger in the heat of the water, but not tonight. Tonight, he wanted to join his wife in bed as soon as he could. With a drying cloth wrapped around his waist, he made his way back to his bedchamber.

He felt his manhood react as soon as he got in bed and wrapped himself around his wife. While he knew he could easily wake her passion, she looked far too peaceful in sleep to disturb her. Tomorrow morning would be soon enough and content with that thought, he fell asleep.

Chapter Fourteen

Sky crept through the keep, doing her best to keep her footfalls as light as she could so as not to disturb anyone, though more so not to alert anyone to what she was about. She had grown accustomed to waking up in her husband's arms these last few weeks and often coupling. However, she presently needed the solitude of watching the sunrise to prepare her for the day to come. She wished she could go into the forest and be joined by some of the animals as was her way back home. Unfortunately, it was not safe for her to venture into the forest alone, so remaining inside the stone wall that surrounded the castle was her only choice.

It was a relief to wake this morning and slip on the clean garments Euniss had left for her last night. A finely spun, soft wool, light green tunic and a freshly washed linen shift to wear underneath it. She did not bother wearing the wool leggings. They were better left for winter, but she was grateful for the finely crafted leather shoes. Unfortunately, with as much walking as she loved to do, she feared they would not last long. She had braided her hair into a single braid, though her hair always had a mind of its own and would no doubt break free of its confines soon enough.

A board creaked beneath her foot, and she stilled, listening. When she heard nothing and no one appeared, she continued through the Great Hall and breathed a sigh of relief once outside. She might not be able to go to the edge of the woods to greet the day, but she would find a spot to enjoy the break of dawn and gather the strength she would need to begin her new life here. She hoped a few animals would seek her out and offer her some comfort as well as making friends with her. Animals would probably be the only friends she made here, not holding much hope that people would accept her.

She set out for the east part of the village where the sun would rise.

With abundant cottages and buildings, it was not easy to find a spot to view the sunrise and time was running out. The predawn light was beginning to rise. She needed to find a spot now. The rising pale light gave her a better view of the village than the few flaming torches situated along the village pathways, and she spotted an area that looked perfect.

She hurried back toward the castle, keeping to the east side of it. There was an animal pen up ahead, toward the back of the keep, but she did not see any animals. A small enclosure also occupied the pen, so she assumed the animals were inside. Daybreak might bring them out since most animals rise early in the springtime, eager to enjoy the warmer days.

Sky came to a stop where the trees cleared, and she was able to see the sky in all its glory just as the sun dawned, painting it in beautiful yellow and orange colors. She breathed in deeply, grateful for a new day and all the beauty, promise, possibilities, and even problems it might hold.

She watched quietly, thinking how much the forest and the animals had taught her and how eager she was to learn more. The sun continued its ascent when she picked up the sound of a low growl that grew slowly and was joined by another growl. It didn't frighten her since she had yet to find an animal who she could not befriend, but she erred on caution, for she was wise enough to know that not all in the animal kingdom wished to be friends.

She turned slowly so as not to alarm the animal and her eyes went wide upon seeing four wolfhounds sitting lined in a row staring at her from behind a wood rail fence. A fence they could no doubt easily jump, though they remained as they were, growling in warning.

The four were no doubt battle hounds. Wolfhounds were a preferable dog to take into battle because of their size and fearlessness. While the look of them could easily intimidate, Sky was not deterred by it. She had befriended fierce dogs before now.

She approached the large dogs slowly, keeping her voice soft as she spoke to them. "Good morning to you all. I am Sky and I would love to make friends with all of you."

The hounds continued to growl.

"I mean you no harm. I hate seeing animals harmed, even ones with teeth as sharp as yours and your penchant to battle though no fault of yours. I would much rather sit and talk with you. I love to watch the sunrise, so perhaps we can watch it rise together each day."

She knew it would take time for the hounds to trust her and she would not mind at all visiting with them daily to talk, assuring them she meant them no harm.

Their growls turned softer.

"I could bring you a treat. A bone or two that the cook has no use for," she suggested with a soft tilt of her head at the hounds.

Their growls stopped and they tilted their heads as well.

"Wonderful," she said with a wider yet gentle smile. "I will see you all tomorrow and we will talk more. Enjoy the sun that I hope will last throughout the day." She waved before walking off, the four wolfhounds staring after her without a growl from any of them.

That she would have animals to converse with lightened her worry some and she continued her trek through the village that was coming quickly to life. Fires were lit under cauldrons and broths and porridges would soon be cooking and people eating, fortifying themselves for the day ahead. Children were busy at play before they would be chased off to get to their chores and women congregated in small groups to share news.

It was a scene she was familiar with, it being similar to her own clan's morning routine. Only her clan was much smaller, and many would at least acknowledge her with a nod. Everyone here who she passed turned away intentionally, fearful of meeting her eyes.

Her confidence began to dwindle from the endless whispers and unfavorable glances, and she found herself anxious to return to her husband. She hurried toward the keep, her head down, paying heed to no one. A sudden frightening screech from what was surely an animal stopped her. She ran toward the terrifying sound to help whatever poor creature was suffering.

It took only a few steps around a cottage to stare horrified at three lads, around ten years of age, throwing stones at a small, black kitten that attempted to shield itself between two barrels pressed tightly together, screeching in fright and pain.

"STOP!" she yelled with fierce anger.

The lads laughed at her and gathered more stones to continue their assault.

"Don't you dare throw any more stones at that kitten," she warned and hurried toward the small ball of black fur.

The lads, busy collecting more stones, didn't see her run to the kitten. Once they were done, they turned in unison laughing and launching the stones at the kitten. Instead, they hit Sky pelting her in the back as she scooped up the kitten to cradle protectively in her arms.

A larger rock caught her in the back of the head, and she cried out in pain.

"WHAT THE BLOODY HELL IS GOING ON HERE?"

Sky shivered at Slayer's vicious roar of anger and turned to see the three lads frozen in place, their faces drained of all color, and fearful tears welling in their eyes.

People came running, one man grabbing one of the lads by the nape of his neck and demanding to know what he did. A woman hurried toward another of the lads poking him in the chest demanding answers, and an elderly woman approached the last lad shaking her head.

"The three of you stay where you are," Slayer ordered, pointing at the lads before he went to Sky. He had to fight to keep his hands off her when all he wanted to do was to take her in his arms.

"Are you all right?" he asked, and he almost lost all willpower when he saw the hurt in her eyes and how she went to take a step toward him then stopped. Her first reaction was to seek his arms just as his was to reach out to her and it angered him even more that they couldn't.

She raised her hand to rub at the back of her head and cringed when her hand connected with a painful lump.

Slayer did not hesitate. There was nothing improper about him seeing to any injury she may have sustained and at that point he did not care what anyone thought. He would see the injury for himself. He pushed her hand away and felt the area she had touched and let loose with, "Bloody hell." He turned to the three lads. "Which one of you hit her?"

The man shoved his son forward. "Answer his lordship."

Sky felt sorry for the lad. He looked terrified and he sent a quick glance to his mates for help, but they were just as terrified and as speechless as he was. She did not condone their actions toward the kitten but she worried what Slayer might do to them, so she spoke up.

"I doubt they know which one of them hit me since they were all throwing stones at the kitten," she said, glancing down at the black ball of fur that cuddled tightly against her. "I got in the way. I do not think they meant to hit me."

Slayer turned an angry glare on each lad. "Did she tell you to stop?"

The wide-eyed lads nodded in unison.

"How many times did she tell you to stop?" Slayer demanded.

The three lads looked at each other and one got the courage to say, "Twice."

"One time too many," Slayer said. "And tell me, do the three of you enjoy harming a helpless animal because I can show you how it feels when someone bigger and stronger than you decides to torment you?"

"Please, my lord, my grandson is just a foolish lad. He will not do it again," the elderly woman begged.

"Aye, Ruth, you are right. Wade will not do it again once he tastes what it feels like," Slayer said, and the woman shook her head and Wade looked about to cry. He turned to signal one of his warriors and saw that Sky was about to speak. "Not a word," he ordered.

The warrior came forward and waited for Slayer to speak.

"Take the three lads and have them work with the Gallowglass warriors today and for the next five days, and they are not to go easy on them," Slayer ordered.

"Aye, my lord," the warrior said and turned to call out to the lads. "Over here, the three of you. NOW!"

The lads rushed to the warrior.

"Follow in a single line behind me," the warrior ordered, and the lads hurried to obey, their heads hanging down and a tremble in their steps,

Slayer called out for all to hear, "Sky is under my protection, the clan's protection. If she is harmed in any way there will be severe consequences to pay. Now go and attend to your chores."

The people hurried off, not a whisper passing among them.

Slayer turned to Sky. "Leave the kitten and come with me."

"Please do not ask that of me, Slayer," she whispered softly. "The clan no doubt believes me evil and responsible for what the lads will suffer, due to their own foolishness. That will only make some intent on taking their anger out on the innocent kitten and make her suffer. I cannot allow that to happen. Please, let the kitten remain with me."

He shook his head. "I had not given thought to that but that is a good possibility."

"Besides, the kitten will provide me with some friendship."

"Am I not enough friendship for you?" he whispered.

Sky was glad she held the kitten, or she would have reached out to touch him gently. "You are my best friend, but you have duties to tend to."

"Once they get to know you, they will think differently."

She shook her head and followed alongside him as he began walking toward the keep. "They will never get to know me since they will not take the chance to speak with me, and you cannot force them to speak with me. Such a decree would only worsen the situation."

"Keep the kitten, but keep him out of my way," Slayer said.

"Cats choose who they will befriend."

"Are you telling me the kitten will not like me?"

"You said yourself that you are not a kind man. The kitten will sense it and avoid you unless..."

"Unless what?" he demanded.

She smiled. "Unless you are not as unkind as you say." He looked about to lecture her, so she hurried to ask, "The wolfhounds, are they yours?"

Slayer stopped abruptly. "Never go near the wolfhounds' pen. They are vicious animals, bred to fight in battle and obey only me. Whatever magic you think you have with animals, you do not have with them. Stay away."

She was glad he continued walking and had not insisted she give her word to him, but then he expected everyone to obey his word so what need was there for a promise?

Seeing Ross sitting at one of the tables upon entering the Great Hall, Slayer asked, "There are a few things I wish to discuss with you before you take your leave?"

Ross went to stand.

"Stay, I will join you there," Slayer said and was quick to call out to Sky when she did not follow him to the table. "Where are you going?"

"To feed the kitten. I will return shortly," she said and hurried out of the room.

"You let her bring the kitten she saved into the keep?" Ross asked.

"You know about that already? You have only arrived from the compound."

Ross nodded. "Word spreads fast throughout the clan. I heard all about the attack and your victory yesterday. The servants are whispering about both, and much blame is being placed on Sky for the kitten incident. To them, she is an outsider, and her affliction does not make it any easier."

"Do I command this clan or not?"

"You command the Gallowglass. You lead this clan."

"And the difference?"

"I imagine more patience is needed with one more than the other."

"One cannot lead without command, and patience is more like indecisiveness and can be fatal to a clan. Patience did not win us endless victories or save the lives of our warriors. I command. It is what I was taught and what I do to keep everyone safe. If I had spared those three lads the consequences of their actions, they would never learn to obey my word. And one day that may cost them their lives."

Ross raised his tankard. "The reason you lead, and I follow."

***

"Cats don't usually stay in the keep," Euniss said, watching the little ball of fur licking up the milk from the bowl she had placed on the floor.

"Why, when they are so good at keeping the mice at bay?" Sky asked and tried to ignore the whispers and stolen glances from the servants.

Euniss appeared hesitant to say, strange for her since she had been blunt with her remarks since Sky had met her.

One of the servants bravely spoke up. "They fear his lordship."

"Nonsense. Cats know better than to get in his lordship's way," Euniss said as if that was an adequate explanation itself.

"We shall see how the kitten fares with his lordship," Sky said, thinking, like most cats, the little ball of fur would have her own way. "Let her enjoy the milk and I will return for her, if that is all right with you, Euniss."

"Aye, the little darling is welcome to stay."

"I am grateful," Sky said and turned and headed for the door.

"Looks like you won't be going anywhere without her," Euniss said with a chuckle.

Sky turned to find the kitten at her feet meowing. She scooped her up and the kitten curled herself in the crook of her arm, letting her know Euniss was right, she wouldn't be going anyplace without her.

"You rescued her. She is not going to trust anyone but you," Euniss said.

"She is such a sweet thing, a little angel," Sky said.

"Angel. A good name for her," Euniss said. "I will send a bowl of milk to the Great Hall for Angel."

"Thank you," Sky said and left. As she made her way to the Great Hall, she gently lifted the kitten, kissed her small head, and whispered, "You are safe with me, Angel, I will always protect you, and I could use a dear friend right now."

The kitten's tiny tongue peeked out to give Sky's cheek a lick and with a smile Sky returned her to the crook of her arm. She no longer had any worries. She had an angel with her.

Slayer watched Sky enter the room, glad she had returned, and glad Ross had taken his leave. He had gotten annoyed when he woke this morning and found her gone. His annoyance had grown when he had gone in search of her and did not find her in the keep. He wanted time alone with her before starting the day. He had never thought of his arms as feeling empty, but they felt that way now, not being able to hold or touch her.

He gave a quick glance at the spot beside him, so she knew to sit there. When she did, the flowery scent that had been on her pillow drifted off her teasing his nose and senses and arousing him as it had done this morning when he turned in bed and it had greeted his face. It worsened as he watched her gently stroke the kitten cuddled in her arm, recalling memories of her stroking his manhood, and he wanted to rush her back to their bedchamber.

Annoyed that he allowed thoughts of her to overpower him, he said gruffly. "I gave you no permission to leave the keep this morning."

"I did not think I needed it. I believed myself safe within the confines of the castle walls," Sky said, her soft smile never wavering.

He loved that she forever wore a soft smile and the way her two different colored eyes gazed upon him with pleasure as if she had missed him and was happy to be there with him. No one had ever been happy to see him.

"With your life in danger, it is wiser that I know where you are at all times, or I can have a warrior follow your every step," he said, an easier solution than constantly worrying as to her whereabouts.

To have her every move watched upset her and she pressed her leg against his beneath the table. "Please don't do that, my lord. I would feel a prisoner not able to move about at will. And would your clansmen not question my trustworthiness if a warrior must forever keep pace with me?"

Feeling her leg pressed so firmly against his made him want to feel more of her. Not being able to touch her, show the simplest of affection or comfort was far more challenging than he expected and that she referred to him so properly annoyed him even more. Then there was her remark that made sense but did not help the situation.

His father had told him that Sky spent much time alone and probably did not possess a bright mind, but he had found just the opposite, sharing the last few weeks with her. Her mind was quick to see things and make sense of them.

"You know from our many talks, I so favored, that I spent much time walking in the woods and, though I know I cannot do that here, I would not mind walking through the village."

"Why, if you feel no one will befriend you or speak with you?" he asked, curious.

"A brave soul or two might, but if not, it still allows me to learn about your people and the village. I do not want to be ignorant of its workings and I cannot learn if I do not see for myself."

"You observe like I do," he said.

He never let anyone have any insight into him, it could prove dangerous if the enemy were to learn his ways. Yet Sky's kind and trusting nature made it easier and easier to share with her.

She smiled. "Observation is the key to learning. The forest teaches, the animals and people teach, the rivers teach, and the sky as well. Knowledge surrounds us if we but take the time to observe it."

How could he confine her any more than he already had by bringing her here and keeping her contained behind the castle walls?

"I would never want to rob you of gaining knowledge, for it is important to learn and better understand things. So, I will allow you to walk through the village unfettered if you agree to one thing."

"What is it?" she asked, hoping it would be something easy for her to do since the idea of constantly being watched, being followed would make her feel like a prisoner all over again.

"That you share your observations with me," he said, and her eyes brightened, and she looked ready to kiss him and he so wished she could.

"I would love to share my observations with you," she said, then whispered, "I wish I could kiss you right now."

He kept his voice to a murmur. "I want more than kisses from you."

She went to lean her head closer to him when she saw two servants staring at them. "They watch us. Reprimand me."

"Aye, I will and give good reason to send you to our bedchamber," he whispered, then raised his voice. "You will heed my word or be sent to your bedchamber to do penance."

Sky bowed her head as if repentant, fighting to keep a smile off her face, and whispered, "I believe I will be doing much penance."

Slayer kept a stern expression on his face. "And make no mistake, I will thoroughly enjoy delivering it."

The few servants there turned away, whispering while one hurried off, no doubt to let others know of Lord Slayer's warning to the guest.

A warrior suddenly rushed into the Great Hall calling out for his lordship and wasted no time in delivering the news. "A troop of mercenaries have been spotted not far from the village. Your men await your command."

Slayer stood. "Ready the men. We ride."

He glanced at Sky aching to kiss her.

She spoke so low that she feared he might not hear her. "Come back to me."

"Always," he said and felt an ache so sharp in his heart at leaving her that he wondered if he had lost his heart to her.

Chapter Fifteen

The faint light of dawn was just beginning to show itself as Sky made her way to the spot close to the wolfhound pen. She was not surprised to see only two wolfhounds, her husband no doubt having taken the other two with him.

Soft growls drew her attention and she realized she had stopped, and the two hounds were letting her know they were impatient for the promised treat. She was cautious in her approach, knowing they did not fully trust her yet and she had yet to trust them.

"Good morning to you both. It is good to see you again. I brought bones as I said I would," she said softly as she approached. "I assume your other two mates are with Lord Slayer."

Her remark had the two hounds glancing into the distance as if keeping watch for their return, which confirmed what she thought. He had taken the two other hounds with him. She glanced in the distance herself, wondering how long Slayer would be gone. She missed him terribly, though he'd been gone only one night.

She had found out where the discarded bones were kept and found four that would suit the wolfhounds. She didn't want anyone to know what she intended to do with the bones, the reason she'd been secretive about collecting them. She would have been subjected to too many questions and speculations, and Slayer would not be happy that she disobeyed him.

The two hounds started growling when she got closer, and she looked down and saw why. Angel was peeking her little head out of the shawl she had tied around her neck and fashioned into a pouch to make it easier and safer to carry the kitten around.

Angel hissed, as much as a tiny kitten could, at the hounds, then ducked back down into the safety of the pouch.

Sky cast a soft smile on the hounds and kept her voice tender with a touch of firmness. "The kitten is tiny and frightened and you two are large and fearless. You must protect Angel, not harm her. She is my friend like you two are my friends."

The two hounds tilted their heads as if attempting to understand and their eyes followed her every move as she slipped two bones out of the sack and walked closer to the fence. She had only met them yesterday, far too soon to think it was safe to get too close. So, she extended the bones out to each hound and each bone was quickly snatched out of her hands.

She spoke softly to them for a while, then said, "Enjoy your treat. Angel and I will visit with you again tomorrow." She glanced up at the gray sky as she walked away. "No sun today, Angel."

She wondered if the sour sky would bring on sour moods. She found people often mirrored the weather. Sunshine brought more smiles, rain brought dreariness, and snow brought worry of survival.

Clansmen were waking and beginning their morning chores as she made her way through the village. Glances were cast her way, whispers exchanged, and no doubt assumptions made, and she did her best to ignore them. A couple of dogs appeared ready to approach her but were shooed away by a man who kept his eyes turned away from her.

She wished she could escape to the forest, feel it slip around her like a shawl that warmed and comforted, and be among animals that would not hesitate to befriend her. But she would not be so foolish and take the chance with her life in danger.

Sky continued through the village, keeping a welcoming smile on her face, hoping that someone might return it. No one did, so she made her way back to the keep, around the side, to the kitchen to return the two unused bones to the basket to collect again another day.

She scooped Angel out of the makeshift pouch and placed her on the ground to explore while she looked over the kitchen garden. It was large and probably took several people to keep it so well-maintained. Growth was well-established in some places while other places sprouts had only recently broken through the ground.

She explored along with Angel until she heard the approach of voices busy in talk. She hastily snatched up the kitten as a small group of men and women came around the corner of the keep. They stopped and stared at her.

She took a chance that one of them might speak with her and said, "It is a lovely garden."

One lass smiled, but a warning look from the others caused it to vanish.

Sky hurried off, hugging the kitten against her cheek to whisper, "At least I have you, Angel."

The day wore on and Sky was beginning to feel imprisoned. There was nothing for her to do and with the forest off limits, she felt trapped. It also didn't help that she had no one to talk with, which made her miss her sisters even more. If she felt this way after only two days here, how would she ever endure spending the rest of her life here as Slayer's wife?

Sky left Angel in the bedchamber sleeping curled in a blanket in a basket near the hearth for extra warmth. Supper had finished, Angel her only company, and night had yet to fall, and Slayer had yet to return. She could not face another sleepless night, another night without her husband to curl around. So, she decided to wander through the village in hopes it would exhaust her enough to sleep at least part of the night.

She made her way through the village, taking note of faces and names being spoken, noticing how the dwellings were well kept, not a hole in any thatched roof, and watched with envy as women congregated in small groups sharing the day's news. None invited her to join them. Her heart heavy, she turned to make her way back to the keep and the company of Angel.

The sudden screams tore her out of her musings and warriors began running past her. Instinct had her following them. She joined the mass of people running, fear shivering her when she realized where they were headed… the wolfhounds' pen.

"Let me go! Let me get Oona!" a woman screamed as two men held her firm, preventing her from going anywhere.

"Nay, Glynis, the hounds will tear you apart," one of the men holding her warned.

"Better me than my daughter," Glynis cried out.

Gasps and wide eyes stared at a young lass who laid unmoving in the wolfhounds' pen. The two large hounds stood over the lass snarling and snapping, appearing as if they were fighting over who would eat her.

"What happened?" a Gallowglass warrior demanded.

Glynis continued to cry as she spoke. "Oona was beside me one minute and gone the next. She is so fast for one so young. I couldn't catch her before she reached the pen and climbed the fence and fell in. Oh God, they are going to rip her apart."

"You've got to save her," someone called out.

"Do something," shouted another.

"They listen to no one but Lord Slayer," another cried out.

Sky did not hesitate. She pushed past everyone and went to the fence and climbed over it before anyone tried to stop her. Not that anyone did. To them, she was not worth saving.

She kept her voice even and soft. Not a tremble or fear could be heard in it. "You have done well protecting the little lass and I am grateful to you both, but you must step away from her now and let me take her. Will you do that for me?"

One of the hounds backed away while the other eyed her skeptically.

Sky turned her hand palm up and keeping it low reached out to the hound. "I mean her or you no harm."

A collective gasp sounded when the hound's mouth looked about to clamp down on Sky's hand, but the large hound sniffed, then licked it, and stepped back.

Sky crouched down slowly to see the little lass' eyes flutter. She would wake soon and if she cried out, the hounds might believe she was hurting her and attack.

She lifted her gently, then glancing at Glynis called out as softly as she could so as not to upset the hounds, "Walk slowly and come take her from me."

Glynis did as Sky said and took the lass from her just as she woke and cried out.

The hounds started growling and rushed at Sky. She had no time to jump the fence. She turned and faced them.

"The lass got a fright from the fall, but she is safe in her mum's arms. You did well in keeping her safe." She lowered her voice to a whisper. "I will bring extra bones to you tomorrow in thanks."

The two hounds stopped growling and their heads shot up and sniffed the air. She heard people suddenly running and crying out in fright and when Sky turned it was to see the people hurrying away from the pen and the two missing wolfhounds racing toward the pen ready to vault it. Again, she had no time to jump over the fence. She stayed where she was, seeing her husband come barreling toward the pen on his stallion.

"SIT!" Slayer commanded as soon as the two wolfhounds with him cleared the fence.

All four wolfhounds sat, their eyes on Slayer.

Sky remained as she was, her eyes on Slayer as well as he brought his stallion to a halt and dismounted.

Dried blood clung to the side of his face and stained the sleeves of his shirt and the front of it as well. A film of dirt and sweat covered him. That he had engaged in battle was evident and she felt an overwhelming relief that he had survived. Though she could tell by the fiery look in his eyes that he was none too pleased to find her in the wolfhounds' pen.

Slayer walked over to the pen, and the wolfhounds' eyes remained steady upon him. He did not say a word. He reached over the fence, grabbed her beneath her arms and with a forceful lift swung her over the fence to land with a solid thud on her feet.

"Are you hurt?" Sky asked, seeing the wound on his head where the blood had dripped from and dried.

Slayer glared at her, having been prepared to unleash a tongue lashing on her for being in his hounds' pen. Yet she robbed him of those words when she showed concern for him rather than defending herself.

"My lord," Glynis called out. "She saved Oona from the hounds. She had fallen in the pen and Sky did not hesitate to enter the pen and keep the hounds from harming her. She saved my little lass, she did, and without any thought to her own well-being."

"And where were my warriors in all of this?" Slayer demanded, sending a scathing look to each one of them there.

"I did not give them a chance to do anything," Sky said, "I jumped over the fence before anyone could stop me."

One of his warriors stepped forward. "There is no excuse for our failure, my lord, we should have been able to stop her."

"You're right and you'll pay for it," Slayer shouted. "And, Glynis," —he turned to the woman— "if you let Oona get anywhere near the hounds' pen again, you will suffer the consequences."

"Aye, my lord, it won't happen again," the woman said, her lips trembling along with her words.

"It better not," Slayer warned. "Now begone, all of you."

All left but his warriors. They remained, waiting to face their punishment.

"I will speak with you all tomorrow. For now, you will do extra duty at your posts. Now go and never disappoint me again," he said with a scowl at each one of them.

Their heads hung low as they walked away, though one of the warriors hurried to take the reins of Slayer's horse to see to his care.

"Take extra good care of him," Slayer ordered.

The warrior nodded. "Aye, my lord."

Slayer walked past Sky to the hounds' pen. "Food will be brought to you soon. Rest until then. We will hunt soon."

The hounds laid down, resting as he ordered, though their attention sparked when Slayer mentioned that they would hunt soon. What amazed Sky even more was that the hounds remained in the pen, though they could easily jump the fence as the two had done upon returning with Slayer. Yet they didn't. They remained there waiting for Slayer's order. It appeared that everyone, even animals, obeyed him without question.

Slayer glared at her, angry at the scene that had greeted him upon his arrival home. He wanted to lash out at his wife for being so foolish while also wanting to wrap his arms around her tightly, grateful she was unharmed.

"You are a foolish woman!" he yelled and reached out to grab her hand and yanked her along to follow him.

When Sky felt him squeeze her hand, she knew he yelled at her for others to hear and to see that he had grabbed her hand to force her to walk along with him when truthfully it was an excuse for him to take her hand. But she also knew that part of him was angry with her, and she could understand why.

Sky cringed at the enormous shout that echoed through the crowded Great Hall upon entering beside Slayer. Praise of his leadership and how he had led his warriors to victory rang out. He stopped to grip hands in solidarity with those who reached out to him and reminded them that victory was not possible without all of them battling side by side fearlessly.

She lost him somewhere in the crowd, maneuvering around the tables filled to the brim with battle-worn warriors. They ate with enthusiasm from the mounds of food in front of them and downed tankard after tankard of ale. While those who had remained behind stood around the tables and in between the aisles, drinking and listening to the praises lavished on Lord Slayer and snippets of the fierce battle.

Sky made her way just beyond the dais, thinking they would not be alone together anytime soon but then she caught his eye, and he sent a glance to the stairs.

She made her way to the stairs, taking a few steps up and stopping out of sight when his booming voice filled the room.

"Eat, drink, enjoy! I have an important matter I must see to."

Cheers of praise once again rang out and Sky smiled and waited on the stairs.

"I have missed you," she said when he appeared, and he eagerly took the steps up to her.

"Not as much as I missed you," he said and nodded for her to continue climbing the stairs. "I would snatch you up in my arms, but I will not stain you with the blood of battle."

She hurried up the stairs, eager to be alone with her husband. When she saw that the tub was already prepared and food and drink covered the table, she realized that word must have reached the keep to prepare for Lord Slayer's imminent and victorious return. If she had remained in the keep, she would have learned of the news, but then she would not have been there to help the little lass.

She turned to her husband, discarding the last of his garments. She had come to know his body well and had come to enjoy seeing him naked. Never had she seen a man with such muscles. There was no paunch to his stomach or lag to his skin. He was firm with muscles everywhere. They rippled and curved beautifully over his body, taut and strong, almost as if they had been sculpted. Even the grime and blood of battle that he wore could not diminish his fine body.

"Did I not warn you to stay away from the wolfhounds?" he demanded more than asked, wanting badly to take her into his arms, but he would not stain her with the stench and grime of battle.

A sigh of resignation preceded her admission of guilt. "You did, but at least they let me approach them and did not turn away from me as everyone here does."

It hurt to hear that his clan purposely ignored her. Why couldn't they see what he saw, a kind and loving soul who would never do any of them harm?

Sky pointed to the tub. "Please hurry and wash so I may feel your arms around me. I have missed you and your touch immensely."

His manhood responded to her remark, rising quickly.

Sky smiled. "I see you have missed me too."

"More than you will ever know," he grumbled and hurried into the tub.

While she wanted him to wash quickly, she could tell from his soft grunt and the way he rested the back of his head on the rim of the tub and closed his eyes that he needed time in the heated water. So, she went to him and picked up a cloth off the stool, wet it, and began to wash the blood off his face.

He opened his eyes and could not stop the soft smile that rushed to his lips, seeing her lovely face and her two different colored eyes that shined with concern for him.

"Close your eyes and rest. We have all night," she said and was pleased when he did as she said.

He kept his eyes closed as she tended to him. Her touch was gentle as she scrubbed the blood off his face, rinsing the cloth repeatedly until he was sure not a spot must have remained. Then she ran the cloth softly over his face. It felt so good that he did not want her to stop. When she did, he thought she would be done with him, but she took the cloth to his neck, then to his shoulders, scrubbing with a firmness that eased his muscles. She took extra care with his arms, stroking and squeezing his muscles until they surrendered to her touch, and he almost sighed with pleasure when she ran the soap over his chest with her bare hands.

"Let me wash your hair before the water loses its heat," she said.

He lifted his head as she scooped up water with a tankard and poured it over his hair and after she lathered his hair with the soap, her fingers began scrubbing his scalp with a firmness that almost had him moaning with pleasure.

Never had he enjoyed a bath like he did now with his wife tending to him and it filled him with a sense of pleasure and peace and the thought that they would share many more moments like this together.

He raised his leg when she tugged at it and kept his eyes closed and loved that she washed his legs with the soap and her bare hands. She squeezed his calf muscles as she scrubbed, and he found himself almost moaning again.

When she finished with both legs, she touched him no more and he opened his eyes to see her standing there with the soap in her hands looking down into the tub and he understood her hesitation.

"No permission is needed to touch me, Sky. I will always welcome your touch," he said, sensing her dilemma.

"I know. It's just that..." Her cheeks turned pink, and she shook her head. "I sometimes think I desire you far too much."

Slayer sat up fast, splashing water over the rim, and cupped her face with his wet hand. "I desire you even more, so you can never desire me too much. Never. Ever. Think that." He leaned over the rim and kissed her gently and groaned low when her hand slipped beneath the water with the soap, and she began to tenderly wash him.

It took only a few strokes before he said, "That's it." He stood, letting the water drip off him before stepping out of the tub and snatching a cloth off the stool to dry himself quickly. "Disrobe," he ordered and was glad she did without hesitation. With parts of his body still damp, and impatient to touch his wife, he reached out and snatched her up into his arms and carried her to the bed to announce, "My turn to touch."

He caught a quick look at the kitten asleep in a makeshift bed by the hearth and almost shook his head. He would let her know tomorrow that the kitten would not be sleeping in their bedchamber. It was for Sky and him alone.

Sky kept her arms around her husband's neck as he placed her on the bed, not letting him move off her and she spread her legs so that his manhood nestled between them just where she wanted it.

"While I would love you to touch me all over, I fear I may explode with passion born of washing you, so I need you inside me quickly, please," she pleaded softly and wiggled beneath him.

He was only too glad to oblige her, being on the edge himself, and said, "As you wish, wife."

He slipped into her, and he was overwhelmed not only with passion as he brought them both closer to the edge, but a sense of something else, something deeper and stronger, something that made him a part of Sky and she a part of him, as if at that moment they became one, forever united together… forever loved.

He looked down at his wife, her eyes filled with passion for him, her grip on him strong as if she never intended to let him go, and he knew at that moment what it felt like to be in love.

Chapter Sixteen

"You cannot do that," Sky admonished Angel, her head peeking out of the pouch as she made her way to the wolfhounds' pen. "If Slayer woke and found you on his head, I fear you would be banned from the keep and we do not want that. So, you will be good and sleep in your bed by the hearth."

Sky sighed, knowing her brief lecture would do little good since cats did as they pleased. She did not want to think what Slayer would have done if he had woken to find Angel sleeping peacefully on top of his head. Thankfully, he slept deeply, exhausted from battle. She would have loved to linger beside him, but Angel needed to see to her needs and be fed and she wanted to visit the wolfhounds before the village woke for the day.

The day was just dawning when she finished tending to Angel and gathered bones for all the hounds. The two hounds she had given bones to the previous day were sitting at the fence waiting for her. The two hounds who had been with Slayer yesterday drifted closer to the fence in curiosity.

"Good morning to you all," she said as she approached slowly. "I wanted to thank you for keeping the little lass, Oona, who fell into your pen yesterday, safe and for allowing me to retrieve her. That was very kind of you." She nodded to the other two hounds who had ventured closer to their mates. "It is good to see you both again. You missed the bones I brought yesterday." Their heads shot up as they sniffed the air while the other two hounds continued to sit in anticipation of the treat. "Fear not, there is enough for all, and I was able to get bones with marrow still in them." She pulled out a bone from the sack she carried. "Be patient. There is one for each of you."

The hounds appeared to understand her and waited patiently as she handed a bone to each of them. The last hound sniffed it, turned, and walked away. His reaction puzzled Sky. She wondered if he was trained not to accept food from anyone but Slayer, or perhaps he simply wasn't feeling well today. She would keep an eye on him.

While the hounds lay enjoying their treat, she lifted Angel out of the shawl pouch and held her cupped snuggled in her hands for the hounds to see.

"This is Angel. She met two of your mates yesterday. She is my friend and helps me bring the bones to you. She means you no harm, so please cause her no harm." Angel meowed and one of the hounds growled. "Nay, you must be nice to her. She helps me gather the bones."

The mention of bones stopped the hound from growling.

"It is good you understand since Angel and I enjoy visiting with all of you."

The way the little kitten trembled she doubted that was true, but she hoped as their visits continued the hounds and the kitten would become friends. This way they could protect Angel if ever necessary.

"We will leave you to enjoy your treat and see you tomorrow," Sky said and tucked Angel into the safety of the makeshift pouch to nestle there once again.

She smiled, seeing the brilliant hues that painted the sky. Sun would warm the land today, hopefully longer than only a couple of hours. She closed her eyes and took a deep breath of the fresh morning air, scents of burning wood from the early morning cooking fires beginning to mingle with nature's own scents. She wished she was in the undisturbed woods where nature's vibrant scents welcomed, and where her mind could be free of troubling thoughts.

"I gave you no permission to leave the keep?"

Sky jumped, turning quickly to find Slayer standing directly behind her. A fresh scent from his recent bath drifted off him and she thought, for just a moment, that she caught a faint scent of their coupling from last night. Or perhaps it was only that it had lingered in her nostrils to remind and tempt her. And it did. It almost had her throwing her arms around him and hugging him tightly. But she refrained with great difficulty.

"I expect to see you first thing in the morning," he said, letting her know he was not happy to wake and find himself alone in bed.

"Aye, my lord, I will make certain I make myself available to you then."

"Make sure of it," he ordered with a gleam in his eyes that quickly turned to a scowl. "Were you by the wolfhounds' pen?"

"I wanted to make sure they were all right after yesterday's incident."

"They are dangerous animals, not cuddly kittens. Stay away from them and I will not warn you about that again," he said.

"But—"

"Not another word, Sky. You will obey me on this. Find other friends. The wolfhounds will never be your friends. They are not even mine. They obey me because of my strength, my leadership."

"Not fear?" she asked, knowing how easy it was to fear him.

He stepped closer to her. "Not fear, wisdom. They, like my warriors, know I am the stronger one, the alpha male of the tribe, and none will dare challenge me."

His brow scrunched and Sky thought for a moment he was going to reach out and touch her and was disappointed when he didn't.

He kept his voice low when he asked, "Do you fear me, Sky?"

She tilted her head, not sure how to answer at first.

"How many times must I tell you I would never harm you?" he asked annoyed.

"I am sure of that, my lord," she rushed to say and watched his annoyance flare and knew it was because she addressed him properly. "But that does not stop me from fearing you at times, though I should clarify that."

"Aye, do clarify it."

"It is the Gallowglass warrior in you that I fear sometimes—" She hesitated briefly. "He can be vicious, snarling and biting, like the wolfhounds—" She hesitated again. "Unpredictable."

He leaned closer to her and whispered, "The very thing that makes a powerful leader powerful. Your foe never knows what to expect of you. Whereas my wife will never need to worry about that."

"It might take her time to get used to," she suggested, careful with her words in case anyone heard, the village having come to life for the day.

"Unfortunately, I am not a patient man."

"Something that she would surely learn upon meeting you and do her best to handle."

"That would be wise of her."

Sky smiled. "I am sure you will find yourself a very wise woman to wed, sir."

Slayer had to keep himself from smiling, seeing that people were watching them. "I will settle for nothing less." He took a step away from her and made his voice known. "You are safe here, Sky. No one will harm you. I will speak with you later."

She bobbed her head. "Thank you, my lord."

She strolled through the village, as usual, hoping someone might talk with her or at least return a smile but instead she heard snippets of talk.

"Why did he bring her here?"

"Why does he protect her?"

"The hounds obey her."

"She must be evil."

"Stay away from her."

She made her way to the kitchen garden and was glad no workers were there. She plucked Angel out of the pouch and placed her on the ground to sniff and roll around, though she did not venture far from Sky.

Her mind wandered to her sisters as she watched Angel play with a small stick. She missed them and wished she could speak with them. There was so much for them to discuss, so much to learn, to make sense of and hopefully discover the truth about their births. But right now, she would just appreciate having them there with her, so she did not feel so alone.

Leroa would advise her not to dwell, to keep busy. But how did she do that? She spotted a small area that had yet to be prepared for planting and she thought about the small garden at the cottage. Maybe she could have her own garden to tend and keep her busy.

"Come, Angel, we go speak with Euniss," she urged the kitten who ignored her at first but seeing her about to disappear into the kitchen, Angel hurried after her.

***

"Finally, I hear from you, Melvin," Slayer said when he entered the Great Hall after being told the man had just arrived.

"Aye, my lord, Cavell and I thought it was time I come speak with you," Melvin said.

"My solar," Slayer ordered, and Melvin followed him.

Tankards were filled with ale and Slayer pointed to a bench for Melvin to sit while he stood. "What news have you for me?"

"The Murdock sisters are in danger," Melvin said and took a quick swig of ale.

"That I know," Slayer said, anxious to learn something he didn't know.

"It has been discovered that the Murdock sisters are not blood sisters."

"I know that as well. I learned that from friends in the Lowlands, a reliable source of information." Slayer went on to explain it all to Melvin. "Why a prominent family searches for this lass, now woman, after all these years or why they or someone else would want her dead, I have yet to learn. The most obvious reason would be that she stands in someone's way. Tell Cavell to remain cautious, and I have sent word to Noble to do the same."

He did not share the news about the woman having reddish blonde hair in case it was meant to mislead, though he did trust the source. But if it was true, Cavell would find out soon enough.

"I will relay it all to Cavell. Elsie asked me to speak to her sister, Sky, and see how she fares. May I speak with her, my lord?"

"Nay, you may not, and is there a reason you do not think Sky would fare well with me?"

"Nay. Nay, not at all and I told Elsie that but that does not stop her from worrying about her sister."

"She has nothing to worry about. Sky is well."

"Just a brief word with her, my lord?"

"You know I do not repeat myself, Melvin," Slayer said annoyed.

"I know, but Elsie worries so much about her."

"Then she will be relieved to hear the news you return with that her sister is doing well and she has nothing to worry about. I will, however, relay the message that her sister asked about her and that is my final word on it."

"Aye, my lord," Melvin said, knowing it was done.

"Have you heard anything at all in regard to my father's and brother's deaths?"

"Nay, my lord. Have you learned anything new?"

Slayer shook his head. "Nothing, though with so many mercenaries descending on the area it could be that a rogue group attacked them, but why they would doesn't make sense. It was known my brother was protected by the Gallowglass. But I will find out who is responsible, and they will suffer greatly."

"Cavell and I are at your service when needed," Melvin said.

"I never doubted that," Slayer said. "I am aware that Clan Murdock requires help in many ways, warriors to help protect the clan and see it grow being one of them. You will take a message to the Gallowglass compound. Twenty-five warriors are to return with you to Clan Murdock to help with repairs and such. If any of those warriors wish to remain and start a new life with Clan Murdock, I will free them of their obligation to the Gallowglass. You will also tell them what supplies Cavell needs and take them with you as well."

"That is generous of you, my lord," Melvin said.

"More wise than generous, Melvin. Is that all the news you have for me?"

Melvin hurried to gulp down what remained of the ale in his tankard.

"What news needs ale to fortify the telling of it?" Slayer demanded.

"Clyde, sir. He is dead, brutally murdered, stabbed repeatedly and his throat cut." Melvin leaned his head back, fearful that Slayer might spew fire from his mouth such fury raged in his eyes and his hands fisted tightly at his sides ready to pummel anyone in his path. "We have no leads, no idea of who may have done this. It could be mercenaries, but why kill one lone man?"

"Blood is going to be spilled for my friend, my brother, and my father," Slayer warned. "I will cover the land with blood if necessary to revenge their deaths."

Melvin rarely feared anything being a Gallowglass warrior, but he was wise enough to fear Slayer, for he had repeatedly seen the carnage Slayer could leave in his path.

***

Anger surged through Slayer over his loss of family and a friend and his failure to have found the culprits by now. He should have had them in hand already, so why didn't he? A question that haunted him and one he would have discussed with Ross if he was here. Yet his first thought was to talk with his wife about it.

His anger slowed with thoughts of her, and he realized he needed to talk with her about both her sisters, Elsie and Leora. He decided to tackle that task first, though it also might have been because he had not held her since last night and his arms ached to take hold of her and hug her tightly. That he had this aching need for her was still foreign to him and he continued to grapple with it and embrace it at the same time.

He was not sure where to find her, so when he entered the Great Hall, he called out to the servants there. "Does anyone know where Sky is?" Slayer got annoyed seeing how frightened they looked to speak, and he lost his patience, what little he had, snapping, "If someone knows they better tell me now."

One brave soul rushed to say, "I saw her go up the stairs a short time ago."

Slayer hurried up the stairs and to their bedchamber, glad he would have her to himself and grew concerned when he found their bedchamber empty. Where would she have gone? Could Euniss have told her about his mum's quarters? But why would she go there?

He shook his head and decided to see for himself before returning downstairs. He stopped to listen when he heard his wife's soft voice coming from his mum's solar, the door slightly ajar.

"I cannot understand how anyone would want to be confined in here for too long of a time, Angel, when the forest has so much more to offer. But what else is there for me to do when I am denied even the simplest thing?"

"What have you been denied?" Slayer demanded, his anger returning as he shoved the door open. His eyes narrowed when he caught her wiping her cheeks before she rushed out of the chair, placing Angel on the floor in front of the low burning hearth, and turned to face him.

"I was hoping you would find me. I miss you," she said, forcing a smile.

He rounded the chair and hooking his arm around her waist snatched her up against him. "You avoid answering me and your eyes shine from shed tears. Why?"

"It is nothing," she said, annoyed at herself for allowing tears to stain her eyes and wishing he had not caught her upset. She worried what he might do if he found out.

"I will decide if it is nothing," he said.

"Here we go. A nice brew and a honey cake to soothe you," Euniss called out before entering the room and stopped abruptly when she spotted Slayer.

"What brought my wife to tears, Euniss, since you say she needs soothing?" he demanded.

Euniss sat the wood tray down on the small table beside the chair. "It is not a good idea for her to plant her own garden. No one will eat anything that grows there, and it will only cause her pain. She can find solace here embroidering as your mum did."

"First, that is not your decision to make. Second, I will eat whatever my wife grows. Third, I will not see her confined to this room. She loves the woods and animals, and since she is presently deprived of that pleasure, she can at least enjoy herself in the garden."

Sky didn't need to force a smile. It came naturally hearing her husband not only defend her but hearing how well he had come to know her.

"Good, then I will assign servants to help her," Euniss said.

"I plan a small garden, so I require no help," Sky said, preferring solitary time in the garden and knowing that whoever was forced to help her would only resent her more.

"It will be there if you need it," Euniss said. "Now I will leave you two to have some time alone."

"Euniss," Slayer called out before the woman reached the door and turned. "Do not test me to see if I would side with my wife ever again."

"I don't know what you mean, my lord. I would never do that... though it is good to know you will defend her," Euniss said with a grin.

"Always," Slayer confirmed.

"I am sure Sky is pleased to hear that." Euniss's grin grew before she left the room.

"Bloody hell but that woman can be annoying," he said.

"I think she is delightful."

Slayer looked at his wife ready to reprimand her for not agreeing with him. But seeing her lovely smile and the joy in her eyes, he kissed her instead, lingering in it until he reluctantly ended it.

He took hold of her chin. "Listen well. I am the only one you need to seek permission from for anything. Do you understand?"

"Aye, I do. Now tell me what troubles you," she said, taking his hand and tugging him to the chair to sit and once he did, she made herself comfortable in his lap.

He tucked his arm around her waist to keep her nestled there. "What makes you think I am troubled."

She pressed her hand on his chest. "I can feel it in you."

"You seldom cry. I do not like it when you cry," he said, kissing her cheek lightly.

"I shed no more than a few tears, too few to matter."

"Your tears will always matter to me, *mo ghaol.*"

Her heart felt like it stopped with him calling her, my love, and she wondered if he even realized he had done so. Not wanting to point it out or fuss over it, she smiled. "Do not think to distract me from finding out what disturbs you."

He did not know where those words, *my love*, had come from, but he found that they fit her perfectly.

"Melvin, one of my men returned today with news from Clan Murdock," he said.

She would have jumped off his lap if he hadn't held her firmly. "Can I speak to him?"

"Nay, he needed to take his leave again, but he said Elsie asked about you and how you were doing, and I told him you were well and doing good and that she had nothing to worry about."

"She is well then? And my da?"

"I forgot to ask about your da, but Elsie does well with her new husband. He is a good man and will treat her well and—" He paused.

"What do you hesitate to tell me?" she asked concerned.

"Something I should have told you earlier. My tracker, Noble, I sent to find Leora… he is her husband."

"Does Leora know that?"

"She will when Noble finds her. You are not surprised at this news?" he asked, expecting her to be shocked by it.

She shook her head. "If my da arranged marriages for Elsie and me, it is only reasonable to assume he would do the same for Leora. I assume you helped to arrange the marriage since Leora is wed to a Gallowglass warrior."

"I did and your da was only too glad to agree to it since Noble is my fiercest warrior and will keep Leora safe."

"Is he patient?" Sky asked.

He nodded. "Aye, he is since tracking requires much patience."

"Your fierce tracker will need plenty of patience to deal with my all too-stubborn sister. And I warn you, Elsie might accept hearing that I am well, but Leora will not rest until she is able to see and speak to me herself."

"In time, I will permit it," he assured her.

She understood the reason for the delay. It could prove dangerous for the three of them. She only hoped it would not be too long before she was reunited with her sisters.

"Noble is a good man?" she asked.

"The finest and most honorable."

She quieted and laid her head on his shoulder.

"Something troubles you now. Tell me," he said and squeezed the curve of her waist gently.

"I wonder if my sisters question who they are like I do. I don't know where I truly came from nor do I know anything about my true parents, or why my mother felt the need to give me away. Who truly am I?"

"You are my wife. You belong to me now and always, nothing else matters," he said, but knew it did to her and one day, when all was settled, he would help her find the truth.

Chapter Seventeen

Sky was worried. The hound who had refused the bone yesterday did so again today and though she tried to coax him to the fence so she could get a better look at him, he wouldn't budge from where he rested. She had told him repeatedly that she would never harm him, only help him, but he continued to keep his distance.

Worried over the hound, she went in search of Slayer after leaving the kitten in the kitchen. Euniss and her workers had taken a fancy to Angel, to Sky's great relief, so she felt comfortable leaving the kitten there at times.

No one paid her any mind as she walked through the village except Glynis. She smiled and nodded at her now and so did Oona, though the woman prevented her daughter from approaching her. But at least it was a start. She spotted Slayer talking with two warriors when a woman's screams brought her to an abrupt halt.

Seeing her husband rushing off, she followed in his direction and again came to an abrupt halt not far behind him.

Some people stood frozen, too frightened to move, women clutched their children, and men shielded their wives with their bodies, and all stared at the wolfhound who stood on one of the paths that wound through the village.

"Fane, back in the pen, now!" Slayer ordered with a fierceness that would have anyone obeying him.

Sky approached slowly to peer around her husband and saw that it was the wolfhound who refused the bone. He stood there growling softly. She was able to get a better look at him. He was ill, drooling profusely and unsteady on his feet. He was looking for someone to help him. She didn't hesitate, she ran around her husband, keeping a wide birth so he could not reach out and stop her.

"Sky!" Slayer yelled, thinking his strong command would be enough to stop her. It wasn't.

Gasps rushed through the crowd when Sky reached the hound and crouched down next to him.

"You're ill. Let me help you," she said, softly and eased her hand out gently to cup his face. He collapsed against her, forcing her to plop on her bottom, and his head dropped to rest in her lap.

Slayer had not waited, he followed her and was at her side. He crouched down next to her.

"He is ill and looking for help," Sky said, then called out, "Are any of the other hounds ill?"

"Nay," someone shouted. "They are fine, though they pace the pen and whine."

"They are worried for their friend," she said and ran her hand gently over him. "He trembles slightly and drools excessively." She had seen such symptoms in a few animals in the forest and had watched them eat something that forced them to empty their stomach. She knew what must be done and turned her head to look at Slayer. "I must force him to empty his stomach. Something inside him is making him ill."

"How can you make him do that?" Slayer asked, seeing how the hound kept himself close to Sky as if he instinctively knew she would help him.

"There are plants that can force one to empty his stomach, but that takes time and I fear if we wait, he might perish."

Anger sparked in Slayer's eyes. "Are you saying the hound was poisoned?"

"Twice now I have offered him bones and he has refused them, and he appears worse than when I only saw him a brief time ago. He ingested something and he needs to purge it."

Slayer's anger flared learning she had visited the hounds when he had warned her not to but now was not the time to debate it. "Do what is necessary to save Fane. He is my best hound, though a stubborn one."

Sky caught the annoyance in his eyes at her for not staying away from the hounds though concern as well. His annoyance would have to wait. Her only concern now was for Fane.

"I must stick my fingers down his throat as far as I can to force him to empty his stomach."

"Absolutely not. He will bite your fingers off," Slayer warned.

"He is too ill, and he knows I mean him no harm."

"I will do it," Slayer insisted.

"Nay, your hand is too large," she said and lifted Fane's head off her lap. "I am going to help you. You must trust me, Fane."

Slayer could have sworn the hound's eyes pleaded for her help.

Sky spoke softly to the hound, letting him know repeatedly as she soothingly stroked along the top of his head that she would never harm him, that he was safe with her.

Slayer understood that she was earning his trust and confidence with her soothing words and comforting strokes, and he offered what little help he could. "I will spread his mouth for you." He did not wait for her to agree, he gently spread the hound's mouth open.

Sky was as quick as she could be about it, the hound not making a fuss as if he understood it was what he needed. She withdrew her hand and he continued to gag until he turned his head away from her to release a bit of what was in his stomach.

"It is not enough," Sky said and did it again. It wasn't until the third try that Fane spewed a sizeable piece of meat. "I believe that is the culprit." She caressed the hound's head. "You did good, Fane, very good. You will begin to feel better. I will get you settled with some water and a soft bed where you can rest."

"He goes back to the pen," Slayer ordered.

"You cannot mean that. He still requires tending if he is to get well. Please, my lord," she said and rested her hand on his arm. "Please let me continue to help him."

In the time since meeting her, she had never shown him an ounce of anger. Her plea was soft, her touch gentle, and he wondered if that, in itself, was what healed.

Slayer stood and cast a glance over everyone there. "There is no more to see here. Return to your chores."

Some hurried a curious look at Sky and Fane, shaking their heads while others whispered amongst themselves. He knew what they thought. What strange powers did this woman with two different colored eyes possess that she could bend a fierce animal to her will?

"Please," Sky pleaded again. "Fane has served you well, please let me care for him."

"Care for him, but when he is well enough, he returns to the pen," Slayer said.

Her happiness and relief shined not only in her smile but her eyes as well. "I wish I could kiss you right now."

He hunched down and scolded softly, "Do not tempt me, wife, or I will be sending you to your bedchamber to do penance."

"I would do it most willingly."

He grumbled to himself, imagining her naked, kneeling at the side of the bed in prayer and what he would do seeing her there.

"Bloody hell, woman," he scolded and scooped Fane up in his arms, to keep his hands from touching her and walked to the keep, swearing beneath his breath as he went.

***

Sky had taken great pains to see Fane made comfortable in the Great Hall, piling blankets so he would have a soft bed to sleep on. She kept a bucket of water close and made sure he drank from it. She kept the kitten with her as well and damn if the small ball of fur didn't go to Fane and lick his face, as if empathizing with his plight, before settling against him to sleep, and Fane was too ill to object.

Slayer checked on the three now and again, spending a good portion of the night in his solar, wondering who could have poisoned Fane. He did not believe anyone in the clan poisoned him and since the hound got sick soon after their return home, he wondered if he had been poisoned before returning home. That seemed the most logical possibility. But why hadn't Boden, the other hound, taken ill? Fane was the dominate of the four and he could have refused to let Boden consume any of the meat. Why the wolfhounds? Unless the meat was not meant for the hounds and how would he ever determine that, not knowing where Fane was poisoned?

He returned to the Great Hall to see his wife had fallen asleep sitting up against the wall, though it hadn't taken long for her to slump to her side, her arm draped over Fane. He had desperately wanted to sit beside her and take her in his arms so she could rest against him, but he couldn't let anyone see them being so intimate. He had reluctantly taken himself to bed after checking on the trio one last time.

In the morning Fane was much better, his eyes alert, his drooling normal, and not a tremor to him. She had gotten to Fane early enough to save him, though it had been Fane who had sought her help. He had instinctively known she would help him. His wife did have a way with animals.

With Fanes' presence in the Great Hall, the servants avoided it. They were too fearful to be near him. Though they were in awe of Sky's courage, but also cautious, not sure if her strange ability to calm and tend the fierce animal came from good or evil. Then, of course, there was the sudden friendship of Fane and Angel that Slayer had witnessed earlier today. He had to admit it was a sight to see the little ball of fur bouncing and swatting playfully at Fane and the hound poking the kitten with his nose to send her tumbling only for her to bounce back on her feet and start the playful game over again. Then, suddenly tired, Angel would curl herself against Fane and they both would sleep.

His wife had moved the unlikely pair outside, the sunny day far too beautiful to remain indoors. He watched the strange pair now curled together sleeping not far from where his wife worked on the small patch of dirt that would become her garden. Those who worked the large garden kept their distance, no doubt, fearful of Sky as well as Fane. She had changed into the garments she was wearing when he rescued her, though they had been freshly washed, and she wore an apron over them. She was bent down focused on something in the dirt.

He approached, keeping his eyes on her. "Did you find something?"

She glanced up at him. "Your healer, do you have one? She would be of help to confirm what I suspect."

"Verina died shortly after my father. I am currently searching for a new one. Why? What have you found?" He stretched his hand out to help her to her feet.

Sky grasped onto his hand, enjoying the comforting feel of his strong touch, and held onto him a bit longer than she should have, but neither did he let go of her.

Wrinkles spread across Sky's brow. "That is odd that she should die not long after your da. Was she ill or simply old?"

"She was not old or young, though she was frail at times. But what is it you found?"

Sky pointed to a green sprout in the ground. "The odor alerted me, though it has yet to grow strong. But if I am not mistaken that is nightshade, a deadly plant that could have been used to poison your father and perhaps your healer as well. Could someone in the clan have poisoned your da?"

"I don't believe so. They all would fear the consequences of such a betrayal."

"But this plant is one you would find in a healer's garden, not the keep's kitchen garden."

"So, a healer would know how to use it?" he asked.

"Aye, a healer would know how deadly it could be if not used properly. How long had your healer been with you?"

"A year at the most. She was here when I returned from a battle and seemed pleasant enough, though she kept her distance from me and my men. We are trained to tend to our wounds and each other's wounds, so we had no need for her."

His brow narrowed and she asked, "You have a puzzling thought."

"Rory, the liar, told me that the man boasting about poisoning my father did so without even meeting him. I wonder if he got Verina to poison my da and she accidentally poisoned herself in doing so?"

"I suppose that is possible. With your father's illness worsening over several days, it seems unlikely that it was someone passing through who sought shelter for only a night or two."

"Not likely at all since anyone seeking shelter is not allowed inside the gates. They are welcome to shelter in the village outside the gates but only clan members are allowed beyond the gates."

"Did he entertain other nobles or chieftains in the Great Hall or in his solar?"

"He did, but none that I would suspect and none that I haven't already questioned. The fear in their eyes alone while talking with me confirmed what I suspected, none had a reason nor the courage to take my father's life."

Sky could only imagine the fear of the men Slayer had questioned. They knew what he was capable of, what horrible revenge he would inflict on whoever was responsible for his da's death. She doubted any one of them would take such a terrifying chance.

Though that had not been her reason for asking. "Would any one of them have hired someone to do the deed?"

"I doubt it since they would know that when I caught the person, I would make sure to get the truth out of him."

"Not if the person was dead," she said.

He was impressed with her questions, for the thought had crossed his mind as well. "As I told each one of the men who I questioned… there is always a link, and I promised them that I would find it."

Sky's concern to solve the mystery of his da's death grew, realizing that if his da could be poisoned so easily so could he and that realization upset her.

"Did your da die quick or did he linger in death?" she asked.

"It was several days before the healer realized it was not an illness that he suffered from but that he had been poisoned." His brow narrowed again. "Though come to think of it, it was Euniss who suggested my da might have been poisoned, not the healer." A puzzling look settled in his eyes. "I wonder why Euniss suspected poisoning when the healer hadn't."

"You cannot think Euniss had anything to do with your father's poisoning?"

"I will not disregard anything," he said.

She tilted her head in question. "Do you trust anyone?"

"Few. Lies fall far too easily from tongues especially when the lie can prove beneficial. Greed can tempt the most virtuous soul."

"And the most desperate and neither apply to Euniss," Sky said and looked past him. "Shall we find out?" She waved, seeing the woman, and called out, "Euniss, a moment, please."

Slayer turned, ready to summon the woman with a snap of his hand but she was already walking toward them.

"Do you need help, Sky?" Euniss asked when she reached them.

Slayer kept tight rein on his annoyance that his wife was not shown the respect due her as his wife, being addressed properly as Lady Sky, even if it was for her own protection. He was impatient to see this matter settled so she could take her rightful place as his wife.

"Was this area of land ever part of the kitchen garden?" Sky asked.

"Nay, this patch of land was for the healer's use. Verina would not let anyone go near it, warning that some plants were too dangerous to touch. It fell into disrepair when she died, and the frigid winter had not helped the few plants she had."

"Her healing garden was small?" Sky asked.

"Far smaller than our previous healer's garden," Euniss said.

"How did my father come by Verina?" Slayer asked.

Euniss shook her head and shrugged. "A question I asked him myself when she arrived. He told me that it was none of my concern. That we needed a healer and we now had one. That, of course, made me even more curious and somewhat suspicious of the healer since she did not seem a knowledgeable healer. But your father continued to dismiss my concerns, so I held my tongue."

"Until my father took ill," Slayer said.

"I did wonder over her healing skills when your father failed to improve no matter what Verina did, and when I suggested poisoning, she did pay heed to it."

"Or so she made you believe," Slayer said.

Euniss's brow rose in surprise. "It did cross my mind, but I and others had expressed concern about Verina not looking well after your father took ill. Do you think Verina poisoned your father?" Her glance drifted off briefly.

"You recall something?" Slayer asked.

"I cannot believe I dismissed it," Euniss said as if disappointed in herself."

"Tell me," Slayer ordered.

"I caught a servant wrinkling her nose at the bedding taken from your father's bedchamber that she was about to wash one day. I went to ask her if the bedding had gone too long before being changed when I caught a whiff of the scent myself. I warned the servant to say nothing that it was none of our concern."

"What wasn't your concern?" Slayer asked already surmising what it was.

"Verina's scent was potent on the bedding. It was an odd, overly sweet scent. I paid it no mind since I was well aware that your father was a potent man who slept with a variety of women and cared little for any of them." Euniss looked with pride on Slayer. "It is good you have not inherited your father's lack of honor and self-serving trait. Your mum had faith that you would be a good, honorable man, and she was right."

"What about Warrand?" Slayer asked, her remark unsettling him.

"She prayed for him but could see from a young age that Warrand would be much like his father, though she was pleased that Warrand had formed a close bond with you. She hoped he might learn from you and become a better man." Euniss turned her head and sniffed the air. "I must take my leave, sir, or your next meal will be served burnt."

Slayer looked at his wife with a mixture of annoyance, concern, and need in his eyes.

Sky felt it more than saw his need for her and she did not hesitate. She spoke loud enough for those in the distance to hear. "Now go and leave me in peace to do as I please. I will not tolerate being dictated to any longer."

Anger sparked in his eyes at her commanding voice until he realized what she was doing, giving him a reason to send her to their bedchamber.

He let his anger surface, knowing his wife would understand it was not directed at her. "Go to your bedchamber and you will remain there until I give you permission to leave it."

The fiery anger in his eyes froze her for a moment.

"GO!" he shouted.

She jumped and hurried off, though not before scooping up Angel and calling out, "Come, Fane."

The wolfhound did not hesitate. He hurried to his feet and with a snarl at Slayer, rushed to follow Sky.

Chapter Eighteen

Slayer waited for a short time then entered the keep with a furious scowl on his face and issued an order for Euniss to bring ale to his solar. When the only two servants there fled the Great Hall, he went and hurried up the stairs to his bedchamber.

Sky rushed to him as soon as he stepped into the room, and his arms closed around her. They stood there silently hugging each other tight, savoring the moment and the warmth and strength of each other. A light rap on the door had them stepping apart.

Slayer opened it, expecting to see Euniss standing there and stepped aside for her to enter.

"I delivered the ale to your solar as directed so everyone believes you are there. However, I thought you could use some wine and a bit of food while you talk." She set the tray on a small table. "There is much for you to consider, my lord, but do remember that your mum had great love for you and greater faith in you."

"You feel betrayed, don't you?" Sky said, reaching out to take hold of her husband's hand after Euniss left.

He looked puzzled. "How did you know that?"

"I feel a touch of betrayal by my father for not being truthful with me and my sisters when he learned we were in danger. I also feel a sense of guilt for feeling that way, yet I cannot help but think that it would have been prudent of him to confide in us."

"Aye, I do feel betrayed by both my father and brother, and I question the bond I thought I had with Warrand. He stood beside my father the day he announced I would train vigorously and join an elite group of mercenaries that was being formed. Warrand listened to me pledge my life to protecting him and his heirs. Both my father and brother claimed it was an honor for me to do this. How could it be an honor when love for my brother and clan would have allowed me to do nothing less? I felt no honor that day. I felt less important as though my life meant nothing to either of them."

"So, that is what turned you heartless," she said, her heart hurting for him as she eased herself into the crook of his arm and wrapped her arm around his waist.

"It was the beginning, battle after battle adding to it until I found myself not caring for anyone or anything. My only purpose in life... die for my brother and clan."

"No more is that your purpose. Your purpose now is to lead your clan wisely, live an honorable life, be a good husband, and produce an abundance of heirs to secure the survival of Clan Ravinsher."

"It is not easy to let go of the Gallowglass warrior in me."

"I believe in time, when the chaos settles, that he will leave you."

He shook his head. "He will never leave me. He was forged with fire and sword and the cry of battle is in his blood, a cry that he will never be able to ignore."

"Then it is time for you to search for something new to be forged inside you. Something stronger than fire and sword and the cry of battle."

"There is nothing stronger."

"Aye, there is, but only you can find it," she said, "and once you do, then and only then will life hold new meaning for you."

"An impossible search."

"An easy one, if you trust," she said, for she had trusted and found the unexpected... love.

She stepped away from him reluctantly when she would have much rather kissed him, but that would lead to coupling, and she knew he needed more time to talk. So, she went and poured them each a tankard of wine.

"Honor has my time better spent tracking down who killed my father and brother and Clyde. I will not waste my time on an impossible search that benefits only me," he said.

"It may not only benefit you," she said, her heart having felt heavy when she learned of Clyde's death. She had not known him but the brief moment she shared with him was enough to see he'd been a decent man and Slayer had confirmed that when he spoke of him.

He took a swallow of wine then thought a moment more. "Rory could be speaking the truth about what he heard."

"With Rory being a known liar, I would assume a partial truth lies somewhere in his words. Perhaps this man and Verina were friends, and he was there to help her if necessary. Or perhaps she was forced or coerced into poisoning your father," Sky suggested.

"So, Verina could have coupled with my father to win his trust," Slayer said with disgust then downed the rest of his wine. He went to the table to refill his tankard. "I believed my father did what he did for the survival of the clan, but I wonder now if there was more to it than only that. I wonder if it was power he was hungry for and in his search for it he got caught up in something that cost him his life and Warrand's as well. He pushed me hard to become a fearless and feared warrior, a leader in the Gallowglass. He told me repeatedly to never accept defeat, to fear no one, to let no one stand in my way, to kill without thought or remorse, to care for no one and not to be foolish enough to let anyone care for me. He got the ferocious beast he wanted until there came a time when he, himself, feared the beast he created." He turned an angry glare at her. "Even you fear me."

She did not see his anger. She only saw his pain. He reminded her of a few of the animals in the forest, leery at first to approach her, not sure if they should trust but so desperately wanting to. He knew she feared him at times, she had admitted it to him. It wasn't that he was looking for her to confirm. He was looking to see if she could care for him.

Sky went to him and took the tankard from his hand to place on the table then she took hold of his hands. "I was given no choice to marry you. But I have a choice whether I will care for you or not. You made that easy by choosing to become my friend, something no one has ever done, so I will always care for you... but—" She felt him stiffen. "I made the choice alone to love you with all my heart and that I will do even beyond my dying day."

Something shattered in Slayer, broke away, released him to be embraced with an intense joy he never thought existed or was even possible. He recalled the one specific time they had coupled and how he had thought of feeling loved. He had been right. His wife loved him, and he so wanted to love her in return, but he wasn't sure how.

Sky saw the joy in his eyes and the confusion, and she pressed her fingers gently against his lips. "In time, you will come to understand love and know you love me as well, for I feel it every time you make love to me."

He did not understand what he felt, he only knew he never wanted to lose it, never wanted to lose her. He swung her up into his arms and kissed her gently. "I think we should concentrate on producing an abundance of heirs."

She kissed his cheek. "And every one of them will be conceived with an abundance of love."

He felt it, though the warrior within him would deny it, think it foolish, but it could not be ignored. It overpowered him, gripped at his gut and heart, forcing him to acknowledge it.

Love.

Did he truly love his wife? Was that what he felt that he could not understand? He did not know but he would find out. For now, he would do his best to show her what he felt.

***

Wakefulness stirred Slayer the next morning, though it was more an urge to come fully awake, to open his eyes. Or was it a warning? He did not debate the matter; he opened his eyes.

Sky lay on her side beside him, her hand stretched out to his face, though frozen in flight, and her cheeks were stained deep pink. No desire stirred in her two different colored eyes. On the contrary, it was fright he saw sparking there.

Then he felt it, a movement on top of his head and he all but growled at her. "Do not tell me the kitten is on top of my head."

"You are on her pillow," Sky said softly.

"*Her* pillow?" Slayer asked none too gently.

"She likes to nap on it," Sky said and quickly snatched Angel off the top of his head and the kitten hurried to bury herself against Sky's chest.

"The animals do not belong in bed," he admonished and received a warning growl from Fane, whose head had suddenly popped up from beyond Sky's side of the bed. Slayer sprung up to lean over Sky and glare at the hound near the hearth. "Never growl at me, Fane."

The hound approached the bed submissively, his body hunched, and laid his chin on Sky's hip and whined.

"He is torn between his loyalty to you and his gratitude for my help."

"His loyalty to me comes before anything else," — Slayer paused, his brow narrowing— "though I am glad to see that he protects you but not from me."

"Then let him know you mean me no harm, or he will remain confused."

She was right about that. His hounds trusted him because he made his commands clear to them. He rested his hand gently on Sky's waist. "I protect Sky, Fane, just as you protect her. She is part of our pack. We will keep her safe and she will see to our care."

Fane licked his hand as if understanding.

"Confirm my words," Slayer ordered with a possessive squeeze to her waist.

Sky turned on her back to glance at Fane, her husband's hand moving along with her as she turned to lay on her back, keeping a possessive hold of her.

"I care for you all, Fane," she said and patted his head.

As soon as his wife turned her attention on him, he said, "The animals do not belong in our bedchamber. They carry bugs and I will not have bugs in our bedchamber."

He remained sitting next to her and she looked up at him from her prone position. Even upon waking, he soothed the eyes though his manner was a bit grumpy.

She reached up to brush a strand of hair off his face. "I rubbed them both with a powered mixture of copious amounts of mint and rosemary to keep the bugs off them and had rosemary and lavender placed around the room. Fane and Angel probably have less bugs on them than the clan's people."

The kitten had crawled over Sky to get to Fane and once at the edge of the bed fell off. Fane quickly scooped up the little ball of fur by the rough of her neck and carried her to the hearth where he plopped down after releasing the kitten only to have her curl against him.

"They have grown fond of each other. They are an odd but loving pair," Sky said with a gentle smile.

Odd but loving pair. Would people think that of him and Sky when it was found out they were wed?

Sky sat up and placed a gentle hand on his arm. "Fane would serve you better if he remained by your side rather than closed away in the pen and Angel is my friend and I prefer she remain with me."

My friend.

He felt a pang in his chest that spread into annoyance, realizing that Euniss was the only person in the clan who spoke with her. No one had attempted to make friends with her. The animals were her only friends.

He hooked her around the waist and fell back on the bed with her. "Keep Angel off the bed. It is for you and me alone." He kissed her and did not stop, so it was sometime later that they left their bedchamber. He left first, though not before stopping at the door to say, "I detest not being able to take your hand or grab you in a hug. This must end soon, for I will not be kept from you. Fane! With me, now!"

The hound got to his feet and the kitten was ready to follow him, but Sky scooped her up and when the door closed behind Slayer, Sky said, "We will go soon and see if my husband heeded my words and kept Fane with him or returned him to the pen. Where, of course, we will rescue him."

Sky made her way to the kitchen, staying out of the way of the busy servants preparing the morning meal and fixed a bowl of food for the kitten and took it outside. She ignored the stares and whispers of those who worked in the garden. She expected both after the incident with Fane. But having her husband to talk with, and Angel, as well as Fane in the last few days, she felt she had an abundance of friendship.

"Angel is doing good. Soon she will no longer fit in the pouch you carry her in."

Sky turned and smiled at Euniss. "She does do well."

"It is your loving heart that grows her strong and it touches more than only Angel."

"Aye, Fane has recovered well."

"It is not Fane I think of, and I am pleased to see it. He deserves it. It has been too long since he has known a loving heart and touch. You are good for him." Euniss said, her eyes tearing. "His mum would be relieved and pleased."

"What was his mum like?" Sky asked, curious to know all she could about her husband.

"Lady Candra was a sweet woman, too sweet for Lord Bannaty. She obeyed his every command. She did not want her son to be named Slayer, but Lord Bannaty insisted that he would grow to be a great warrior. She was not strong enough to defy him and he cared nothing for her. Theirs, like most, was an arranged marriage. Lord Bannaty was not an easy man to be wed to. His concern was always for the clan, the land, and sustaining it beyond his years. The two lads spent little time with their mum thanks to their father. Lady Candra spent time in her solar and would retreat in prayer often to Whitehall Abbey, not far from here. I believe she died of a broken heart."

Sky's heart broke for the woman. She understood the isolation and loneliness she must have suffered, having experienced some herself. But at least she had had her sisters. Lady Candra had had no one, not even her sons. Lord Bannaty had been a cruel man, and she did not want to think about what life may have been like wed to Warrand if he had inherited his father's traits.

"Did the clan favor Lord Bannaty?" Sky asked.

"He was respected and tolerated since he took good care of the clan. All had shelter, no one went hungry, and the clan was well protected, even more so when Slayer became part of the Gallowglass. So, there were no complaints just as it is now with Lord Slayer."

"Yet someone poisoned Lord Bannaty. Why, if he was at least respected?"

"A question we all ponder," Euniss said.

"Do you recall any visitors he may have had before he took ill?" Sky asked, aware Slayer had probably asked the very same question of her but thinking it would not hurt to ask again. More importantly she loved her husband and wanted to keep him safe just as much he wanted her kept safe.

"The usual chieftains and lords that visited with him, some seeking his counsel on matters, others requesting help. Lord Slayer spoke to every one of them when they arrived to pay their respects to him after his father was buried. Most left pale or shaken, others so frightened, you would think they had just spoken to the devil himself. It was obvious every one of them were far too frightened of Slayer to harm his father."

A shout from the kitchen summoned Euniss.

"I must go tend to my duties unless there is something else you need from me."

"Nay, you have been most generous in helping me and I am grateful."

"Oh, I just remembered," Euniss said, turning around after reaching the door. "After Lord Slayer spoke to me about our healer, Verina, and the possibility of her poisoning Lord Bannaty, I recalled a cleric that had arrived here just before Lord Bannaty had turned ill, then he vanished just before Lord Bannaty died. I recalled Verina speaking with him often."

"Was the cleric known to Lord Bannaty?"

"Nay. He never entered through the gates. He always kept a pious stature, keeping his head bent, his hood pulled down, and his hands clasped in prayer. I must tell Lord Slayer right away. He will want to know and see if he can find the cleric."

"You are busy. I can tell him, and he can seek you out to question you further," Sky offered.

"That would be most helpful," Euniss said and lowered her voice for only Sky to hear. "Thank you, Lady Sky."

It was good that Sky's back was turned to those working in the garden or they would have seen her surprised look. With her marriage to Slayer a secret, she had not fully grasped her position here and what it meant to be his wife, to be the lady of the castle. It quite intimidated her. However, she was learning, first from her time imprisoned in the abbey, then rescued by Slayer and their time at the cottage, and now here at the castle, that locking herself away would not serve her well. It was time she freed herself, especially after hearing about Lady Candra's plight.

She recalled when Euniss showed her Lady Candra's solar. There was a small hearth that kept the room comfortably warm, and a single chair and table where the woman would have sat. She remembered seeing a large basket piled with various pieces of embroidered cloth left unfinished. She imagined Slayer's mum sitting there before the hearth, embroidering in peace and silence day after endless day, heartbroken, never having the courage to free herself.

"Never. Never will I be like her, Angel." Sky smiled, thinking how her sisters would have freed her from such a horrible situation, but believing now that she not only had the strength but the courage to free herself. Oddly enough, she owed that discovery to a powerful Gallowglass warrior.

"Let's go find Fane, Angel. We'll check the pen first and bring the other hounds some bones," she said, hoping Slayer had kept Fane with him.

She slipped Angel into the pouch, thinking she would not need to carry her around soon, though the kitten did seem to enjoy it, peeking her head out in interest as they walked through the village. Suspicious glances were cast her way, but she paid no mind to them while keeping a keen eye on her surroundings, continuing to hope she would see Fane with Slayer.

The hounds greeted her with eager barks, and she smiled seeing how happy they were to see her. Angel leaned further out of the pouch anxiously searching for Fane.

The wolfhound was nowhere to be seen and Sky was pleased. It meant Slayer had kept Fane with him.

The hounds' tails wagged with such excitement that their whole backsides shook, letting her know they were thrilled to see her, and she need not fear them.

"It is good to see you all again," she said and pulled out bones from the sack she carried to hand one to each of them. They eagerly snatched her offering out of her hand and went to lay down to enjoy their feast.

"Enjoy, my friends. I will see you tomorrow, and I will see what other treat I can find for you."

The hounds' heads went up at the mention of a treat and after she sent them a wave, they returned to enjoying their bones.

"I believe Fane is with Slayer, Angel, so let's find them both," she said, after turning away from the pen and Angel agreed with a strong, for her size, meow.

She kept her eyes peeled for Fane and Slayer as she wandered through the busy village. It wasn't until she approached the gate that she caught sight of her husband. He was speaking with a warrior and Fane stood by his side until he caught sight of Sky.

"Sit, Fane!" Slayer ordered when the hound went to run and Fane immediately obeyed him, plopping down on his bottom beside him.

People watched in awe and Sky heard some of the whispers of those nearby.

"He commands the hellhound and the witch."

"Even evil fears him."

"He has the power over her."

"She cannot harm us."

Sky had heard such whispers before but that didn't mean it did not hurt to hear them again. Though she was more concerned with the way her husband glanced her way while speaking with the warrior and a chill ran through her. Whatever they discussed had something to do with her.

Her sisters.

Had something happened to her sisters? She hurried toward him, but he reached her first. "Tell me," she pleaded anxiously.

"When we get to the keep," he said.

"Please, I cannot wait to hear. Tell me. Is it my sisters? Has something happened to them? My da? Is it my da?"

"Your family is safe."

"Then what is it?" she asked, refusing to move until he told her.

"News that took some time to reach me. First, Elsie has discovered who her true parents are, and her mum is the woman responsible for placing you and Leora with the two you believed were your parents and sometime after that Leora arrived home."

He did not tell her that Elsie had almost lost her life and that Leora had saved her. That was best left for her to discuss with her sisters.

Sky's heart burst with joy. "That is wonderful news. I am so relieved that Leora is home safe and unharmed. She is unharmed, isn't she?"

"Aye, Leora is unharmed and has settled in at Clan Skirling with Noble."

"How did she take the news about having a husband?"

"I don't know, but I am sure she will tell you all about it when you are able to meet. She is, if anyhing, persistent about seeing you. But until both your safety can be secured that is not something that will happen anytime soon."

Sky would not think of putting her sister's life at risk even if she was eager to see her again. When the time was right they would be reunited. She was just glad Leora was safe and she hoped the best for her marriage to Noble.

"I am so pleased for Elsie and for Leora and myself since Elsie's true mum can now tell us about our true parents."

Slayer wished the news he was about to tell her was far different. "Unfortunately, she cannot. She is dead."

Chapter Nineteen

Sky sat in her husband's solar trying to digest the news and a soft smile suddenly lit her face. "Though this is sorrowful news for Elsie, it truly is wonderful news for the three of us. While before we had little information about our past, we now have a place to start. Elsie's mum must have left a trail of sorts that we can follow. That reminds me. I spoke with Euniss only moments ago." She reiterated what Euniss had told her about the cleric.

"You smile yet your brow wrinkles. Something disturbs you about this cleric?" Slayer asked, wondering how his wife was able to find a bright side to the surprising news.

"Euniss said he was a pious man, keeping his hands steepled in prayer and his hood pulled down over his head. What if he wasn't a cleric? What if he posed as one to meet in secret with Verina?"

It continued to amaze him that they thought so much alike. "A thought that came to me as soon as you told me. I will see what I can do to find him."

"Did your father share anything on his deathbed that might help us?" she asked. "Surely, if he was worried about the clan's survival, he would have shared all his plans, even his doubts and suspicions, with you to make certain they saw fruition."

"My father was a stubborn man. I truly believe that he did not think he was on his deathbed. He believed whatever ailed him would pass and he would live on as leader of Clan Ravinsher. It was only when he could barely talk that he attempted to speak with me and by then it was too late." He scowled and drew her into his arms. "Your brow continues to pucker. Something still troubles you."

"It all troubles me," she said and rested her head on his chest, though hard with muscle, served as the perfect pillow day or night. She reluctantly lifted her head to look at him and could not help but smile. Though it was not his fine features that brought the smile to her face, it was more than that. It was that he was her friend, her husband, and that she could talk freely with him. "It is a mystery that grows and defies solving and keeps us apart far too much." She stretched up to reach for his lips, but they were already descending on hers. A bolt of pleasure struck her and raced through her.

Slayer did not intend to linger in the kiss. That would be dangerous since it would not be long before he bent her over the table and satisfied them both. Instead, he held onto her, refusing to let her go, keeping her as close to him as he could. So close that she felt part of him. That was how the kiss made him feel—that she was part of him.

"Lord Slayer!"

The shout from just beyond the solar's door tore their lips apart and Slayer cursed beneath his breath, irritated that their kiss had been interrupted. His arm, however, lingered around her waist. He did not want to let her go. Not now. Not ever.

"Lord Slayer!"

There was a tremor in the shout and Slayer reluctantly released Sky to turn around and see Fane sitting in front of the closed door growling, warning the person beyond the door to stay away.

Slayer could not stop himself from grinning. The hound deserved a treat for protecting their privacy. His wife was right. It would be prudent of him to always keep Fane with him.

"We will finish this later, *mo ghaol*," Slayer said, reluctantly releasing her and going to the door.

Sky's stomach fluttered, hearing him call her my love for the second time. She loved the way it rolled off his tongue so easily and with such strength as if confirming it for himself, and she smiled.

"What is it, Reed?" Slayer demanded after opening the door.

Reed hesitated, seeing Sky there.

"Tell me!" Slayer ordered sternly.

Reed's head snapped to the side to look at Slayer, and he spoke quickly. "Two of our sentinels were found dead as were several mercenaries when it came time for our sentinels to change their posts. Fearing for the sentinels stationed further out from the castle, a troop went to warn them and came upon what was left of the mercenaries. They battled and returned with prisoners in tow. They have been secured outside the gate."

Sky had come to understand that her husband did not like losing any of his men. One glance at him now confirmed that. She could see that the news angered

Slayer. He fisted his hands at his sides and his brow narrowed. But mostly, it was the way his body grew taut, intensifying his muscles, his chest expanding and his arms bulging. Any sane man would walk away from him, and any wise woman would hide.

As was the way of the Gallowglass, all captives were immediately questioned, defeat making for looser tongues in hope of being spared torture or death. So, Slayer asked with confidence, "Has any of the captured mercenaries provided us with any new information, something that we don't already know?"

"Nay," Reed said with a quick shake of his head. "The promise of abundant coin is what drew them to the mission. Though it was learned that some retreated when told it was the Gallowglass they would fight. More left when it became known that it was Lord Slayer and his warriors they would face. One other thing, I thought not to mention it, but you always said even the smallest detail should not be ignored."

"That's right. The smallest of details could be the most important, so tell me," Slayer urged.

"It could be nothing more than a mistake," Reed said. "Glen took count of the captured men, as usual, once we had them all secured. I counted them again once they were settled to confirm the number. I got one man less than Glen did. I had Glen count again and it agreed with mine."

"It is not like Glen to make a mistake," Slayer said, his brow pinched in concern. "Let's go count again." He turned to Sky to order her to remain in the keep. Her eager smile halted his remark, giving her time to speak.

"I am good with numbers. I will help with the count," Sky said, her smile brightening.

Reed's face lit with a smile and his cheeks flushed, Sky's lovely smile captivating him.

"Lead the way!" Slayer snapped at Reed, though he knew where the captives would be held. He wanted the warrior's eyes off Sky.

Reed jumped at Slayer's gruff command. "Aye, sir."

They reached the area where the captured mercenaries were being kept corralled in a circle surrounded by Gallowglass warriors. Some men lay on the ground groaning in pain, their bandages soaked with blood. Others had minor wounds, and a few had no wounds at all. But every eye there focused on Slayer as soon as he came to a stop in front of them. The groans soon ceased, some men paled and some trembled. Their fate lay in the hands of the man now looking from one captive to another until he had met all eyes there.

"We count now, Reed," Slayer ordered and once again looked from man to man.

"I counted twelve," Reed said when finished.

"I counted the same," Slayer agreed and looked to his wife.

Sky had waited to see if he would permit her to join in and she was pleased that he did. "I got twelve as well."

"You say Glen got one more than you," Slayer said.

"Aye, thirteen was what he counted," Reed confirmed.

Slayer looked over the captives and called out, "The first who tells me who escaped from your group will be freed."

They all started yelling out names and Slayer waited, not saying a word, letting them call out name after name until the voices died and no one spoke. They stood staring, waiting for Slayer to speak.

Sky watched fascinated. Her husband had to know they all would attempt to throw a name at him in hopes of being freed. Yet he stood there and did nothing but listen. She pondered what his plan might be, then one man spoke up.

"He snuck in and snuck out. He's not one of us."

All heads turned, their eyes going to an older, grey-haired man. A blood-stained bandage was wrapped around his leg, and another circled his arm.

Slayer waved him forward. "Come we will talk."

Chapter Twenty

Sky expected to be dismissed upon entering the Great Hall with her husband and was pleased, though surprised when informed otherwise.

"You may join me at the dais while I question the man, but you will remain silent," Slayer said and with a light touch of his hand on her lower back guided her around the dais to sit. "Not a word," he reminded and only after she sat, did he settle himself in the chair beside her.

Jugs of cider and ale were brought to the table and tankards filled while bowls of food were sat in front of them. Sky's stomach gurgled reminding her that she had yet to eat this morning.

"Eat," Slayer ordered. "The morning meal has been delayed long enough."

Sky did not hesitate. She reached for a quail egg and a piece of bread just as Reed entered with the prisoner. She was reaching for another quail egg by the time the man reached the dais, his wounded leg leaving him with a slow gait and a visible limp.

"Your name?" Slayer demanded when Reed forced the man to a stop a few steps away from the dais.

"Lester, sir," the man said, staring at the food with hunger in his eyes.

"Tell me of the man who snuck in and out of the prisoners' circle."

"I did not see him sneak in. I did not even give it any thought until you asked about him and I looked around and did not see him there."

Sky now understood why Slayer had handled the situation as he did. He knew someone would think to look around and see who might be missing.

"He looked no different from us, though talked more with a grunt of sorts. He was about my height, though younger than me. Common enough features, at least from what I could see through the dirt and sweat worn on his face. He hadn't been injured. He sat beside me, worried over our fate and if more mercenaries would attempt to kill the woman." Lester went to nod at Sky and stopped when she raised her head. He stared, not able to look away.

"Take your eyes off her," Slayer ordered.

Lester turned his head away and shifted his injured leg with a grimace.

"What else did this man say to you?" Slayer demanded.

"He told me the coin was not worth it and blamed a friend for talking him into joining the mercenary group for this mission alone."

"So, you're a motley crew that was hastily thrown together for this mission," Slayer said, having realized that upon first seeing them and learning that his two dead warriors had managed to kill twelve more of them before losing their lives. If the fools had planned well and worked in unity, the outcome could have been vastly different.

"When you're hungry, sir, you'll do just about anything for food," Lester said. "I have nothing left, no family, no home—"

"No clan?" Slayer asked.

"Nay, sir. It was swallowed up in a quick battle and the new chieftain made it clear that if you could not do your share, you were no longer welcome in the clan. My leg had been damaged in a previous battle and never healed right." He glanced down at the bloody cloth around his leg. "It's probably worse now."

"What else did this man say to you?"

"He said women weren't worth the trouble they caused, especially the beautiful ones."

Lester barely shook his head, but Slayer caught it and demanded, "What have you not said?"

"The man said something odd but now getting a closer look at one of the Murdock sisters his words make sense."

"What words?" Slayer asked, the annoyance in his voice warning that he was losing his patience.

Lester hurried to respond. "He said, 'Beauty or not, it is good the woman with the strange affliction dies.'" He shook his head in a way that questioned. "No mention was ever made about a Murdock sister with an affliction. So, how was he aware of it?"

Sky placed her tankard back on the table without taking a swallow and contemplated the question. How could that single mercenary know about her affliction when none of the others did? A quick glance at Slayer caught deep wrinkles at the corner of his eyes and told her that he questioned it himself.

"You did not see this man leave?" Slayer asked.

"Nay, sir. I was exhausted from the battle and the pain from my wounds. I closed my eyes and when next I opened them, he was gone."

"What were you told of this mission?" Slayer asked.

"That there was a large bounty for the death of the two Murdock sisters with the light-colored hair."

"Do you know who offers this bounty?"

"Nay, the men answer to the fellow who leads us, and he answers to someone else from what I could tell. I did not care as long as I got some of the coins. Those who were wise enough to have fled when your men descended on us probably joined the small band of mercenaries that waited for news and, no doubt, they have already fled."

"Where would they go?" Slayer asked, though the answer did not matter to him. He would send warriors to track them down.

"Somewhere they believed safe for a few days at least. Men joined us along the way and talked of being moved around to different mercenary groups. Some talked about men leaving to try the mission on their own so they could keep the coins for themselves. Others mentioned some mercenary leaders killing those who attempted to go off on their own. It is chaos out there and all for the sake of generous coins."

"The top mercenary leader would keep the majority of the coins for himself and share little, if any, coins with his men," Slayer said.

Lester tilted his head slightly and squinted in question. "Are you saying the men will get no coins for their help as promised?"

"Why do you think the Gallowglass was founded?" Slayer asked of the gullible man. "Nobles were searching for warriors who could be trusted, honorable warriors who would fight for honorable issues, and who would keep their word and not steal from or lie to the nobles."

"There is no honor among the men I fought alongside," Lester said, sadly.

"Then you were a wise man to speak up."

"Your word was that I am a free man, my lord," Lester reminded.

"Free to remain here at Clan Ravinsher," Slayer said, tapping the table hard with his finger. "When I can confirm what you say is the truth, then you are free to leave."

Lester's eyes showed worry. "That might be difficult to do, my lord."

"Not as difficult as you may believe, Lester. I have eyes and ears everywhere in the Highlands. I will know soon enough if you speak the truth or lie to me. The truth will bring you freedom. Lies will bring you death." Slayer turned to Reed. "Have his wounds tended to and see that he is fed. House him with the warriors so they can keep an eye on him and make certain he does not go outside the castle walls."

"Should I assign him a chore, my lord?" Reed asked.

"Not yet, and make sure he is watched closely," Slayer ordered and returned his attention to Lester. "A warning. If I find you lied to me or you try to escape before I set you free, I will find you no matter how long it takes and when I am done with you, you will beg for death, but it will not be forthcoming."

Sky shuddered along with Lester, who also paled when hearing Slayer's ominous warning.

Lester bobbed his head and turned away as quickly as his injury would allow and followed slowly behind Reed.

With his eyes still on Lester, Slayer waited. Once the door closed behind the two men, he turned to his wife. "What do you think of Lester's story?"

"I cannot say for sure if he speaks truthfully or not," she admitted, a bit perplexed. "It is difficult to tell when a person lies, and Lester has good reason to lie… freedom. So, you are wise to keep him around until you can find out the truth. However, I agree with Lester's question of how the man knew about my affliction when Lester did not know anything about it until he saw me. And another thing that gave me pause was that the man asked if Lester thought more mercenaries would pursue the hunt for the woman, not two women since no one knows whether it is Leora or me who is the true target? And why would this man even care if he claimed it wasn't worth it?"

Once again, his wife impressed him. She had a sharp mind and listened well. He had found issue with the same things Lester had told them as she did. Issues he intended to pursue as they searched for the truth.

"What are your thoughts," she asked, more relieved than pleased that he continued to think of her differently than others. Most people not only thought her two different colored eyes evil, but many thought it also left her brain lacking, not able to comprehend like normal people.

"It makes me wonder if two different people search for you and your sisters and for different reasons."

"I did not think of that, but you could be right." Instinct had her reaching out to lay her hand on his arm when she realized what she was doing and dropped her hand in her lap. "That might make it more difficult to keep me safe."

Slayer slipped his hand beneath the table to grip her hand that lay in her lap. "Nothing will stop me from keeping you safe."

The voices of servants not far off reminded them that they were not alone, but Slayer kept his hand gripped on hers beneath the table, not willing to let go, not just yet.

"I must go talk with my warriors," he whispered, and his hand slowly fell off hers and he gave her leg a gentle squeeze before standing. "Stay close to the keep," he ordered gruffly.

Sky smiled softly at his gruff manner, knowing it was for the benefit of others there and her reputation. "As you say, my lord." She saw in his eyes what she felt that he wanted to kiss her as much as she wanted him to.

"With me, Fane," Slayer ordered, and the hound followed his rushed steps out of the keep.

She hurried to her feet. Time to keep herself busy and rid herself of thoughts of her husband, not a likely endeavor. He invaded her thoughts constantly in ways that made her smile and ways that stirred her desire. There were far more important matters for her to dwell on. She smiled. What could be more important than her husband? She shook her head again.

"Many things," she scolded herself and hurried to find Angel and take her with her to the garden.

It didn't take long to find the kitten sound asleep in a makeshift bed by one of the two hearths in the kitchen. She looked far too comfortable to disturb her and feeling a lovely breeze drifting in from the open door, she eagerly sought the outdoors.

"Join me," a voice said.

A bit startled, after only taking a few steps outside, she turned her head.

"I did not mean to frighten you, but the day has turned lovely, the sun peeking out from behind the clouds now and again," Lester said, sitting on the long bench, which sat against the outside wall of the kitchen, holding a wood bowl, the food in it almost gone. "I love the sun and we don't get enough of it."

She was going to refuse his invitation not sure she would be safe with him. But with two Gallowglass warriors nearby keeping watch on him, what was there for her to worry about? Talking with him could help determine if it were truth or lies, he had told.

She joined him on the bench, though kept a good space between them.

"You are safe with me. Freedom is more important to me than coins," Lester said with a smile then gave a nod at the bowl in his hand. "Your cook is not only a good one but generous with her portions."

"That she is, but you should have had your leg tended to before you ate," Sky said with a nod at the bloody cloth.

"The wound can wait. It has been too long since I have eaten."

Being this close to the man, she noticed he appeared far fitter for an older man. But there were some older men fitter than most so she could not be sure about his age. There were also some men whose hair turned gray when young. So how old was he actually?

"You are Lord Slayer's wife?" he asked.

"Nay," she said, wondering why he would ask.

"But you sat at the dais with him."

"I am a friend, no more than that," she said, keeping their marriage secret as Slayer had warned. She decided to be blunt, having no intention of lingering there with him. "Did you lie to Lord Slayer, Lester?"

"Why would you think that?" he asked, surprised by her question.

"The better question is,+ why wouldn't I question the word of a stranger?"

He nodded slowly. "A wise assumption."

Sky looked and saw the two warriors whispering among themselves. She wondered if they were just as suspicious of her as they were of Lester.

"You are in more danger than you know, Sky," Lester whispered with a quick glance at the warriors. "I hoped I would have time to explain, but I don't. You are not who you think you are. Trust no one. The truth will reveal itself soon enough."

His words stunned her, and she quickly asked, "Who are you?"

"A friend, please trust that I am a friend," he said and suddenly dropped the bowl, yanked her to her feet and with a strong hold on her pulled her along with him toward the garden.

Sky did not waste a minute. She screamed out for her husband, "SLAYER!"

The two warriors were rushing toward them and when they got close, Lester shoved her at them, sending her crashing into them and tumbling to the ground.

Fane came running around the corner of the keep moments before Slayer. The hound rushed to Sky, snarling and snapping, ready to attack the stranger. Fury sparked in Slayer's eyes when he saw one of his warriors helping Sky to her feet and the other one chasing Lester who had managed to climb the large tree on the other side of the vegetable garden and was disappearing up in its branches.

"Silent, Fane," he ordered when he reached the tree and the hound stopped barking and stood beside him, his eyes, like Slayer's, looking up from where they stood under the tree branches.

"You won't get away," Slayer yelled.

"You will not find me," Lester called back, sounding a distance away.

Slayer's face turned red with fury. "I will find you and make you pay."

"Save your strength, Slayer. He will come for her. Save her."

Chapter Twenty-one

"Ready a troop, Reed, we hunt him," Slayer ordered.

"Aye, sir, with his wound he should not get far," Reed said with a bob of his head and hurried off.

"My lord."

Slayer turned at the sound of his wife's voice and he took hasty steps to her, seeing her limp toward him. Without thought, he swung her up into his arms as soon as he reached her.

Fane stuck close to his side as Slayer hurried her to his solar., yelling as he walked through the kitchen, "A bucket of water and cloths, Euniss."

Sky saw Angel run toward them and before she could warn her husband not to step on the kitten, Fane's mouth scooped her up with his mouth for her to join them.

Slayer sat Sky in a chair near the hearth and went to grab a nearby bench while Fane deposited Angel in Sky's lap then sat beside the chair.

"Which leg?" Slayer demanded, after placing the bench in front of her.

She pointed. "The right ankle."

He crouched down and lifted her right leg gently and placed her foot on the bench. He pushed her garments out of the way and slipped off her shoe.

"There is no swelling," he said as he caressed her ankle with a tender hand. "Does it pain you?"

Euniss entered then to Sky's relief since she did not want to lie to her husband.

"Keep everyone away from here, Euniss," Slayer ordered.

"I have taken care of that already. Everyone believes you are admonishing her for speaking to the prisoner. They will avoid you not wanting to catch the tail end of your anger."

"Wise of them," Slayer said.

"They know you well, my lord," Euniss said and left them alone.

Slayer dropped a cloth from the small stack into the water-filled bucket and looked at his wife. "You need admonishing for putting yourself in danger as you did."

"I thought I might learn more from him and I did. He said he would not hurt me. That he was a friend I should trust."

"Friend? Trust?" he asked incredulously and twisted the soaked cloth tight until not a drop of water fell from it. Then he shook it out and placed it on Sky's ankle. "How do you trust a liar to be a friend? The other prisoners say that Lester only recently joined them and that none of them trusted him. He would disappear at times and suddenly return with a poor excuse of where he had gone. The mercenary leader didn't care since Lester was a skilled swordsman, and he didn't want to lose him. Just learning that, I was on my way to question him some more when I heard you scream for me."

"He told me that he had hoped to have more time to talk with me—"

"Bloody hell," Slayer grumbled. "He knew his time here was limited and that when I found out more about him, he would once again be a prisoner."

"That was why he ate before having his wound tended to. His stomach would be full, and he would not need to worry about food, only his escape." Sky shook her head. "Seeing how fast he climbed that tree, I suspect he never suffered a wound."

"I believe you're right," Slayer agreed. "What else did he say to you?"

"He told me that I was in more danger than I knew—" She stopped talking suddenly.

"What is it, Sky? Tell me," he urged.

Her brow wrinkled, recalling Lester's words, and she shook her head slowly as if not believing what she was about to say. "He told me I was not who I thought I was but that the truth would reveal itself soon. He must know who my parents are."

"Or he lies to you as he did to me. But I will catch him, and he will have no choice but to confess everything to me."

"His last words sent a chill through me. Who will come for me? Why will he come for me? And why do I need saving from this man?"

"You could be the one the Lowlander family searches for and with there being no love lost between Lowlanders and Highlanders, it could be why he warns you against trusting anyone. I would linger and discuss this with you and try to make sense of it, but I cannot wait to hunt him. His tracks will be fresh and when I catch him, I will get the truth from him."

"What if others wait for him and you ride into a trap?"

"That will not happen. The trackers and riders have already been dispersed and will send word to me, so I know what I face. It is Lester, if that is his name, who needs to worry and fear what awaits him." He stood. "You will rest and heal your ankle while I am gone, and you will not go beyond the gate." He leaned down and kissed her firmly, then pressed his cheek next to hers to whisper, "I will miss you, wife."

Sky was off the chair when she heard the door close and thought about running after him and reminding him how much she loved him and that he was to stay safe and return home to her. She almost reached the door ready to do just that when it swung open. She did not wait. She threw her arms around him.

"I love you with all my heart. You will stay safe and come home to me. I will have your word on it," she insisted, even though she knew fate would have the final word.

"Your ankle healed quite fast," Slayer said with a slight smile.

Sky's cheeks turned a warm pink. "It was the only way I could get you alone."

"Yet when you had me alone you still allowed me to believe you were injured."

"I gave it thought, but then your hand felt so good on my ankle, I found myself remaining silent."

He kissed her gently. "I am glad you did since I very much enjoyed caressing your ankle."

"We think alike, husband," Sky said. "Now please give me your word that you will return to me."

"Nothing will ever stop me from returning to you. Even a wound will not stop me. I will make my way home to you, for if I am meant to die it will be in your arms."

"Nay! Do not say that. You will not die. We have a whole life to live together," she insisted, keeping the tears that sprang to her eyes at simply the thought of losing him from falling. "Why did you return? Did you forget to tell me something?"

"Aye, I forgot to tell you that you, *mo ghaol,* belong to me and only me and I will let no one ever take you away from me. You are mine and always will be."

His hand cupped the back of her head as his lips came down firmly on hers in a kiss that left no doubt that he meant what he said in the only way he knew how… that he loved her.

***

Sky kept herself hidden as best she could while watching her husband in the practice circle. She had noticed how empty the village seemed today and had asked Euniss if something was going on beyond the stone walls. She told her that Slayer was challenging his warriors today. He did so every now and then, though mostly when his anger lingered. It was a way for him to rid himself of it. Unfortunately, most of his warriors did not want to challenge him when his anger simmered, though the clansmen enjoyed watching their leader go undefeated.

Sky was aware that her husband's temper had lingered and been simmering for the last couple of weeks. It was because Lester had not been found, not even a single sign of him had been spotted. Slayer had been withdrawn, spending more time in his solar, not talking with her as much as he usually did. And it had been several days since they had coupled, or he had shown her much affection and she missed the closeness they shared. He purposely avoided her, even in their bedchamber. The last few nights he had joined her in bed after she had fallen asleep, and he was gone before she woke in the morning. She was not sure what to do about it, although she knew it could not go on like this much longer.

He struck quite a figure in the circle, no warrior coming near to his size nor to his skill. He stood shirtless, a sheen of sweat covering his broad chest and muscled arms and suffering no breathlessness. Not so for the six warriors he had engaged separately in a sword fight. They all sat beyond the circle breathless and dripping sweat, except for one. He suddenly dropped back on the ground, his body prone, as if he had no strength left to hold himself up.

Clansmen cheered for Slayer, and Sky wondered how many more men he would need to fight to assuage his anger. He did not wound anyone who fought him, though he could have several times. He won by exhausting them into surrender. He paced the circle like a caged animal waiting for his next opponent to step forward. His warriors glanced amongst themselves waiting for the next brave soul to volunteer.

She went to turn away when he caught sight of her and the intensity in his eyes sent a shiver racing through her. It was not her husband who fought in the circle. It was the fearless Gallowglass warrior and leader. Not only did anger spark like flaring embers in his eyes, but passion swelled there as well. She understood now that it was not her husband who had been avoiding her but the fierce Gallowglass warrior.

For a moment, she thought of turning away and avoiding the warrior in him that at times frightened her, but she stopped herself. How could their marriage grow stronger and survive if they both did not reconcile the two?

She needed to get him alone and there was only one way to do that... defy him. It would force him to punish her, and all knew she was sent to his solar for a tongue lashing or her bedchamber where she would spend time in penance for her disobedience. When truly, it gave them time alone. But how did she accomplish that with all eyes on him?

The sudden cry of a hawk had her tipping her head back to look up. The bird circled overhead, then abruptly dropped down, disappearing into the forest of trees. She silently thanked the hawk for his help and, with her stomach twisting anxiously, she cast what she hoped resembled a defiant glance at her husband, then headed toward the woods.

"SKY!"

She cringed at how he could make her name sound like a forceful command, thinking any wise person would stop abruptly. And she almost did, but caught herself and kept walking, slowly since she had no desire to truly disobey him. She only wanted to get him alone even though that thought worsened her already anxious stomach. It was time she faced the Gallowglass warrior whether she wanted to or not. Though recalling the consequences of the one time, in the thunderstorm, against the tree that Slayer had let the fierce warrior loose, she wondered if it was wise to do so again. But things were different now. She knew more, understood more about intimacy, and had grown to love every intimate moment they shared.

"STOP, SKY!"

This time she stopped since he sounded closer, and she was getting too close to the edge of the forest. She turned and took a step back as his powerful strides made him appear that he was set to devour her once he reached her.

"You are not permitted to go into the forest," he said, slowing his steps to keep a distance between them, and keeping his voice loud enough for all to hear his command.

Sky cast a glance past him to see that all who had gathered stood silently watching them, so she did the same as her husband. She kept her voice loud enough for all to hear and kept her defiance clear, leaving him no choice in what he must do.

"I want to go into the woods," she said with a tilt of her chin, though hoped he did not notice the quiver that raced through her.

"Nay! I forbid it. You will go to the keep and stay there," Slayer said at first surprised by her outright defiance before he realized what his wife was up to. He stepped closer to her and kept his voice low, though failed to keep his anger in tow. "You are being foolish. You will stop this now, Sky."

She briefly thought of doing as he said, dismissing this foolish plan of hers and obeying him. When suddenly she was flooded with memories of the endless times that she had dismissed plans because someone deemed them foolish for her. If she was ever to escape the fearful and unsure woman she once was, then she had to start now by confronting the Gallowglass warrior.

Sky tilted her chin higher, a gesture of defiance when actually it was to look him straight in the eye, and say, "Make me!"

Slayer was not sure he heard her correctly, although it was more likely that he never expected to hear such defiant words from her.

"I will warn you one last time. Go to the keep now!" he ordered, his eyes narrowing and his gruff voice threatening. He lowered his voice quickly to add, "Do not defy me, Sky."

This was the moment. She either backed down or stepped forward and stood firm.

She stepped forward and poked him in the chest. "Nay. I will not."

A chorus of gasps filled the air and Sky almost expected to see fire spewing from his mouth, the anger in his eyes expanding tenfold. He latched onto her arm so tight that she cringed, but he appeared not to notice or was too angry with her to care since he propelled her forward, forcing her to keep pace with his powerful strides.

"Get back to your chores!" he ordered the crowd.

Sky was not surprised to hear snippets of talk as the crowd dispersed around them.

"He should beat her good."

"She will hold her defiant tongue then."

"Lock her away."

Slayer stopped suddenly, tightening his hold on Sky when she lost her footing. "Watch your tongues or I will see the same inflicted on you. The next one I hear say a word about her will find himself or herself put in the stocks for two days. Now go do your chores before I change my mind and see that those I heard say such disparaging remarks locked in the stocks."

Everyone there rushed off, keeping a wide berth around Slayer.

Sky held her tongue as well, as he hurried her to the keep and into the Great Hall.

Servants froze and stared at him, fear filling their eyes and Sky understood why. Slayer's anger was on display for all to see.

"STAY!" Slayer shouted when Fane stood to approach him from where he had been sleeping by the fire, Angel halting along with him to scurry under the hound's front legs in fright.

Slayer continued to the stairs, the servants not moving or flinching, but following him with their eyes.

Sky stumbled when Slayer shoved her into the bedchamber but did not close the door. "Never. Ever. Challenge me like that again. You will remain here until I say otherwise." He turned to leave.

She could not let him go. She had to keep him there. She had to help him release his anger. "Are you too cowardly to remain here and talk with me?"

He turned back, his nostrils flaring. "You have pushed me far enough, woman."

"And what has your anger done to me? You barely talk with me, barely touch me, barely couple with me." She went to him, and he backed away from her. "I miss you."

He fisted his hands as if fighting to keep control of them. "Trust me. You don't want me touching you right now." He went to leave the room again.

"I love the Gallowglass warrior in you as much as the man I came to know at the cottage."

Slayer fought the urge to turn around, grab his wife, and plunge his stiff manhood into her, make her scream in pleasure and fill her with his seed until it flowed out of her. But it was such an overpowering need that he feared he would hurt her as he had done that time in the rainstorm when he made her lip bleed and took her against the tree with the rain pouring down on them. The memory further ignited his already fiery passion as did her words of love and if he did not leave the room soon, he worried what he might do.

Sky took advantage of his silence and slipped out of her garments and shoes to stand naked. "I love you, Slayer, and I need you."

He turned to warn her, and seeing his wife naked, a low growl started in his chest. His hands were eager to touch her, and his manhood ached to plunge into her.

He let loose a growl that shivered Sky and she wanted to scream at him to come back when he walked out of the room and slammed the door shut. Her heart hurt, for him and for herself. How was she ever going to get through to the Gallowglass warrior inside him?

Sky jumped when something pounded at the door so hard that she heard it crack. Then the door flew open, and her husband stood there, his one fist scrapped and dotted with blood. He stared at her, fire in his eyes, then suddenly slammed the door shut.

"Tell me to stop, Sky," he warned as he slipped out of his boots then began to yank his garments off. "Tell me now before it is too late."

All Sky could do was stare at him, the hearth's flickering light highlighting the sheen of sweat on him and the small smudge of dirt on his brow. And his muscles where so taut from fighting that the veins in his arms were visible. But it was his manhood rock-hard that made her take a much-needed breath.

"Too late," he said as he descended on her and grabbed her around the waist to lift her off her feet and fling her down on the bed, although he did not drop down with her. He quickly flipped her over to lay on her stomach. "On your hands and knees. It is time to do penance."

"I trust you," she said, reminding him and herself.

He leaned down and whispered, "You might want to think twice about that."

"I don't have to think twice," she said and gasped as her body swelled with passion when she felt his teeth sink with gentle force into the back of her neck, sending gooseflesh rushing over her.

"Mine. Always mine," he said, slipping his hands beneath her to squeeze her breasts and tease her nipples before he positioned himself behind her.

He reminded her of that often or was he confirming it to himself repeatedly to understand what it was he was feeling for her?

She sighed with pleasure, feeling his shaft poking between her legs as he caressed her backside slowly and firmly. Then he suddenly grabbed tight hold of each cheek and entered her with such a hard and fast plunge that she gasped loudly not in discomfort but delight. It felt so very good. He needed this and so did she. He needed to know that her love for him, all of him, was unconditional.

Slayer lost himself in the strong rhythm he set and in the intoxicating melody of his wife's moans of pleasure. This was where he wanted to be, what he ached to feel, ached to get lost in, ached to share with his wife. With every thrust his pleasure grew and he could feel it overpowering his anger, forcing it to retreat, only allowing pleasure to prevail.

He had been so lost in overwhelming pleasure that he had not realized his wife had been close to release until she screamed out his name. But he was not ready yet. He wanted more. When he felt her begin to go limp beneath him, he pulled out of her and with one arm around her waist flipped her onto her back and entered her quickly, driving into her to ignite her passion all over again.

Sky gasped and grabbed her husband's arms, needing to hold on to him, the renewed passion that hit her overwhelming her.

He leaned down over her, his arms taut on either side of her to hover slightly above her as he drove in and out of her.

"Mine. Tell me you're mine," he ordered, slipping closer to the edge with each thrust.

"I will always be yours," she confirmed and stretched her head up to kiss him.

She claimed the mighty Gallowglass warrior with that kiss, and they burst together in a mind-shattering climax that chased his anger away, leaving him satiated but more so, loved unconditionally.

Chapter Twenty-two

"To my solar now," Slayer ordered.

Sky followed behind him as did Fane and Angel.

As soon as he shut the door, he pulled his wife into his arms. "Are you sure you are all right?"

"You continue to ask me that even though it has been a week since you ravished me," she said with a slight chuckle. "And have done so twice since then."

"It is all your fault," he said with a feigned scowl. "I cannot resist you."

"Nor I you," she said and kissed him gently and tapped his chest afterward. "There is something I have been meaning to discuss with you."

"Is there a problem?"

"Nay. All is well. I keep busy in my garden—"

"And with my hounds," he said, raising his brow. "I have not stopped you from visiting them since I know they, as well as you, enjoy the visits."

"I truly appreciate that, and the hounds are what I wanted to discuss with you. Fane trained well. He stays by your side and keeps a close watch on everything and everyone in the village. You waste the other three hounds' abilities by keeping them secluded in the pen until needed. If you assigned a warrior to each hound and have them train the hound to obey, then they can patrol or take watch with them. Hounds are so much more intelligent than people know. The hounds will get to know the scent of those in the village and will alert when an unfamiliar scent is found."

"You just want to free them from the pen," Slayer accused.

"They have become my friends and I hate seeing them confined when they have so much to offer you."

He gave her waist a light squeeze. "I suppose you also have warriors in mind who might work well with the hounds."

"I do, and Reed is one of them," she said excitedly. "Haven't you noticed how well he does with Fane, not fearful of him? I believe he would do just as well with one of the other hounds. Boden would be a good fit for him. I can tell he is eager to leave the pen like Fane."

"And the other two hounds, Dirk and Quinn?"

That he did not quickly dismiss her suggestion gave her hope. "Glen will do well with Quinn. He is the most easily compliant of the four. Dirk has a mind of his own and can be stubborn and will need a firmer hand."

"Angus may do well with Dirk, he is just as stubborn as the hound," Slayer suggested.

Sky jabbed his chest lightly. "You have given this thought as well."

"You should know by now how much we think alike," he said and playfully kissed the tip of her nose. "Besides, you have shown me with Fane how helpful the hounds can be while waiting for the next battle."

"I am pleased that in time the hounds will no longer be confined to the pen," she said, her thoughts drifting.

"Then why the worry lines?" Slayer asked, caressing the deep lines between her eyes.

She sighed softly. "I am eager for Ross' return from Clan Skirling, Leora's new home, and what reply she may have sent to my message that he took to her."

"Do not worry he will deliver the message correctly. You had him repeat enough for him to remember it and he repeated it enough to me that I still recall it." Slayer tempered his powerful voice to sound more like Ross as he repeated the message. "I am to tell her that you are doing well and are being well cared for, though you miss her and Elsie terribly. She is not to worry over you, though she knows you will ignore her words, but she is to trust that you are safe and well-protected, and that when it is safe, the three of you will reunite and have much to discuss and you look forward to that time And most importantly I am to tell her that you have found the love with the animals at Clan Ravinsher that Snowball had given you at home."

"You sounded much like Ross. I only hope his memory is as good as yours."

His voice turned powerful once again. "Ross has an excellent memory, so have no worries your message will reach your sister. I have been meaning to ask you, who is Snowball?"

Sky smiled softly. "A beautiful, precious, white cat I loved with all my heart, and I had since I was young."

Slayer did not hide his surprise, understanding what that part of the message actually meant. "You are letting your sister know that you have found love here."

"With the animals, as I said, though she might realize I mean more since Snowball meant so much to me." Her smile faded. "Although, I do wonder if she would even give it thought since it was assumed I would never wed let alone fall in love because of my affliction. Elsie and Leora often told me that they would always look after me."

"They no longer need to. You have me now," Slayer reminded, "and you have yourself. You have grown in strength and courage since I first met you. You had no choice being wed to me, but you had a choice whether you would accept the marriage and find a way to make it work rather than do nothing more than tolerate it. I am proud to call you my wife."

His words filled her heart with joy. Never had she expected to hear such meaningful words from a man, let alone a husband and she was quick to respond. "And I am proud and overjoyed that you are my husband and I love you with all my heart."

Slayer went to speak and stopped. Instead, he kissed her, a gentle, lingering kiss, then he rested his brow to hers. "I feel for you, wife, like I have never felt for another. You have become a part of me I cannot live without, like a breath or a beat of my heart. I want to say I love you, but I don't know or understand love, I don't even know if those words would suffice for what I feel for you—"

Sky kissed him softly. "Your words say more than you know, and they fill me with even more joy."

"Don't you be growling at me, or you'll never get another bone. That's right, hang your head. I know you have been getting bones on the sly."

Sky and Slayer turned their heads toward the door, hearing Euniss reprimand the hound, who stopped growling at the threat of receiving no more bones.

"That woman fears nothing," Slayer said.

Sky smiled. "I think that is why I like her so much."

"You are needed, Lord Slayer," Euniss called out.

Sky slipped out of her husband's arms reluctantly and he reluctantly let her go. "I will leave first. I am eager to work in my garden today and I am already eager to see you later."

She blew him a kiss before she opened the door and he thought he felt it graze his cheek, though it could have been the light breeze that swept through the room. However, he allowed himself to believe it was her kiss and touched his cheek gently sealing it there.

"Come on, Fane," he commanded. "We have a busy day ahead of us."

***

Sky was surprised when she reached her garden to see the young lass, Oona waiting there for her.

"For you," she said and brought her hand from behind her back to offer Sky a small, yellow wildflower. "You helped me."

"It is beautiful. Thank you," Sky said. "I shall wear it in my hair." She tucked it in the braid that lay over her shoulder and on her chest.

"Pretty," Oona said with a smile and tilted her head, staring at Sky. "Why do your eyes look like that?"

Sky smiled and shrugged. "I don't know. I was just born this way."

"Oh," Oona said. "Can I play with Angel?"

"I believe she would like that," Sky said, the kitten rubbing herself against the little lass' legs. "But you must stay here to play with her."

"Aye," Oona said without a second thought and plopped down on the ground and giggled when Angel began to crawl all over her.

"To be young and pure of heart again, before life tarnishes the mind and soul."

Sky turned to see Ruth, Wade's grandmother, walking toward her.

"Oona had the courage to do what I should have done weeks ago, offer my thanks for your help. You did not speak against my grandson, and I am grateful for that. I am also grateful for Lord Slayer's punishment. After Wade spent time with the Gallowglass warriors he changed. He now joins the other lads in sword practice daily after his chores are done. He wants to be a warrior so he can protect me and the clan." Her eyes grew shiny with tears. "He makes me proud, and I know his parents would have been just as proud. He lost both within a short time of each other."

"I am sorry to hear that, though I am glad to hear that he is doing so well," Sky said.

"Could we sit and talk for a bit?" Ruth offered.

"I would love to," Sky said and walked with Ruth to the bench that appeared near her garden one day. She knew it was her husband's doing, although he never mentioned it to her.

"I hope you do not mind me saying, but your eyes are beautiful, strange yet beautiful."

Sky could not hide her shock. She almost told the woman that Slayer was the only one who had ever told her that, but she caught herself. "Your words surprise me since I have never had anyone tell me that."

"More fools they, but then I have seen such strange eye color like yours before."

Again, Sky could not hide her surprise. "You have?"

Ruth nodded. "Aye, when I was young my da and I traveled to his sister's clan after my mum died. He left me with her and took off. I never saw him again. It was on our travels there that I saw the young woman with the strange eye color. My da and I traveled a well-worn path to get here and met fellow travelers along the way. He would nod pleasantly to some and ignore others. Those, he would tell me, are not our kind and it was best to avoid them. One day we encountered a group of three men and two women. The younger woman had eyes like yours. They approached from the opposite direction we traveled. My da cautioned me not to look at them."

"But being a child and curious, you could not help but sneak a peek," Sky said, understanding.

Ruth chuckled. "Aye, I could not help but look. I had never seen anyone as beautiful as she was and to me her different colored eyes only made her more beautiful. And with my child's imagination running wild, I believed her to be a magical creature. Especially once it was confirmed for me by a strange occurrence. I glanced back for one last look and saw a small bird land on her shoulder, and it looked as though he whispered in her ear. The next thing I knew they all disappeared into the forest."

"Your da never said anything more about them?"

"Only that they were foreigners and not to be trusted. The incident faded with time, and I never saw them or anyone like them again until you arrived here, and the memory of that day returned more vividly. I wondered if perhaps you are related to the woman I saw, but then I learned you were one of the Murdock sisters and realized it was not possible. Although I cannot get over how much you resemble her and that you have the same different colored eyes as she did."

"It is good to know that I am not the only one with such eyes," Sky said, wondering if it was possible she somehow was related to the woman.

"And then there is the way animals so easily trust you as the bird did with the woman," Ruth said. "I do hope you make Clan Ravinsher your home. It would be nice to have someone with your beauty and kindness reside among us." She lowered her voice. "But be careful. I see the way Lord Slayer looks at you. It is obvious he favors you and he will need to find a wife soon enough and produce an heir."

Sky recalled that Slayer introduced her as a guest at Clan Ravinsher. Was Warrand's forthcoming marriage to her never made known?

It was a question she hoped Ruth might know the answer to, although she did not ask it directly. "I thought I recalled hearing something about a marriage being arranged for Warrand."

"Aye, it was time for Warrand to wed but Lord Bannaty had yet to decide on a union that would benefit the clan."

So, the clan was never told of Warrand's forthcoming nuptials, but why? Why would Lord Bannaty hide it?

"Lord Bannaty always did what was best for the clan and Lord Slayer is doing the same. The clan will always come first to him and that is the way it should be," Ruth said. "I should be going. I promised Wade oat cakes today. You must visit me soon. We can share a hot brew."

Never had Sky been invited for a hot brew with anyone and her face lit with a smile at the invitation. "I would love to."

Ruth stood and Sky stood with her.

"Midmorning is a good time for a visit on any given day," Ruth said.

"I will see you soon," Sky said, looking forward to it.

Ruth stopped after taking only a few steps and turned around. "I just remembered something about that encounter with the woman who shares your eye color. She carried a pup with her in a pouch, much like you carry the kitten at times." She shook her head. "It was probably a young lass' imagination, but I could have sworn it was a wolf cub she carried."

Sky remained where she was, lost in thought. Was there any significance to the wolf cub and her repetitive dream about the wolf she had when she was young? Could it possibly have something to do with where she came from and who she truly was?

"Oona, you should not be bothering the lady," Glynis scolded her daughter.

"She is my friend. Angel is too," Oona said, hugging the kitten.

The young lass' words touched Sky's heart, and she smiled. "Oona is no bother, and she is right. Angel and I are her friends."

Glynis glanced around, seeing that the garden workers had ceased working and were staring at her.

"I understand," Sky said, drawing Glynis's attention. "It is difficult to be dismissed by your clan because you do not think as they do."

"Mummy, look." Oona pointed to Sky's braid. "The flower. I picked it for her. She put it in her hair." The lass giggled. "It looks pretty."

Glynis smiled. "It does look pretty, Oona, and that was very kind of you to do."

Oona abandoned the kitten to scurry over to Sky and attach herself to her leg with a hug. "I like her. She is nice. Be her friend too, Mummy."

"Aye, Oona, Sky is nice," Glynis said and looked at Sky. "And I would like to be her friend."

"I would like that as well," Sky said.

"We will chat the next time Oona plays with the kitten," Glynis offered.

"I look forward to it," Sky said, amazed that she had made three friends in such a brief time. It filled her heart with joy and gave her hope for the future here at Clan Ravinsher.

Sky thought of seeking out her husband after Oona and her mum left, but she needed time to think, clear her head, make some sense of things before she spoke with him. Working in the garden would help with that and while Angel settled herself under the bench to sleep, she went to work in the garden.

She was pulling weeds, thinking on the plants, allowing nothing else to interfere with this moment of peace and clarity when a shadow fell over where she knelt. She turned her head, tilting it up to see who it was and was surprised to see one of the lasses who helped tend the kitchen garden.

"Wild pottage for your garden," the young woman said, stretching her hand out, offering Sky the plant.

Sky took the plant from her. "Thank you for sharing it with me."

"It grows abundant in the woods," the lass said, "but we grow it in the garden, so the cooks have plenty to add to the stews. It was a favorite of Lord Bannaty's. I can show you where it grows one day if you'd like."

"That would be most kind of you," Sky said, not actually accepting or refusing her offer since she knew Slayer would never allow her to go into the woods just yet.

The lass smiled, nodded, and hurried to return to her task, the other workers quick to gather round her.

Sky wondered over the sudden interest in her. Had Ruth and Glynis speaking with her turned people curious enough to talk with her and judge her for themselves? Or had she been here long enough for them to see that she posed no threat to them? Whatever the reason might be, she chose to remain hopeful.

She worked in the garden until the eagerness to talk with her husband could no longer be ignored. After cleaning the dirt off her hands and leaving Angel to eat in the kitchen, she went to find her husband. There was much she had to share with him.

She walked through the village and not spotting him, she approached one of the Gallowglass warriors to ask, "Would you know where Lord Slayer is?"

The young warrior looked her directly in her eyes as if showing all that he was not afraid of her, unless it was because her husband had ordered his men not to turn away when speaking with her.

"Lord Slayer is beyond the gate."

"Thank you," she said with a smile and the warrior's cheeks heated red and he hurried off.

Sky hurried to the gate and quickly left the confines of the castle's protective wall. She stood still after only taking a few steps to see if she could spot her husband among the buzz of activity in the village. He would be easy to spot, standing a good head above most men. She spotted him speaking to Reed. Impatient to reach him, she kept a quick pace and had to force herself not to let others notice how eager she was to see him. He, however, had no problem turning a scowl at her. She recalled then that she was not to go beyond the castle walls without his permission. He had reiterated that order once things had settled down after that day on the practice field when she had followed others outside the castle walls. She could not wait for the time to come when such confinement was no longer necessary.

The blaring horn froze her as did the shouts of the villagers.

"ATTACK! ATTACK!"

Chapter Twenty-three

"Run to the castle! We have only so much time before they reach us. Run!" a woman warned the children, and they took off.

Sky hurried a glance at her husband, and he pointed at the castle. She turned and ran, heeding his command and realizing the outer sentinels had alerted to the approaching hoard, giving them time to prepare.

She had almost reached the castle wall when she spotted a frantic Glynis calling out for Oona.

Sky stopped when she reached her. "What's wrong, Glynis?"

"Oona, she was out here playing with some of the children, and I cannot find her. Oona!" Glynis cried out again.

"I will help you find her," Sky said.

"We haven't much time," Glynis warned.

"Then we shouldn't waste it. I will search this side. You search from the other side." Sky squeezed the woman's hand. "Worry not, we will find her."

Women and children rushed past her going in the opposite direction. A quick glance showed that her husband and his warriors were gathering weapons and preparing to take a stance. Why did he remain outside the walls instead of seeking their safety? The answer came easily enough. He was Gallowglass and they feared nothing.

Sky turned her attention away from the scene, needing to continue to search for Oona. She worried for the little lass when another horn signaled that the attack was imminent, and she saw her husband and some of his men mount their horses. There was a huge group of warriors, and they were a remarkable sight with their weapons drawn and their faces raging with fury. Only fools would battle them.

"Hurry!" a woman shouted. "The gate closes."

Sky looked to see that Glynis was still frantically searching and she did the same. When she thought all was lost, she spotted a piece of cloth peeking from behind a large rock. She hurried over and found Oona huddled behind it, tears flowing down her cheeks. She scooped her up and the little lass wrapped her small arms tightly around her neck.

Glynis spotted them and came running, tears flowing down her cheeks as well.

Sky handed the lass over to her. "The gate is closing, hurry."

Glynis took off and Sky went to follow when she was suddenly grabbed from behind and dragged backward.

Glynis turned, and her eyes went wide with fright.

"Run!" Sky urged. "Run!" When she saw Glynis hesitate, she cried out, "He'll come for me!"

As Sky was dragged into the woods, she watched Glynis and Oona make it through the gate doors just before they closed shut.

It was not until they were further into the woods that the man let go of her and two other men joined them.

"We don't have much time," the man who abducted her said. "That troop that attacked will be defeated soon enough and once he discovers her gone, he will search for her."

The man was right about that. Her husband would come for her, and she needed to survive until he did.

"Did Olin escape?" another man asked.

"I'm here," a voice was heard before a man emerged from the woods.

"Good job, Rory," one of the men said with a laugh.

Sky recalled the name only her husband referred to him as Rory, the liar. It seemed he was a good liar since he was not the man he had claimed to be.

"There is no time for laughter. This mission must get done," Olin said, "Iver is right. We don't have much time. We need to get out of here."

Fearful beyond belief, Sky forced herself to ask, "Who are you? What do you want with me?"

Olin ignored her and turned to Iver. "Where are the horses?"

"Not far from here and out of sight of the sentinels."

Horses. Once they got on horses, they could easily distance themselves from Slayer, taking longer for her husband to find her. There was also the chance of more men waiting to wherever they took her. Her fear grew and her stomach roiled. She had to escape them before they reached the horses to give her husband a better chance of finding her.

At least she was somewhere that she was familiar with… a forest. And she knew the secrets of the forest well.

"We need to get to those horses and keep moving," Olin said. "It will take us no more than a day's ride to reach the meeting spot, get our coins, and be done with this."

Iver was the man who had dragged Sky into the woods, and he gave her a shove. "Get moving."

"She stays unharmed, or we could get less coins for her," Olin warned and turned to one of the men as they walked. "Go a distance ahead and make sure no surprises await us."

She could not take the word of a liar that she would be left unharmed and that encouraged her even more to escape, and soon, since there would be one less man to hunt her. She was not familiar with this area of terrain which could prove dangerous, but the trees would help guide her and rock formations would provide her with places to hide. It also helped that they had not bound her wrists. It would make escape that much easier.

"Keep pace," Iver ordered with a slight shove when she slowed after only a few steps.

"Throw her over your shoulder, Iver, if she slows again," Olin called out, several steps ahead.

She could not let that happen, so she kept pace and feared their hasty steps would get them to the horses before she had a chance to make her escape. That meant she could not wait. She had to make her escape soon. But how?

It came to her when she spotted a sizeable stone ahead and when she reached it, she purposely stumbled, falling just enough to grab the stone.

Iver grabbed her by the arm. "Stay on your feet."

Sky didn't wait. She slammed Iver in the head with the stone and his hand fell off her as he collapsed to the ground. She took off, knowing she had little time, Olin and the other man having kept their quick pace. That had put enough distance between them for her to dash into the forest and hide.

It was only a few moments later that she heard Olin yell, "You idiot!"

Sky ran as if the devil was on her heels, keeping watch for places to hide and places to avoid.

"Spread out," Olin yelled.

His strong voice sounded close. She needed to find a place to hide and fast or they would find her.

The forest thickened, making it difficult to keep a good pace. She spotted towering pines grouped close as if they hugged each other. If she could squeeze through the thick branches, she just might be able to hide among them. She might suffer some scratches but that would be the least of her worries. She heard the cries and screeches of some of the forest animals. They were cries of distress. They were warning her. The men must be close.

Once she reached the bushy pines, she closed her eyes, leaving barely a slit to see from, so no pine needle could poke her eyes and make things more difficult for her.

"I see her!" one of the men shouted.

Sky hurried her way through, knowing she would have to run fast once she passed the trees. The pine needles poked and prodded as she maneuvered her way through and as soon as she broke free of them, she ran. Too late she realized she was at the edge of a cliff and, try as she might to save herself, momentum had taken hold, and she went tumbling off the side of a steep cliff.

Olin was the first to breach the pine trees and caught his steps, stopping himself from tumbling off the edge. He called out, "Go slow! There's a cliff."

The other two men stepped carefully past the trees and looked down to where Olin glanced.

"She's not moving," Iver said.

"We'll never get her out of there," the other man said.

"We wouldn't have enough time even if we wanted to. Slayer will be on our trail soon enough." Olin looked at Iver. "I should force you to go down there to make sure she is dead."

"I don't think that's a good idea," the other man said, pointing. "Wolves."

The three stood staring as two large wolves inched close to Sky.

The one man gasped. "She's moving."

"Not for long she won't be," Olin said. "We need to get out of here fast before Slayer finds out what happened to her and feeds us to the wolves."

***

"Go to the keep, Fane, and find Angel. You have earned a rest," Slayer ordered the hound and turned to

Reed as Fane hurried off. "How many of our prisoners escaped during the attack?" Slayer glanced around at the few that were there.

"Three. We found two but the liar is still missing," Reed said. "I've never met anyone who could spin a tale the way he does or how fast the tales grow with each telling."

"Did you pick up his trail?" Slayer asked.

"We did," Reed confirmed.

"Ready a small troop to follow," Slayer said.

"It is already done, sir," Reed said then shook his head "It was barely a battle. The fools did not stand a chance against us, so why attack?"

"I doubt they were meant to," Slayer said, seeing his men start to collect the dead to dispose of them. "They were an expendable troop which makes me think they were meant to distract."

"But from what?" Ross asked.

Slayer wondered the same, his wife's safety immediately coming to mind, but she was headed to the gate when he last saw her. But he never saw her go through the gate.

"Lord Slayer! Lord Slayer!"

Slayer turned to see Glyniss running toward him and terror gripped him.

"A man took Sky and dragged her into the woods."

Slayer hurried toward the woman, his heart beating wildly. "What happened?"

"I couldn't find Oona after the horn sounded its warning. Sky helped me search for her and she found her. The gate was near to closing and she urged me to run with Oona. I thought she was behind me, and when

I turned to look, I saw a man grab her and drag her into the woods."

"Why didn't you alert someone sooner?" Slayer snapped harshly.

"I tried but I couldn't reach your warriors. I was shoved into the keep and none there would listen to me."

"You mean that no one cared what happened to Sky," Slayer said, his anger mounting.

"I tried, sir, honestly, I tried, but only Ruth and Doreena, a young woman who works in your garden, showed any concern. When we were finally let out, I immediately came in search of you." Tears pooled in Glynis's eyes. "Sky is a kind and generous woman. She cared more about mine and Oona's safety than she did of her own. When she saw me hesitate to leave her, she cried out, 'He'll come for me.' I knew she was right. You would never let any of us in the clan be taken captive."

His wife had said that for one reason alone… he had given his word to her that he would always find her. She had let him know that she had no doubt he would search and find her, and she was right.

***

Sky groaned as she woke. Pain struck her whole body as she attempted to move. It took her a few moments to clear her fuzzy head and recall what happened. She froze, recalling the fall and feared what injuries she may have suffered. Knowing it would do her no good to delay finding out how seriously she was hurt, she moved one arm. She felt no pain in it though her body ached in protest, so she waited before moving her other arm. It was in that stillness that she heard the soft growl. She prayed it was only her imagination and lifted her head to find out it wasn't.

Not far from her, two large gray wolves stared at her, one growling low.

The fierce, growling face of the wolf in her recurring dream assaulted her and she shivered with fear. Then she recalled what Ruth had told her about the woman who resembled her and that she carried a wolf cub in a pouch. If by chance she was in some way related to the woman, then she should not fear wolves.

She forced a smile. "I am sorry to intrude on your den, but I took a fall and fear I am hurt."

The wolf stopped growling, although both remained as they were.

She wanted to maintain eye contact with them, but she ached too much to continue holding her head up.

"I need to rest a bit," she said and dropped her head on a bed of pine, realizing she had landed on a fallen pine tree that probably cushioned her fall some. Hopefully, it had prevented her from suffering any serious harm.

Sky felt a wet nose touch her hand on the arm she had stretched out. That the wolf was curious and not hostile boded well. She lay there unmoving, letting the wolves get to know her, as she drifted back into unconsciousness.

She stirred awake to gray clouds hovering overhead and wondered how long she had laid unconscious? She needed to move, keep herself awake, and find out the extent of her injuries and find some type of shelter since the dark clouds promised rain.

"Slayer," she said softly. "How will you ever find me?"

She raised her head to see the two wolves lying nearby. "Thank you for staying with me."

She tried to move but the pain that ran through her body forced her to cease all movement. She feared what damage she had suffered and told herself the only thing she could do right now was rest and get up when the pain finally eased. With the two large wolves nearby, she need not worry of being harmed… she hoped.

When next she woke, it was to feel something poking her, and she smiled as she said, "Slayer."

But when she opened her eyes, it was to see a wolf poking at her arm and the other she felt poking at her leg. She understood what they were trying to tell her. They were urging her to get up, but why? She felt it then, the pine tree trembling beneath her. Horses were headed her way.

***

The four men were on their knees in front of Slayer, six of his warriors standing behind them and more warriors surrounding the area.

"I knew you would show your true worth eventually," Slayer said as he approached Rory.

"It is the coins. Olin promised us lots of coins."

"Shut up, Iver," Olin ordered, a furious look on his face.

Slayer nodded. "So, the lie started with your name. What else did you lie about?"

Before Olin could answer, Slayer grabbed the man's hand and snapped his wrist back, breaking it.

Olin screamed out in pain.

Slayer grabbed a hunk of his hair and yanked his head back, forcing Olin to look only at him. "That is just the beginning. I am going to break every bone in your body until I get the truth from you." He let go of his hair, giving him a shove and nodded to the warriors behind the men. "And what I do to you will also be done to them."

His warriors stepped forward and one by one broke the wrists of two men, but before they reached Iver, he shouted out, "She escaped us. She hit me in the head with a rock and ran."

Slayer nodded at the warrior standing behind the man and he quickly snapped his wrist.

The man screamed and cradled his broken wrist in his arm.

Slayer grabbed Olin's other hand and snapped that wrist and as he screamed in pain, the others begged for mercy.

"Tell me the truth and I will spare you," Slayer said, his face twisted in fury.

Iver rushed to speak up. "She ran and we followed." He hesitated, but when the warrior reached for his other hand, he spewed out the rest. "She fell off a cliff."

A fiery rage twisted Slayer's face and he snarled, "And you left her there?"

"She was dead, not moving," Olin said and gasped when Slayer rested a dagger against his throat.

"She moved," Iver cried out.

Slayer's anger spewed out with his every word. "And still you left her there?"

Iver was quick to explain. "We had no choice. The wolves got to her first."

Slayer felt a tremendous pain pierce his body as if one of his limbs had been severed, as if he lost a part of himself. "They attacked her?"

"We didn't stay to see," Iver said. "We feared you would catch us if we didn't take our leave fast."

"You will take me to this cliff," Slayer ordered, praying his wife survived the fall and that her unique way with animals just might have saved her.

"Aye. Aye. I will take you," Iver said eagerly, cradling his broken wrist.

Slayer turned to Reed. "Keep them here in case they have lied to me. Besides, I have more questions for them." He looked at Olin. "Afterwards they will suffer a slow death."

Olin made the mistake of saying, "Why should we tell you anything if you plan to kill us anyway?"

Without hesitation or warning, Slayer swept his dagger across Olin's arm. He screamed and Slayer grabbed his face, squeezing it. "It is the difference between a fast or slow death. Your choice." He turned to Iver, who was more than willing to talk. "How far is it?"

"You caught us not far from the cliff."

"Show me," Slayer commanded.

***

It did not take long to spot the line of pine trees not far in the distance or for Iver to beg for his life.

"Please, my lord, spare me. I did not want any part of this," Iver pleaded. "I will help you any way I can."

"Aye, you will help me willingly or not," Slayer said. "But why take part in this if you did not want to?"

Iver sputtered as he searched for a response.

Slayer answered for him. "Greed."

"I will not deny I wanted the coin, but I gave better thought to it after I watched men brutally kill a large Gallowglass warrior. I never saw a man fight so fearlessly and continue to do so with so many wounds." Iver shuddered. "I have seen evil things done by evil men, but never did I truly look on evil until that day when I watched a man step out of the woods to deliver the final blow to the Gallowglass warrior. One glance and you could see the pleasure he derived from slowly driving his dagger into the warrior and twisting it before he slowly sliced his throat." Iver shivered at the memory. "I never saw such bravery as the Gallowglass warrior lay there unable to move yet not crying out in pain. He even managed last words." He shook his head. "I didn't understand why he said, 'I won.'"

Slayer was nearly brought to an abrupt halt upon hearing that, but he was far too anxious to get to his wife. Clyde would have to wait. However, he would find the man and avenge his friend's death.

"Did you and the other men with you partake in this attack?" Slayer asked.

"We're here and the edge of the cliff is only a few steps beyond the pines," Iver warned, coming to a stop in front of the tall pines.

"Lead the way," Slayer commanded and grabbed him by the back of the neck and shoved him roughly to push through the pines. That Iver ignored his question was answer enough.

Slayer's heart thundered in his chest, fearing what he might find and not wanting to think of a day without Sky. He did not know when she had become so essential to his life, but she had and if that was love then his love for her was stronger than anything he had ever felt in his life.

Slayer kept a firm hand on his captive as they maneuvered through the trees. When they broke past the pines and he saw how little distance there was between the trees and the edge of the cliff, he could almost picture his wife breaking through on the run to escape her captors and tumbling off the edge.

"Take him," Slayer ordered one of several warriors who had followed behind him, and Iver was grabbed by the neck once again.

Slayer approached the edge, his heart pounding, and his stomach twisting, and leaned over the edge to peer down.

His wife was nowhere in sight.

Slayer released a ferocious roar that would frighten the most powerful beast, and, in the distance, wolves howled.

Chapter Twenty-four

Slayer turned to Reed. "Take another man and have him bring a large troop of warriors here. You remain behind and oversee the safety of the clan until I return, and have a message sent to Ross to return home immediately and let him know why. And tell him that Noble and Cavell may be needed."

Reed did not hesitate to take his leave.

One of his warriors pointed to a narrow stream. "That stream must connect with another body of water. If we find it, it will lead us down there."

Slayer looked to the warrior who had pointed it out, one of his best trackers. "Take two warriors with you, Devlin, and go find the waterway that connects with that stream while I go down and see if I can find anything that can tell me what may have happened to Sky."

"How will you get down there?" a warrior asked as Devlin disappeared into the bushy pine trees.

"I'm going to climb down the cliff."

"But what if the wolves return, my lord?" a warrior asked.

"They will be distracted," Slayer said.

The warrior looked puzzled. "How, my lord?"

Slayer turned to his warrior who had a grip on Iver. "You never answered me, Iver. Did you participate in the attack and brutal killing of the Gallowglass warrior you told me about?"

Iver paled, seeing the fury in the eyes of the Gallowglass warriors standing nearby. "Please, I beg you."

"Clyde was not only a fellow Gallowglass warrior but a good friend." Slayer nodded to the warrior who held Iver and without delay he gave Iver a hardy shove that sent him flying off the cliff screaming. His screams died when he hit the ground. They all looked down to see his limbs bent unnaturally and blood pooling beneath his head.

Slayer turned away and made ready to climb down the side.

One warrior expressed concern. "If you fall—"

"I won't," Slayer said, and tossed his sword off the cliff before he lowered himself over the edge and began to make his way down.

Nothing would stop him from reaching the bottom and finding anything that might help him locate Sky. With that being the only thing on his mind, he continued his descent, reaching for crevices and sturdy trees that grew out of the rocky cliff here and there.

After a while, the strain of the climb had his arm and leg muscles burning like they were on fire, but he did not slow or stop to rest. He needed to find out what happened to his wife.

Once he reached the bottom, he retrieved his sword, slipping it in the sheath on his back, then he hurried to make certain Iver was dead before surveying the area. He would find the others who made Clyde suffer, especially the evil man Iver mentioned, and see that each one of them paid the price for killing his friend.

He turned away from Iver, glancing over the area and spotted a fallen pine tree, its branches crushed, and he hurried to it. He squatted down beside it looking for any signs of blood or pieces of garment but saw none. Yet something told him that this was where Sky had landed and if so that meant there was a good chance she survived the fall. The question was, did she walk out of here on her own, or did someone take her out of here? He rejected the thought that the wolves could have gotten to her. If that were so, there would be some evidence of it, and he saw none. So, what had happened to her? Or was she still here?

He surveyed the area with a fine eye finding paw prints—the wolves—then he spotted a strange pattern in the dirt. Someone had covered tracks, and he carefully brushed the soil away in rutted parts of the terrain and discovered hoof prints. Horses had been here. Someone had taken Sky.

Slayer was ready to kill, to rip off limbs and tear out hearts to find his wife, but he tempered his rage, saving it for when he found the person who took her. He set his own tracking skills to work, following a trail he was able to find. Unfortunately, they were on horses, and he was on foot. He feared they had already outdistanced him. He had dismissed the thought that he would find her dead along the way. If they intended on killing her, they could have already done so. But they had not. They had taken her with them.

The tracks took him into the forest, and he kept following them. He could not take the chance and wait for his warriors. Every moment mattered and he had no doubt his warriors would find his tracks and follow.

Slayer kept a good pace, the horses' tracks showing a slower one. He wondered if it had anything to do with Sky and if her injuries required a slower pace. He kept alert to his surroundings as he hurried along.

He almost roared with anger when the tracks divided, and he stood at the crossroads of a decision that could mean life or death for his wife. He turned his head from side to side as if each path might reveal something to him when suddenly a small red squirrel appeared on the path to the right. He released a piercing chirp and titled his head at the path as if telling him to go that way.

If his wife trusted the animals, then so could he. He looked at the squirrel and ordered, "Lead the way."

He followed the squirrel for a good distance until he suddenly stopped not far ahead of him. He went up on his hind legs and sniffed the air, then the little fellow barked and scurried off. He remembered Sky saying that squirrels communicated by the different sounds they made. What was it she had said about a bark? *Threatened.* That's what it was. The squirrel felt threatened.

Slayer tempered his steps, keeping them light and cautious, making as little sound as he could. He was about to return to his fast pace, hearing or seeing nothing, when he heard voices ahead. He crouched down, keeping out of sight until he found an area thick with foliage where he could keep himself hidden and peered carefully through the branches.

His eyes narrowed and his heart slammed in his chest, seeing at least six bodies on the ground. Only one moved and a warrior stood over him, a bloody sword in his hand and Slayer counted five more with swords in hand and there was no telling if more warriors lingered nearby.

"Where is she?" the thick warrior demanded.

"Don't know."

The warrior prodded the wounded man with his foot. "Lie. Where did you hide her? We know you made it to the bottom of the cliff before us."

"She was gone," the man said, struggling to speak.

The warrior spit on him. "Another lie. She fell off the cliff. She could not have gotten up and walked off on her own."

Another warrior spoke up, "If he's telling the truth then he could be leading us away from wherever she's hiding."

The thick warrior prodded the wounded man with his foot again, though stronger this time and the man cried out in pain. "Are you doing that? Leading us away from her?"

Speaking in short breaths, the wounded man said, "Never. Saw. Her."

"He's going to be mighty angry if we don't find her," one warrior said.

"He'll kill one or more of us for failing to find her," another said.

"Then we better find her," the thick warrior warned. "We will backtrack and see where we can pick up her tracks."

"What about him?" a warrior asked, pointing his sword at the wounded man.

"Leave him," the thick warrior commanded. "He deserves a slow, painful death for not helping us."

Slayer remained where he was until the group of six warriors disappeared into the woods before he, silently as possible, approached the wounded man. He was shocked to see it was Lester, the man who had escaped him.

Lester's eyes went wide when Slayer crouched down beside him. "Find her. Before they do."

"You didn't see her?"

"Nay. Gone. When we got there." Lester cringed, shutting his eyes for a moment. "Found footprints. Covered them. Alive. She must be alive."

"Did you mean her harm?" Slayer asked to determine the man's fate.

"Never. Sky—" He cringed in pain again. "Daughter of the Wolf clan."

That surprised Slayer and he knew it would thrill Sky to learn about her origin. "There is much I want to ask you, but I have no time. I need to find Sky."

"Aye. Go. Keep her safe. Do not let him get her. Blames her," Lester fought to say, "Revenge."

"Stay alive," Slayer ordered. "You have much to tell me. My men will be here soon. Tell them we spoke, and you are to be kept safe." He went to stand, and the man managed to lay his hand on Slayer's arm.

"Wo-wol-wolves."

The man's eyes closed, but there was still breath to him. Slayer tore off a strip of cloth from the hem of Lester's garment and wrapped the wound on his side to try and stop the bleeding. There was a chance he would survive if his men reached him in time.

Slayer stood and gave Lester's last word thought. *Wolves.*

There had been no wolves in the ravine, but there had been paw prints. Had they guided Sky to safety? But where would that be? Where would the wolves take her?

Slayer shook his head at how easily he understood. The wolves would have taken his wife to their den.

***

Sky examined her ankle. The walk here had not helped it. It had swelled, though not badly but it did hurt her. It was her only injury from what she could tell. Her body ached but she had found no other wounds except for the scratch on her face she had felt after feeling it sting there. She had been lucky. She could have suffered far worse wounds or died from the fall. It had not been easy getting here with her ankle hurting her and her own worry about trusting the wolves, but they had proved to be trustworthy, especially when they offered their den as protection for her.

The incident of when she faked an ankle injury came to mind and she wished she felt her husband's tender touch on her ankle once again. He was no doubt already searching for her and his skilled trackers were sure to locate her. However, she worried that whoever else was searching would find her first. She hoped the wolves were enough to deter them and hoped no wolf lost his life protecting her.

Sky's head shot up. She heard something. Growls. The two wolves outside the cave-like dwelling were growling. Someone approached.

The space was not tall enough for her to stand, so she shifted herself along her bottom to reach the entrance and peer out. Aches and pains attacked her body, but she did her best to ignore them, needing to find out if friend or foe approached.

But wouldn't a foe have already killed the wolves so they could reach her? Hope had her stomach fluttering, and she was careful to peer out the opening to look, though not be seen.

"Sky!"

She rushed her hand to her chest at the sound of her husband's voice and called out softly so as not to alarm the wolves, "Slayer."

"Curb the wolves," he called back.

"Friend. He is a friend. Here to help me. Friend," she repeated in a gentle tone.

She spotted her husband then, bravely stepping forward to show himself and approach the cave.

"Friend. Friend," Sky kept repeating as she made her way out of the wolf's den, worried they would not allow a dominant male to enter their home.

Relief so strong hit Slayer that he thought for a moment his legs would buckle as he watched his wife emerge from the cave. He forced himself to remain where he stood and forced strength to return to his legs. Though he desperately wanted to rush to her and take her in his arms, especially when he saw how she struggled to get to her feet. But he knew if he rushed toward her the wolves would view it as a threat and attack.

Sky smiled and after she managed to stand, she glanced at each of the two wolves there and spoke softly. "Slayer is a friend and will help me get home now. I am grateful for your help, and I will be here for you if you are ever in need of help."

Slayer almost took a quick step forward when his wife cringed as she took steps toward him. She had suffered an injury, her leg or ankle most likely from the way she limped, but he saw no other visible injuries on her. No blood stained her disheveled garments, though debris from the pine tree clung here and there to her and pine needles stuck out of her hair that had fallen loose from its braid.

"Reach out and claim me, so they know I belong to you," Sky said when she got near him.

Slayer was only too happy to do as she said. He eased his arm around her and drew her to rest against him, then he looked to each of the wolves as she had done and said, "My thanks for protecting my mate."

The largest of the wolves approached them, his eyes on Slayer.

"Stay as you are," Sky whispered.

The wolf came to a stop beside Sky, his eyes remaining on Slayer. He pressed his body against Sky's leg, and she brought her hand to rest on his head.

"Again, I thank you, my friend," she said, and the wolf stepped back, his eyes never leaving Slayer.

Though it was difficult for him, Slayer kept silent as they walked away. It was not until they neared a stream that he went to speak, but Sky spoke first.

"I hurt my ankle and I ache from the fall but other than that, I am good."

"You knew what I would ask," he said, not surprised, they both having come to know each other so well.

"Just as I knew you would find me," she said and stopped to turn and rest herself against him.

"Always," he said and held her close, though not tightly, worried he would cause her more pain. "We can take a quick drink from the stream and then we need to move and not stop until my men reach us."

Sky nodded, eager to quench her thirst and even more eager to return home.

He took hold of her arm and lowered her gently to sit by the stream and he almost cringed along with her when he saw the pain it caused her.

"You will rest when we get home," he ordered and could not stop himself from kissing her lips ever so gently after sitting beside her.

"I look forward to it and more of your kisses," she said and cupped her hands to take a drink and gasped lightly at the chilly water stinging the scratch on her face.

Slayer took a gentle hold of her chin and turned her face toward him. "You landed on the pine tree, didn't you?" He ran his hand gently over the minor scratch.

"Aye. It saved my life as did the wolves. I kept drifting in and out of consciousness. They poked me with their nose to wake me and warn me someone approached. Not knowing who it was, I tried to hide, so I could see if it was you, but the wolves kept urging me away, so I trusted them."

"It was Lester and a few of his men."

"Oh, he told me he meant me no harm. He would have helped me."

"Nay. The wolves were right in urging you away. Lester and his men were attacked. He was the only one to survive, though not for long if my men do not reach him. The group who attacked him were searching for you to take to someone. Lester says you are a daughter of the Wolf clan and this person looking for you blames you for something and seeks revenge."

Sky was stunned. "Lester knows who my parents are?"

"I imagine so since he is from the Wolf clan."

She reached out to grab her husband's arm. "I do hope he survives. There is so much he could tell us."

"Hopefully, my men have reached him. I did what I could for him, but I could not stay with him. I needed to find you."

Sky rested her brow to his. "And I could not have been happier to see you."

She kissed him gently this time, lingering a bit until Slayer ended the kiss reluctantly.

"We need to go. Drink your fill for we will not be stopping again," he said, annoyed that he had to rush her when she needed to rest.

Her brow narrowed in worry.

He knew what concerned her for it concerned him as well. "I will keep you safe."

"Not at the cost of your life," she cautioned.

"Drink. We must leave," he ordered.

Sky did not argue with him. It was futile to do so. He would have his way, though not if she could help it.

They had barely left the stream when the large wolf appeared in front of them, blocking the way.

"He is warning us. We need to go back to the wolf's den and hide." Sky shook her head when her husband looked ready to argue. "We must go. Now."

"The wolves may not let me enter," Slayer said.

"He will. He senses the danger."

Slayer went to argue when he heard the thundering roar of horses' hooves. It was no small group headed their way. He scooped his wife up in his arms and ran.

The two wolves paced in front of the cave once Sky and Slayer entered, and Sky worried what might happen to them while trying to protect her.

"A large troop approaches," Slayer warned, sitting cramped in the confined cave with his wife tucked tightly against him.

"Not yours?"

"Nay. Not mine," he confirmed, and his mind ran wild with what he could do to keep his wife safe and grew furious when he was unable to find a solution.

The horses suddenly sounded as if they stopped in front of the cave. But the horses were heard braying and pounding their hooves, unwilling to get near the wolves.

"Archers!" a man yelled.

"NAY!" Sky yelled before Slayer could stop her.

"Come out or we kill the wolves," a man demanded.

"Do not respond," he whispered.

"A daughter of the Wolf clan would never allow a wolf to die for her," the man called out.

Slayer shook his head.

Sky kept her voice to a whisper. "They do not know you are here with me."

Slayer shook his head again, knowing what his wife was thinking.

Sky pressed her finger to his lips. "Please. We have no choice. You must let them take me. It is the only way you can save me. Otherwise, you die here. And my fate? We do not know. Would you really leave me to suffer?"

"I grow impatient, woman!" the man yelled.

"Give me a moment. I injured my ankle," she yelled out. She quieted her voice once again. "You will find me. You will always find me." She grabbed hold of his face and kissed him.

"Nay!" Slayer said when their kiss ended. "I cannot let you—"

"You must. It is the only way we both have a chance of surviving and having a future together." She placed his hand on her stomach. "I feared the fall would take the bairn from me, but so far it has not. If he can fight to survive, then so can we."

How rage and happiness could exist together, Slayer did not know. There was so much he wanted to say to her but there was no time.

He kissed her hard so she would have part of him to hold onto, then whispered. "I will find you."

"I know," she said, moving toward the opening.

"I love you, Sky," he said before she reached it.

She turned her head and smiled. "I know that too."

Chapter Twenty-five

"Chase the wolves!"

Slayer heard the man yell as he moved closer to the opening of the cave to listen, fighting to stop himself from rushing out to protect his wife and unborn bairn. But that would be foolish, and Sky's sacrifice would be in vain. He would wait, find her, and have his revenge.

Sky turned her head as she pointed to the cave behind her and whispered, "Protect and help him."

The wolves did not hesitate, they entered the cave.

The two wolves lay by the entrance, watching Sky, and ignoring him.

Bloody hell, if his wife did not continue to protect him while sacrificing herself, sending the wolves to protect him so that the men would not come near the cave and find him. She was foolish, stubborn, and brave.

"She commands the wolves!" a man called out sounding frightened.

"Don't look at her!" another man ordered.

"Cover her eyes so she cannot curse us," another yelled.

Anger had Slayer clenching his fists and his jaw, the thought of her blind while with her captives infuriating him.

"It is how she commands the wolves and other animals, you fool," a man called out.

Slayer had not given thought to that and wondered if it was the reason for her strange abilities with animals.

"We head home," the man commanded. "Get her on my horse."

"Let her walk," someone called out.

"She will slow us down with that limp," another said.

"I did not ask your thoughts on it," the man said with a snarl. "Now do as I command."

Slayer did not like that his wife would ride on a horse with the man, but it was better she did. Her injured ankle would only get worse and then there was the bairn to consider. He hoped whether it was a son or daughter who nestled within her that he or she would continue to fight and survive.

"Halfdan will be pleased that we have been successful in finding her."

"We have yet to reach home."

"Once we join the other two troops no one will be able to stop us."

Slayer listened, glad to hear what the men were saying as they rode away. He knew who Halfdan was, Chieftain of Clan Scylding. A clan to the north comprised of a mixture of Northmen and Scots that settled there after raids from the north stopped. Slayer's father traded with him from time to time and he wondered if the old chieftain had anything to do with his father and brother's deaths.

When the men and horses could be heard no more, Slayer attempted to leave the cave, but the wolves growled and would not budge. So, he waited, trusting them. Only a short time later, he heard two voices.

"I told you no one else is in that cave. Come on, let us go. I do not trust those wolves even from high up here in the trees. Let us get to our horses and get out of here."

Slayer remained where he was until the wolves moved, then he cautiously left the cave and made his way back toward the ravine, hoping to meet his warriors on the way. He did not need anyone to track his wife. He knew where they were headed. Besides, he knew the wolves would follow her, leaving their tracks for him to follow.

***

Slayer was pleased when it wasn't long before he spotted his men and joined them. It also pleased him to hear that Lester's wound had been tended to and he had been taken to the village. Whether he would survive was still unknown. He returned to the top of the cliff where Olin and the other two men were being held. He was already forming a plan in his mind on how he would rescue his wife. He did not know if Olin had any more information that might help his plan, but he intended to find out.

Once he was done with that, he would return to the keep and set his plan in motion and be ready to leave at dawn tomorrow. He wanted to follow now, not wait, but that would not be wise. He needed the Gallowglass with him. He needed to ensure victory.

Angus approached Slayer as he headed toward Olin. "I see the other two men are gone. I assume you discovered that they were just as responsible for Clyde's death as Iver?"

"I did and they wait to go to the Gallowglass compound to meet the same death Clyde was made to suffer and where there will be no lack of volunteers to take part in their punishment and death."

"You did well, Angus. Clyde would be pleased that the Gallowglass revenged his death, though the one who delivered the final blow has yet to meet his fate," Slayer said, intending to find out who the culprit was and see to the man himself.

"As soon as you give the word, my lord, I will send them off to get what they deserve," Angus said.

"First, I need to know one thing from them, then you can take them away," Slayer said, and Angus followed alongside him to the three men. He stopped in front of the two men, their heads tilting back to look up at him, their faces bloodied and bruised. "Tell me about the man who delivered the final blow to the vicious attack on the Gallowglass warrior."

"He was a big, wide man" one man said without hesitation in an effort to save himself.

The other man spoke up just as eagerly. "He had a few old scars on his face, and he had long gray hair."

The man who had spoken first shuddered. "He was an evil looking one, snarling and snapping like a dog."

"I have heard enough. Take them away," Slayer ordered.

"He tried to poison one of your hounds," one of the two men called out when Slayer turned away from them.

Slayer turned back.

"I did not," the other man protested. "He did. He thought it a funny thing to do, killing the hound of the mighty Gallowglass warrior."

"Nay! Nay! It was him," said the other man with a nod to his cohort. "He thought it would make you look like a fool that you could not protect your hound."

"You two truly are fools if you think trying to save yourself by accusing the other of attempting to kill my hound would work. Since I cannot be sure which one of you it was, you both will die as planned." Slayer said, ignoring their pleas for mercy as he walked away, too busy thinking about the man the two men had described... Halfdan. Now he had another reason to see the man dead. Though he could not help but think how pleased his wife would be to learn how Fane had been poisoned, having worried over the incident. And he was pleased as well to know that Fane's poisoning attempt would be avenged.

"Ready to tell me the truth, Rory or Olin or whoever you are?" Slayer asked, approaching the man sitting on the ground bent over in pain, his broken wrists resting at his sides while blood soaked his sleeve and shirt from the wound on his arm. His face was bruised and battered, his mouth bloody and one eye swollen shut. One ankle was twisted at an odd angle as were a few of his fingers. His men had made sure he would be ready to talk.

"I will tell you anything you want to know," Olin said and spit blood along with a tooth from his mouth.

Slayer grabbed his hair and yanked his head back. "Make sure it's the truth this time or I'll have my men start pricking your body with their daggers." He shoved Olin's head as he released his hair and stepped in front of him, waiting with his arms crossed over his chest and a furious scowl on his face.

Blood dribbled from the corner of Olin's mouth as he spoke. "I sign my fate with what I am about to tell you." He paused for a moment as if questioning if he should continue, then shrugged and winced in pain. "It matters not. I am already a dead man." He attempted to grin but only caused himself to wince again. "I was hired to kill your brother and father."

Slayer took a swift step forward, keeping his hands fisted tightly.

Olin cringed waiting for the blow he was sure to come and was surprised when it didn't.

"Who hired you?" Slayer asked, containing his anger so that he would not do anything foolish before he got what he needed from him. "Why did this person want my father and brother dead?"

"You know it does not work that way. Mercenaries are given a mission but not a reason and seldom, if ever, is the person behind the mission revealed."

"Tell me everything," Slayer demanded.

Olin was quick to explain, his pain worsening by the minute. "My mission was to see both your brother and father dead. The attack on your brother was swift and brief thanks to the skilled warriors I hired. Your father on the other hand presented a problem." He paused in pain.

"You got help," Slayer said.

"I did."

"Verina, our clan healer."

"Aye. Verina, but she was no healer. She posed as one, going from clan to clan. I posed as a cleric who sought shelter for a few days and spotted her when she was outside the castle walls. I saw soon enough how your father favored her." He paused again due to the pain.

"And threatened her if she didn't help you?"

"And chance exposing myself? Nay."

"You promised her coins," Slayer said, having learned most people could be bought for a price and knowing those who had coin barely parted with it which meant. "Coins you never intended to give her."

"You are wiser than I'd been told," Olin said with a bit of admiration.

"You had her poison my father and unwittingly poison herself," Slayer said.

"I did. I gave her two mixtures of herbs, one to sprinkle on a favorite food of his. Wild pottage, I believe she said he favored, and another mixture for her to take in case she received the poison accidentally. I knew she would take it out of fear, not need."

"Who approached you about this mission?" Slayer asked.

"A monk, though like me it was a disguise. I was offered far more coins than seemed reasonable, so I asked why such generosity. He only had to say one word. *Gallowglass*. I warned myself to refuse the mission, but I thrive on challenges, and it certainly was a challenge to go against the Gallowglass."

"So, when you finished your task, you decided to add to your wealth by going after the coins offered for one of the Murdock sisters?" Slayer asked, assuming his greed got the best of him.

Olin looked puzzled. "Nay. The sister with the two different colored eyes was part of the task."

That news stunned and enraged Slayer, though his expression remained unchanged. That meant Halfdan was also responsible for his father and brother's deaths. But why?

"It would have been an easy task and a successful one if I had reached Dundren Abbey before you."

Never. Never would he have allowed that to happen even though he had never met Sky. It was his duty. She was his wife. Besides, no one took what belonged to a Gallowglass warrior and lived. And no one, not a soul alive, would take the woman he loved from him. He would have his wife back in his arms and soon.

"Tongues carried news throughout the Highlands about you searching for any word on your brother and father's deaths. All I needed to do was spin a tale that your men would eventually hear, and you would come to me."

"And you played the fool once you were found."

"I did. A fool is less likely to suffer torture since he answers endless questions without much prodding. Though I did worry when you had me taken to the Gallowglass compound. But once you had me brought to Clan Ravinsher, I knew I had a good chance of success. The others who hunted her were too foolish to succeed. Besides, they would never get past you. I was so close to the end of my mission and wealth."

"Who were you to turn Sky over to?"

"I do not know, and I don't care. I was given a location where a man would be waiting for us. I would go with him to collect the rest of my fortune."

More than likely it was where Olin would have met his death. Halfdan was not known for parting easily with his wealth.

"That is all of it, though I do hate dying without accomplishing my mission. But that was my own fault for hiring idiots to help me. Instead of sticking to my plan and waiting until I signaled them to free me, they took it upon themselves to take advantage of the attack. And I paid dearly for their stupidity. Grant me a swift death and I will share my thoughts on who I believe is behind it all," Olin offered.

Slayer was far too concerned with rescuing his wife to care if Olin suffered any more pain than he already had and he was curious as to what the man thought. So, he granted his request. "You have my word."

"The one thing said about you is that you are an honorable man, so I trust you to keep your word," Olin said. "I believe it was—"

Olin fell to his side, an arrow lodged in his back and not another arrow fired.

"Find the archer!" Slayer yelled, his warriors already in motion.

He quickly crouched down by Olin, seeing the man struggling to speak.

"Hal-half," Olin said with his last breath.

Slayer stood.

"Did he say anything, my lord?" Angus asked.

"Not a word," Slayer said loud enough for whoever hid in a nearby tree to hear him. News would reach Halfdan's men that Slayer did not know who had the woman or where they were taking her, which meant they would not be prepared for his arrival.

***

"Everything was seen to, Reed?" Slayer asked the next morning in his solar.

"Aye, sir, all is ready."

"And the hounds?"

"Stand ready, sir," Reed said.

"Good. You know what to do," Slayer said and turned to Fane waiting patiently beside him after Reed took his leave. "We go to rescue Sky, Fane."

Angel jumped up on the table next to where Slayer stood and meowed soulfully at him.

Slayer scooped her up. "Worry not. Fane and I will bring Sky home."

She rubbed her face against his and he thought he caught the scent of Sky on her, and a wave of sorrow and anger washed over him. He missed his wife. He ached to hold her in his arms, wrap himself around her in bed and feel content as the sweet scent of her hair tickled his nose. More so, though, he worried about reaching her in time.

He found little sleep last night, though he would need it, too busy fighting with himself for not having followed her when she had been taken. A foolish thought and one Sky would have agreed with. Following her would have wasted precious time, his warriors not knowing what had happened to him would have prevented timely help from reaching him. And hearing that the men who took Sky were to meet a larger troop would have made it unlikely that he would have been able to rescue her without help. He needed a contingent of Gallowglass warriors to set his plan in motion.

Raised voices outside Slayer's door caught his attention and he placed Angel on the floor just before the door opened and Ross entered. Storming in behind him was an attractive woman with red, blonde hair and he knew immediately who she was and the words she shouted at him proved it.

"Where is my sister, Sky? Why isn't she with you? I was told you would keep her safe."

Fane snarled, baring his teeth in warning.

"Nay, Fane!" Slayer ordered and the hound stilled, though kept one side of his mouth raised in warning.

"I demand to know what happened to Sky!" Leora shouted at Slayer.

Slayer grabbed the woman's arm. "You demand nothing from me."

"Take your hand off my wife, Slayer," Noble warned, having hurried in behind her.

Slayer shoved Leora toward Noble. "Tell her to mind her tongue around me, Noble, or I will see you both put off my land."

Noble took hold of his wife's arm and pulled her against him. "Enough, Leora. Your angry tongue will not help Sky."

"You assured me he would keep her safe," Leora said, her lovely face flushed with anger. "The message said Sky was abducted, yet here you stand without her." She threw her hands up in the air. "I doubt many here even care if she does return. What if she was treated so poorly while here that she prefers to remain with her abductors?" Leora shook her finger at Slayer. "Everyone knows you are a brutal warrior without an ounce of kindness to you. What harm have you brought upon my sister? What have you done to her?"

Slayer lurched forward and Noble quickly stepped back, pulling his wife along with him.

Slayer gritted his teeth as he spoke, fighting to contain his anger. "I have fallen in love with Sky."

Not a sound was heard in the room as Noble and Leora stared in shock at Slayer.

"Hear me well, woman," Slayer said, his eyes intent on Leora. "Sky is my wife and I love her, and she carries our bairn. I will not rest until I hold them both in my arms again. On that you have my word."

"Bloody hell," Noble said. "I didn't think you were capable of love."

Ross smiled. "He didn't have a chance against Sky's kind nature and her loving heart."

"Are you saying my sister loves this savage in return and agreed to the marriage?" Leora asked, shocked at the thought.

"Sky had no choice in marrying me. It was done before I rescued her from the abbey. She wisely chose to accept the marriage and make the most of it. She chose to love me of her own accord, though I still cannot understand why but she does, and I am grateful for her love."

"And you did not think to tell us this?" Leora asked, annoyed.

"I ordered the marriage kept secret, fearing it could place her in more danger than she was already facing. Ross and Euniss, the woman who runs the keep, are the only two who know about it." Slayer pointed a finger at Leora. "And I expect you to hold your tongue until I say otherwise."

"Is she happy with you?" Leora demanded to know.

"Very much, but I do not know how she can be and again I am grateful that she is."

Tears clouded Leora's eyes. "The message said she suffered a great fall. Do you know if she and the bairn are well?"

"An ankle injury, a scratch on her face, and, so far, the bairn remains safe inside her."

Noble's brow creased in question. "How do you know this?"

Slayer looked directly at Leora. "Sky chose to save me so that I could rescue her, and we both could live. She told me if our bairn was strong enough to survive the fall and fight to stay alive then we could do no less. Your sister is not only kind. She is courageous as well."

"Aye, she is," Leora said, her tears beginning to fall as she stepped forward and reached out to poke Slayer in the chest. "You better bring her home safe and sound."

"I intend to and never, ever, poke me again, woman," Slayer ordered.

Leora lifted her chin, not an ounce of fear in her eyes. "I will have your word as a Gallowglass warrior on that."

"You have my word as a Gallowglass warrior, and you have my word from the man who loves your sister from the depths of his heart and soul that I will bring her home unharmed." Without another word, Slayer left the room, Fane following at his side.

Leora looked at her husband. She need not say anything, Noble knew what she wanted.

"I will go with him and make sure he and Sky return home safely."

She hugged him and went to tell him to stay safe when a horn sounded alerting the clan that an attack was imminent.

Chapter Twenty-six

Sky was exhausted barely getting any sleep last night after they had finally stopped. Her body ached worse today than yesterday, though her ankle had not swollen any more than it already had. Not that it would be easy for her to run, if necessary, a thought that disturbed her.

What if she had no choice but to attempt an escape? How would she ever manage to run?

She had no doubt Slayer was on his way to her, though she feared he might have followed directly behind her when she had been taken. She dismissed the thought quickly enough. He had to have heard the men talk about meeting up with a larger troop of warriors. Her husband would have been wise enough to realize he needed help to rescue her. That meant he would not come alone for her. His Gallowglass warriors would be with him. That thought brought her hope and relief.

She had tried to find out what she could while riding with the man yesterday. She learned his name—Borg—from his men calling out to him. She was unsuccessful in learning anything more than his name since any time she spoke, he warned her to hold her tongue.

"He'll never reach you in time," Borg said with a laugh, grabbing her arm and yanking her to her feet. "He and his clan are too busy fighting, defending themselves against the swift and unexpected attack of Halfdan's army of warriors. Slayer will find you too late. That is if he survives." He laughed again.

Fear churned her stomach. Fear for all at Clan Ravinsher and fear that her husband could perish in battle and fear that it left her no choice but to escape and survive and pray that her husband survived as well.

Borg gave her a shove and a sharp pain tore through her ankle causing her to cry out.

"You'll not delay us," Borg ordered and gave her another shove. "Hurry your pace. He waits for us."

Sky was deposited roughly on the horse and Borg mounted behind her.

"We don't have far to go," Borg said.

That worried Sky since it would leave little time for her to escape. She kept alert, trying to think of ways she could get away. Her thoughts were repeatedly interrupted with worry for her husband. He was a superior warrior, and she should not worry. But battle and death played no favorites. He could die like any other warrior on the battlefield.

Her heart felt as if it broke thinking she could lose him and that made her even more determined to survive along with the bairn inside her, for she knew her husband would do the same. He would not give up. He would survive and find her.

Several soulful howls echoed through the woods and the horses grew upset, their riders trying to calm them.

"The wolves followed her," one man said.

"They will see us dead," another said, glancing around nervously.

Another leaned his head back to look at the sky. "That hawk has been following us for some time now."

Sky tilted her head back to see a hawk circling overhead. The hawk probably was hunting and had spotted prey. Or could he be helping someone to find her?

The men continued to express their concern, one saying, "She commands the animals just like her grandmother."

"She'll call them down on us," another cautioned.

"They will get us just like they got him," another cried out.

"And he will see her dead just like her grandmother," Borg called out. "Now shut up and pay heed. We are almost there."

Sky felt the loss. It hurt to hear that she would never get to meet her grandmother and it made her wonder if it would be the same with her mother and father. Were they not alive as well? Was there nothing left of her true family?

It was not long before they entered a small clearing and as soon as she spotted the post planted in the ground, she knew it was meant for her. Once they tied her to it, she would have no chance of escape. But then with six men there and an injured ankle she had little chance of escape anyway. Her only hope was Slayer, but she could help him by giving him more time to reach her.

"Tie her to the post," Borg ordered once he yanked her off his horse.

Sky was glad when only one man approached her. She formed a quick plan and when they reached the post, she jabbed the man so hard in the eye that he screamed out in pain and stumbled. She ran, her ankle screaming in pain. She knew she did not have much time to hide or much time before they found her, but she did not let that stop her. Any extra time she could give her husband to reach her was worth it.

"Get her, you fools!" Borg screamed.

If she kept running, she would be caught easily, so she dashed behind some thick foliage, hunkering down so she could not be seen and watched as the men ran past her. Borg was right in calling them fools, though he should have included himself.

When she could barely see them, she turned and went in the opposite direction, thinking they would discover their mistake soon enough and return. She needed to put more distance between them and more time.

It was difficult to ignore the pain in her ankle and more difficult to keep herself from slowing her pace. She did her best, but she would have to find a spot soon to hide or she would be caught.

She almost cried out in relief when she saw two wolves running toward her in the distance. They would help her, and she hurried toward them only to stop abruptly when they did. When they began to growl, she knew they alerted her to someone nearby.

"Send them away or I will see them dead."

Sky shuddered. She never thought evil could be heard in a voice, but she was wrong. The voice exuded evil in the pleasure that she heard he would get in the deaths of the wolves.

"GO!" Sky called out, frantic the man had no intention of keeping his word, and he didn't.

Arrows sailed through the air and her breath caught briefly until she saw that not one arrow hit its mark. The wolves were safe. She raised her chin, drew her shoulders back and turned to face the man who meant her harm, and an icy chill ran through her.

He was a large and heavy man. His meaty fists looked powerful enough to kill a man with one punch. Old scars marred a face that held no appeal, and his eyes were so dark they appeared soulless.

"You look just like your mother, and I will take great pleasure in seeing you suffer the punishment and death that was due her but that your birth robbed from me."

She felt the sting of another loss and guilt that her mum had lost her life after giving birth to her.

"Chieftain Halfdan," Borg said, nearly breathless as he and his men suddenly appeared.

"You let her get away," Halfdan accused without looking at the man.

Sky saw then that Halfdan was not alone. There were at least a dozen warriors with him.

"We would have found her," Borg said anxiously.

"You let a woman with a limp play you for a fool," Halfdan said, his hand going to rest on the hilt of his dagger in the sheath that hung from the belt at his thick waist.

Sky pressed her arms at her sides to stop herself from shivering, Halfdan's remark sounding as if he condemned Borg.

"We outwitted the Gallowglass and braved the wolves to get her here after Olin failed you," Borg said with a tremor in his voice.

Halfdan drew his dagger from its sheath so fast that no one had a chance to move, and Borg paled and visibly shuddered with relief seeing the dagger land in the chest of the man she had poked in the eye.

"It will be you and your whole troop who die next if you fail me again, Borg," Halfdan said.

"Aye, my chieftain. Aye," Borg said, his face remaining pale.

"Get her tied to the post," Halfdan ordered.

"Will you at least tell me why I am to suffer and die?" Sky asked, hoping to gain time.

"I will tell you the tale so that you know what a worthless woman your mother was and what a dishonorable man your father was and why they deserved their fate."

Halfdan turned away from her and Borg rushed toward her.

"I hear one cry of pain from her, and you will cry out in pain as well. My hands will be the only hands that make her suffer."

Fear churned Sky's stomach. Fear of what she would suffer before her husband arrived and fear that she would lose the tiny bairn inside her that had barely begun to grow. She felt close to tears, but she refused to show him any fear.

She was shoved back against the post and her arms drawn back behind her to hug the post, then her wrists were tied. Another rope went around her waist and her ankles were tied to the post as well. Her body would remain erect no matter what punishment he inflicted on her.

Sky watched Halfdan fist his hands, a glee on his face that turned her stomach. He was going to enjoy this.

Borg made his way cautiously to Halfdan. "She is ready."

Halfdan nodded and without warning threw a punch at Borg that launched the man up into the air, his body impacting the ground hard when he landed. Borg did not move, though blood ran from his mouth.

"A taste of what to expect, but then with you being tied to the post you will remain as you are making it easier for me to deliver blow after blow," Halfdan said. "But first I will tell you about your mother and your father and why they deserved to die."

Sky's heart ached over more loss. Both her parents were gone along with her grandmother. She would never get to know them.

"There was a family in the Wolf clan much revered, the first-born daughters possessing the skill to understand the forest creatures. It was believed that the women possessed this strange skill because they were born with two different colored eyes. Such a skill could benefit a clan and so I arranged for my only son to wed your mother. Your mother, Fawn, refused the proposal, claiming she loved another man and had promised herself to him. Neither I, nor my son, Rainor, could allow such an insult to stand. My son did the honorable thing... he went after your father." Halfdan's face turned red with rage. "Your father killed him, and your mother called the forest animals to feast on my son.

There was barely anything left of him by the time I got to him. I swore that day I would revenge my son's death no matter how long it took. Your father and mother fled but I discovered that your mother was with child. I tracked her to Whitehall Abbey. It was Slayer's mother, Lady Candra, who helped deliver the bairn, born dead. She was there when I arrived and showed me Fawn, the lifeless bairn cradled in her arm as they lay in repose. I was furious that your mother would not be made to suffer but glad they both were dead. I only wished it had been at my hands. It was not until years later that I discovered I had been lied to. I was too busy searching for the man your mother loved. Your grandmother died refusing to reveal his name, leaving me no choice but to hunt for him." He shook his head. "She was the bravest and most foolish woman I had ever known."

Sky realized then that love could be as powerful as it could be destructive.

Halfdan snarled with pleasure as he continued. "It took years, but I found out who your father was. I learned he was there when your mother gave birth, and he held her until she took her last breath. He made sure you were sent to a family who would keep you safe and would keep your affliction as quiet as possible. He left and returned when he believed it was safe enough to do so. He joined the Gallowglass so that he could protect you if necessary. I finally found out who he was, and I finally had my revenge. He was a good friend of Slayer's… Clyde."

Sky fought not to shed a tear but one escaped as she recalled the one and only time she had spoken to

Clyde, never knowing he was her father. Her heart shattered for her parents and all they had lost.

"I rejoiced the day word reached me of Warrand's impending marriage to a woman with two different colored eyes. I sent someone who knew your mother to see if you resembled her. There is no mistake that you inherited her beauty. I bargained with Bannaty for you, but he had no interest. He insisted the deed was done and that you were perfect for his son that you would not get in his way."

"Why kill Warrand and Lord Bannaty? Why not just abduct me?" Sky asked.

"Revenge. Not only did Bannaty's wife lie to me but Bannaty himself dismissed my offer with a laugh. I had plans of abducting you after that but before I could reach you, your father had sent you away and I did not know where. Then there were the mercenaries who descended on the area to earn the enormous fee a foolish Lowlander was offering for the Murdock sisters. I had to make sure none of them got to you before I did. Olin was well worth the coin I gave him until he took too long to deliver you. Then the Wolf clan interfered, planning to see you kept from harm. I did not want to make myself known since I knew nothing would stop Slayer from coming after me if he ever discovered I was responsible for his brother and father's deaths. And it would not only be him who hunted me. It would be the Gallowglass."

"But he will come after you now for abducting me," Sky said.

Halfdan laughed. "Slayer is a warrior before all else. He fights to defend his clan at this moment with no thought of you. And I was wise enough to hire mercenaries to attack. He will never know it was me."

"He will find out," Sky said, sure her husband had heard the men talking as they rode away from the wolf's den.

"No one can track it back to me. I made sure of that," Halfdan boasted. "You are all that is left for me to revenge my son's death. And I am going to take immense pleasure in making you suffer."

Sky wanted to shut her eyes against what was to come, but hearing how her grandmother had been so brave, she raised her chin and stared directly at Halfdan as he approached her, tightening his fist with each step he took.

A savage roar echoed through the woods. Birds took flight and animals hid as Slayer emerged from the woods in a fierce run, his face twisted with such fury that he appeared like a demon rising from the depths of hell.

More roars filled the air as a bevy of Gallowglass warriors burst out of the woods, completely surrounding Halfdan and his men.

Halfdan ran toward Sky as swords began to clash. She knew what he intended. He might not be able to make her suffer but he could see her dead. Her fear was confirmed when he pulled his dagger from his sheath.

She spotted Fane on the run toward her, heard the wolves growling as they approached from behind her, but she feared none of them would reach her in time. She almost closed her eyes but thoughts of her mother, father, and grandmother's courage kept them open. She was glad she did, or she would have missed seeing her husband sail through the air as he launched himself at Halfdan with such force that he sent them both tumbling to the ground.

Fane rushed to stand in front of Sky, snarling and snapping, ready to tear anyone apart who dared approach her. The wolves protected her from behind, their snarls as vicious as Fane's.

Sky could not take her eyes off her husband, watching as both men scrambled to their feet while the Gallowglass warriors quickly overtook Halfdan's men.

Fury raged on Halfdan's face when he finally stood and saw that defeat was imminent. He hurried to grab the dagger that had been knocked from his hand, then pulled another dagger from its sheath and lunged at Slayer.

Slayer avoided the dagger just in time and managed to slice Halfdan's arm with his own dagger.

It took only a few minutes of watching her husband to realize he toyed with Halfdan like prey did with its catch before killing it. Blood began to stain various areas of Halfdan's shirt, sleeves, chest, and back. His cheek was also bleeding, not that Sky saw the slash, it had been delivered so fast.

"You honestly believe I am going to let you die fast when you had my brother and father killed, and my good friend brutally attacked then made him suffer even more when you twisted your dagger into him? Even worse you were about to torture and kill my wife and the bairn she carries?"

Halfdan roared with anger, spittle flying from his mouth, the news enraging him even more.

"You are going to die slowly and then I'm going to deliver the same finishing blow to you that you did to Clyde," Slayer said.

Sky saw no glee or pleasure on her husband's face. He appeared more resolved that it was his duty, and he would not flinch from it. And he did not. She turned her head unable to watch as Slayer sliced and jabbed Halfdan with his daggers repeatedly until the man collapsed to his knees, his daggers falling from his hands.

Slayer grabbed a clump of his hair to tilt his head back and to keep him from falling over. "You can thank my wife for your suffering going faster than I would have preferred since I want to get her home so she may rest and recover. And where we will await the birth of our first of many bairns. You should also know before I gut you and slice your throat as you did to Clyde that since Clan Scyling is without a leader, I intend to claim it for my own. Clan Scyling will be no more."

Halfdan struggled to speak. "My clan will never accept you."

"Your clan will have no choice." He shoved Halfdan to the ground and placed his booted foot to his throat. "You die along with your clan's name today never to be remembered and knowing that the blood of your enemy will now rule over your land."

Halfdan's screams brought tears to Sky's eyes. They were shed for Clyde, her da, realizing what he had suffered in his final moments. She closed her eyes in silent prayer for her da.

"What is wrong? Are you in pain? Did he harm you?" Slayer asked, his hand capturing her chin with a light squeeze.

She tried to smile but her heart was too heavy.

Slayer grew alarmed seeing her struggle to smile. Even at the worst moments she had managed a tender smile. "What is it? Tell me."

With all there was to say to him at this moment, she found herself saying, "I miss your arms around me."

Slayer made quick work of the ropes that bound her, feeling the same. It may have been barely a sunrise since he had held her, but that was too long for him.

Sky collapsed in his arms, her limbs somewhat numb from being constrained and sighed softly when he lifted her into his arms. He walked over to a large oak and sat beneath it, keeping her snug against him as he settled her in his lap.

Fane did not waste any time parking himself next to them, his eyes on the wolves in the distance.

She kept her head rested on his chest, his steady heartbeat and the strength in which he held her reassuring, but it was the words of love he whispered near her ear that made her feel the safest she had ever felt.

She raised her head to rest her brow against his. "I am good now that I am in your arms, wrapped in your love."

"And in my arms is where you will forever remain along with my love for you that is neverending."

"It is exactly where I want to be," Sky said, and went to kiss him when a sudden pain made her wince.

"You need to rest," he ordered, annoyed that he had been so anxious to get her in his arms that he had not considered her injuries.

"Aye, I do, and after I rest, I need you."

"After you have an extended rest and not before then," Slayer said and kissed her in a way that laid claim to her so that anyone who looked upon them had no doubt that she belonged to him.

"I want to go home, husband," she said, "and tell you what Halfdan told me."

"I heard part of it as I got close."

"Then you know Clyde is my da?" She got teary-eyed again thinking about it.

Slayer did not stop his surprise from showing. "That I did not hear, but I want to know all about it."

"I am eager to share the news with you, but what did you hear?"

"I heard him admit he was responsible for my brother and father's death, though I did not understand what he said about my mom."

"Take me home, husband, and I will explain everything to you."

"There is something you should know before we arrive home," Slayer said, his brow narrowing.

Sky grew anxious. "What is wrong? Did the clan lose many in the attack?"

"None in the clan was lost. I suspected what Halfdan might have planned, and I had troops waiting. They never reached the clan. I had the attack horn sounded, knowing he would have men nearby and once they heard it, they would run and tell Halfdan."

"Then what must you tell me?"

"Something much worse," he said with a scowl. "Your sister Leora is at the keep."

Chapter Twenty-seven

Slayer entered his bedchamber with Noble not far behind him. "You have had enough time together. I want time alone with my wife."

"I have not seen her in—"

Slayer did not let Leora finish. "I do not care. I allowed you—"

"Allowed me?" Leora glared at him.

Fane sat up from where he was resting by the hearth, his lips going up ready to snarl. Angel joined, hissing from where she sat between his front legs. Both stopped and laid back down when Sky shook her head at him, Angel returning to snuggle against Fane.

"Aye. I allowed you to tend to your sister's care when we arrived home to give you time to talk as I knew my wife would want to do. Now you will leave us be for the night."

Leora went to argue.

"We will talk all day tomorrow, Leora," Sky said, grateful to her husband for giving her and her sister time alone. She had been amazed at learning about Leora's true parents and Elsie's as well. She looked forward to the three of then reuniting soon so they could share their stories. "Now, I would like time with my husband."

Leora looked at her sister while she pointed to Slayer. "I do not know how you ever managed to fall in love with that heathen."

Slayer turned to Noble. "I regret condemning you to marriage with this woman."

Sky placed her hand in front of her mouth, attempting to hide her laughter.

Noble stifled his laughter as he approached his wife so he could say, "Would you not want time with me if it was you in that bed?"

Leora looked ready to argue and stopped, and rested herself against her husband when he slipped his arm around her waist to pull her close.

"I look forward to talking with you tomorrow," Sky said, seeing that her sister had reluctantly capitulated.

"We have plenty of time to talk since Noble and I will be staying here for a while. I sent word to Elsie for her and Cavell to travel here. I have missed my sisters, and it is time we got together again."

Slayer appeared ready to command otherwise and Sky sent him a silent plea, her two different colored eyes saying it all for her.

"You and Noble and Elsie and Cavell are welcome to visit, but don't forget, I command here," Slayer reminded.

"How could I possibly forget that when you endlessly remind me?" Leora said, her glare returning.

Slayer returned her glare. "And yet somehow you keep forgetting."

Noble looked at Sky and smiled as he shook his head, and Sky chuckled.

"Let's go, wife," Noble said and with his arm firm around her waist and with a firm nudge he got her moving toward the door.

"Sky needs rest, not a demanding husband tonight," Leora called out.

Noble's hand rushed to cover his wife's mouth as he forced her out the door, and he called out, "Sleep well."

"Please don't," Sky said and stretched her hand out to her husband when he looked ready to go after them.

Slayer blew out a frustrated breath before he walked around to the side of the bed, took her hand, and sat. "Your sister is exasperating."

Sky's smile bloomed softly. "You two have quite a bit in common."

"Bite your tongue, woman."

Sky grinned. "You both protect me." She chuckled. "And you both can be overbearing." Her laughter faded and she squeezed his hand. "And you both love me."

"I suppose she has some good points," he said. "So, I will learn to tolerate her. Please tell me Elsie is different."

"You will get along with Elsie. She is reasonable."

"Thank the heavens for that," he said, knitting his fingers with hers. "Before you grow too tired, tell me about what Halfdan had to say to you."

This time Sky's smile consumed her face. "I was shocked to learn that your mum helped deliver me."

Slayer could not hide his surprise. "My mum?"

"I believe there was more to your mum than anyone knew. Euniss once told me how your mum would retreat to Whitehall Abbey now and again. I imagine it was not a retreat for herself but to help other women since Leora told me that women in need often sought help at the abbey."

"My mum was adamant about a yearly stipend to Whitehall Abbey and my father never fought her on it, probably because she retreated there leaving him unbothered."

"Your mum bravely lied to Halfdan about me dying along with my mum in childbirth. Another newly born bairn must have died that day since your mum showed him my mum laying in repose with a deceased bairn cradled in her arm."

"So that is another reason for Halfdan's revenge against my family."

"Aye, but he also feared of you learning that it was him who was responsible. He did not want the Gallowglass brought down on him. You were right in keeping our marriage a secret. There is no telling what Halfdan would have done if he knew that." Tears gathered in her eyes. "I wish I knew Clyde was my da. I would have spent time with him and got to know him."

"I can tell you what I know about Clyde."

Sky attempted to sniffle her tears away. "I would like that. However, there is no one to tell me about my mum, da, or my grandmother. They are gone."

"Lester fights to live. He may be able to tell you about them."

A rap at the door had Slayer ready to order the person away, but the door opened before he could say a word.

"Did I bid you to enter, Euniss?" he snapped, annoyed.

"Nay, my lord, but Lady Sky could use a nice, relaxing brew and some oat cakes," Euniss said, placing the overfilled tray on the chest beside the bed. "There is ale and cheese and bread for you as well since you have yet to eat."

"Euniss, you knew my mum well. Did you know her retreats to Whitehall Abbey were made to help other women and not taken to escape my father?"

"Found out about that, did you?" she asked and did not wait for him to respond. "Your mum was a wise and brave woman. Her time spent in her solar was time she plotted to help the many desperate women who sought help at the abbey. Your father would have been furious if he ever found out what his yearly stipend was supporting. She kept the secret well as did I, just as I promised your mum I would." She sniffled. "I miss your mum, but I am glad to have Lady Sky here and I'm looking forward to the keep being filled with a gaggle of happy bairns."

"I will make sure of it," Slayer said, smiling at his wife.

Euniss went to leave, calling out when she reached the door, "Your wife needs rest for the next few days."

The door shut before Slayer could say a word. "Have I lost complete authority in my own home that two women dictate what I can and cannot do with my wife? Do they believe me that much of a heathen that I would demand you submit to me before you have healed?"

"In time they will come to understand how much we love each other, and they will question it no more."

Slayer rested his hand lightly on her stomach. "Truthfully, you are feeling well?"

"Surprisingly so," she said laying her hand on top of his. "How I and the bairn survived that fall I will never know. Fate. Luck. Who is to say or question? I have a few aches here and there and my ankle is doing well now that I am resting it, and Leora has applied a salve that should help as well." She patted his hand that remained on her stomach. "And our bairn remains tucked safely away. If I had been further along, it may have turned out differently. We have much to be grateful for."

"I am grateful to my father for insisting I wed you and I am grateful to my mum for bringing you safely into this world and I am grateful to Clyde who made sure you remained protected, but mostly I am grateful that you chose to love me."

"Forever and always, husband," Sky said just before his lips met hers.

***

Sky snuck out of the keep, needing time alone. It had been nearly a whole moon cycle since her abduction and she was feeling wonderful, better than ever, happier than ever, but she missed her time alone in the woods. Slayer still would not allow her to go into the woods alone. Leora and Elsie had gone with her a few times, and she had enjoyed it, but she longed for the time she could go alone so the animals would visit with her.

Her sisters would leave soon and while she would miss them, she looked forward to beginning her life openly as Slayer's wife. The clan had accepted the news of her marriage to Slayer better than she had expected, though she wondered if it had helped that her two sisters were there when it was announced. Their presence gave more credence to Sky being no different from any other sister or woman, and people soon began to speak to her. Though it could have been that tongues wagged about her being from the Wolf clan, and it was her two different colored eyes that enabled her to understand animals, which finally laid to rest the belief that she was evil.

She had hoped to learn more about her family and the Wolf clan from Lester, but unfortunately, he succumbed to his wounds. Slayer had his body returned to the Wolf clan for burial. She had mourned his loss and her only chance of learning about her family. Slayer had promised that he would take her to visit the Wolf clan one day but not until he had Clan Scyling under control. Though that did not seem to be presenting a problem from the messages Slayer was receiving from the large troop of Gallowglass warriors he had sent to claim the clan. The clan members had displayed no sorrow over Halfdan's demise but rather relief that they had a new chieftain.

It was early, the village just stirring as she made her way through it. She did not hurry, being lost in her thoughts. She also did not want to catch anyone's attention since they would be sure to alert Slayer, wondering if something was wrong because she rushed.

The gate was open, men making their way to the fields and warriors busy in practice. With few people about and with none paying her any mind, she made it into the woods without being stopped.

She did not walk too far in, knowing her husband would be upset enough with her for being here alone. She found a comfortable spot to sit under a large oak. As soon as she sat, a squirrel presented himself, sitting in front of her and chatting away. She smiled and told him she was pleased to speak with him. He suddenly sprang up on his hind legs and barked, then rushed up the tree. He warned of a threat and before Sky could get to her feet, she saw what had threatened the squirrel.

A wolf approached. He was large and gray, and he held his head high. He showed no sign of attack, and she felt no threat from him, so she remained sitting under the tree. When he got close enough, she recognized the wolf as one of the two who had helped her after her fall.

"Thank you for helping me and I am pleased you visit to see how I am doing," she said softly. "I am quite well and feeling good thanks to you and your mate. I am also pleased to learn that I am from the Wolf clan and have a special bond with wolves. I hope to learn much about you and from you."

He turned his head as if hearing something, then he turned his head back to Sky, gave her a nod, and hurried off.

"Do come back and visit with me," she called out.

"He will."

Sky turned with a smile, recognizing the voice. "Ruth."

"I am sorry to disturb you, but I have been trying to find time to speak with you alone."

"Not an easy task with my sisters here and with everyone now knowing Slayer and I are wed and that I am with child," Sky said and patted the spot beside her. "Please join me."

"The clan is more pleased with the news than you know." Ruth braced her hand on the tree trunk to help lower herself to sit beside Sky. "Lord Slayer remains a formidable man and fierce warrior but there is also a calm about him when he is with you and people are pleased to see it."

"I am glad to hear that. Now what is it you wanted to speak with me about?"

"Do you recall me telling you about meeting a young woman with eyes like yours?"

"I could never forget it. I wonder if perhaps I was related to her."

"You are. She was your mother and my niece."

Sky stared stunned at the woman.

"I was shocked when I first saw you. You look just like her. I wanted to tell you when I first met you, but I had made a promise to my sister, your mum's mother, that I would never reveal the truth about your birth. That tale I told you was far from the truth. It troubled me to see the clan think so poorly of you and I thought if you knew of another woman who had eyes like yours it might help, and I purposely included the wolf cub as a nod to your origin."

"Tell me more, Ruth, please," Sky said, her heart a flutter that the woman was her aunt and she had not lost her whole family.

"I used the story of a young lass we met on our journey here. Her father was not at all pleased that she spoke with us. I accompanied Willa, my sister and your grandmother, and Fawn, your mum, here for her to hide, Halfdan intent on finding her. Once the bairn was born, your da and mum had plans to flee and never return here. No one expected your mum to die shortly after you were born. Slayer's mum arranged for you to be placed with a family who she trusted would keep you safe. Terena, the woman you knew as your mum, was good friends with Lady Candra." Ruth wiped tears from her eyes. "It was so difficult for your da to let you go and so amazing to see such a large man cradle you so lovingly in his arms. He is the one who named you Sky, he and your mum spending time in the fields lying in each other's arms and staring at the beauty of the sky. Those times together brought them much happiness and he wanted you to be part of that happiness."

Tears rolled down Sky's cheeks, happy tears mixed with sad ones, thrilled to know the importance of her name yet sorry her da was not able to tell her himself.

"When it was done, Willa and your da insisted that I remain here fearful of what Halfdan would do to your mum's family in his search for your da and mum. Lady Candra arranged for me to live with a nearby clan so I could send word if Halfdan was spotted anywhere near your clan, though Lady Candra's idea to place a bairn that had died that day with your mum was what kept him away all these years. I met my husband while at the clan and we had a good life together raising two sons. One son left to seek his future, and another fell in love with a lass at Clan Ravinsher. After my husband died, my son insisted I come live with them. On a visit with him, I asked Lady Candra if that would be all right with her and she was thrilled that she would have someone she trusted to talk to. So, I accepted my son's offer, and it is a good thing I did since both my son and his wife perished shortly after each other when a sickness struck the clan. I was left to raise Wade alone and I was here for your arrival." She wiped away her tears again, the past stirring painful memories. "My sister was brave returning home, though Clyde warned her not to, but she insisted she could not abandon her clan. I am so grateful to Lord Slayer for avenging her and Clyde's brutal deaths. Your father did not want to leave you, but he knew he would put you in grave danger if he did not leave. He said he would return one day and make sure you continued to stay safe."

"You both must have been surprised to see each other here at Clan Ravinsher," Sky said.

Ruth smiled. "We were, though we, along with Lady Candra, were careful not to let anyone know we knew each other. I so wish you had gotten a chance to meet your da."

Sky's tears kept falling. "We did meet briefly at the cottage where I stayed for a time. I wish I had known he was my da. I wish I had time to know him." She brushed at her tears. "Now I know why he called me by my name."

"Aye, he thought often of such a time he could do so. I am glad he got the chance. Your da had spent his life making sure you were kept safe, and he would not have done anything to jeopardize your safety. He no doubt intended to wait until he was certain the news could not harm you before letting you know he was your father." Ruth placed her hand over Sky's. "Sadly, your mum and da had no part in Rainor's death. Unfortunately, it was your mum and da who came upon his body. What was left of it after the forest animals feasted on him. Halfdan's warriors spotted them and assumed your da killed him and that your mum called the animals to feed on him. Your grandmother believed it was one of Rainor's own warriors who killed him, since it was common knowledge that Rainor treated people worse than his father."

"Sky! Sky! Where are you? Answer me, woman!" Slayer yelled, his powerful voice sending birds to take flight.

"I should go," Ruth said, and Sky hurried to stand and help her as she struggled to get to her feet.

"We will talk again," Sky said, wanting to learn all she could about her family.

"Aye, we will talk again for there is much for me to tell you," Ruth said, "though you should know that Lady Candra would be thrilled that you and Slayer are wed. She worried what would become of you."

Sky was pleased to hear that and reached out and hugged the woman. "Thank you so much… Aunt Ruth."

Ruth smiled, her cheeks wet with tears. "It is good to be reunited with family." She walked a few steps before turning and saying. "Your da cannot tell you so I will tell you. Your da loved you with his whole heart and then some."

"SKY!"

Slayer's shout had Ruth rushing off and Sky calling out to her husband, "I am here."

She quickly wiped away her tears, though to no avail, he would know she had been crying.

"What is wrong? Why are you crying? he demanded more than asked, taking her into his arms and holding her tightly. "And why are you here in the woods alone?"

"Walk with me," Sky said, easing out of his embrace to take his hand. "I have things to tell you."

"And one of them better be why you are in the woods alone."

She kissed his cheek and smiled, his gruff, demanding manner a familiar and oddly enough soothing melody to her ears. "Aye, that and so much more."

Chapter Twenty-eight

Nearly nine months later.

Slayer plowed through the snow, nearly half a foot having fallen since last night. He silently berated himself for not listening to his own warnings. He did not care if his wife wasn't due to deliver their bairn for another month, he wanted Mother Abbess here in case anything happened sooner, but Sky had thought it unnecessary. After all, her two sisters would arrive in a week to be here for the birth. Elsie's son, barely a month old, would be with her and Cavell. And though Leora was two months away from delivering her first bairn, there was no stopping her from attending Sky's delivery.

Yet who had been right about Mother Abbess arriving early... he was. A lot of good it would do him now with this snowstorm. There was no way Mother Abbess would be able to travel here now and possibl;y not even her sisters.

He practically flew up the steps and into the Great Hall and stopped abruptly when he spotted his wife, her hand braced on a table, bent over, rubbing her back, and grimacing.

"Bloody hell!" Slayer cried out and rushed to his wife, having received word while in the village seeing that everyone would be safe from the storm that she had started labor.

Sky leaned back against him when his arm wrapped around her, and her hand shifted to rub her stomach.

"Now what do we do without Mother Abbess?" he asked, feeling utterly helpless and not liking it.

"Women have been having bairns with the help of other women for ages. We will do just fine," Euniss said. "Besides, I have sent for her Aunt Ruth. She helped your mum deliver Sky and many other bairns. Now she will help Sky deliver her bairn. Now get your wife to her bedchamber."

Slayer glared at Euniss but lifted his wife gently into his arms.

"You can berate me later for dictating to you. The only thing that matters now is your wife," Euniss said.

"I would much rather see you smile on this day," Sky said with a tender smile of her own as her husband carried her up the stairs.

"When it is over and I see that you and our bairn are well I will smile," he said, letting his worry be known. Her mum had died giving birth to Sky. He did not want that to happen to his wife.

"I will be fine," she assured him.

Her confident remark, however, did nothing to ease his worry.

"Nay, not the bed. Not yet," Sky said when he went to place her on it. "I want to walk a bit yet." She rubbed her arms after he placed her on her feet. "It is chilly in here. Can you stoke the fire?"

He wondered if she was truly cold or if she was keeping him busy so he would not worry, but when he saw her shiver, he hurried to add logs to the hearth and get the room warmer.

His arms went around her again once he was done, knowing it would not be long before he was chased out of the room. She shivered again and he realized the problem.

"You are fearful," he said softly.

"A bit," she admitted, "but it is not the birth itself I fear."

"Then what?" he asked anxiously.

"What if I deliver a lass with eyes like mine?" she asked. "The first lass to be born in my family to one like me is doomed to the same fate."

Slayer went to dismiss her fears, letting her know it would make no difference but realized she knew what life could be like for their daughter if she was born with two different colored eyes.

"I would say it doesn't matter but I know it does to you. But look how different things are for you now. The clan has come to know you and they care for you. No one turns their back on you. No one refuses to talk with you. When travelers or merchants stop here and dare make a disparaging remark about your eyes, the clan is quick to defend you. Our child will be well-loved and accepted by the clan and that will become known throughout the Highlands, unlike how the color of your eyes had to be kept hidden. Besides, do you really think anyone would go against a Gallowglass warrior and not just one. Our daughter would have a whole army behind her."

"You promised you would not fight as many battles now that you lead the clan," she reminded, the thought of him riding into battle terrifying her.

"I promised, but I told you that there may be times I cannot avoid that, but I will do my best." Slayer kissed her cheek. "I love you, Sky, and I will love our daughter just as much. So, there is nothing for you to fear."

"Nothing to fear? Of course, she is going to be fearful. She is about to endure a whole lot of pain," Euniss said, entering the room and Ruth following in behind her. "Now go and leave us women to our work."

Another pain struck Sky and she grabbed her husband's arm tightly, trying to breathe through it.

Once again Slayer felt helpless, keeping hold of her, the only thing he knew what to do.

When the pain finally passed, Sky managed to smile at him.

He rested his brow against hers and whispered, "I love you and I have loved your different colored eyes from when I first saw them. They grow more beautiful to me every day."

"Out! Out!" Euniss ordered, giving him a shove. "We have to get her ready."

"I love you always," Sky said as his arms slipped off her and he stepped away.

Ruth gasped. "Those are the very words your mum said to Clyde before we chased him out of the room."

"You will not leave me, wife. I will not permit it," Slayer ordered as Euniss kept shoving him to the door. Before Euniss closed the door on him, he grabbed her hand. "Do not let her die, Euniss. I beg of you, do not let my wife or bairn die."

Euniss stared shocked. The mighty Gallowglass warrior never begged, not ever. Yet here he humbled himself to save his wife and bairn.

She tried to reassure him the best she could. "Lady Sky is strong and brave. If she and the bairn can survive a horrible fall, they both can survive childbirth."

Slayer stood staring at the closed door, praying that Euniss was right.

***

Hours passed with no word from Euniss or Ruth. Ross sat at the dais with him waiting but as the day wore into night and Ross' eyes kept closing, Slayer sent him on his way. Once Ross was gone, Slayer went upstairs to sit on the floor outside his bedchamber door, needing to be as close to his wife as he could get. He would have liked to have had Fane and Angel with him, but he was warned both animals would not do well hearing Sky cry out in pain and so he had shut them away in his mum's solar.

He cringed each time he heard her suffer through another pain and he could only imagine what Fane and Angel would have suffered hearing her. He was glad he had paid heed to Euniss's warning. He continued to cringe, hearing his wife cry out and did not think he could take it much longer when finally, he heard the cry of a bairn. It was finally over, and he could not be more relieved and ready to see his wife and meet their bairn, lass or lad. But his wife cried out again in pain and fear gripped him. He bolted to his feet and swung open the door.

"Get out!" Euniss ordered. "She delivers another bairn."

"Two?" he asked as if he did not understand and grimaced seeing how exhausted his wife looked.

"Two, thanks to you," Euniss said. "Now out!"

"You can do this, Sky," Ruth encouraged. "It will not be long now."

Slayer was about to leave when his eyes met his wife's eyes, and he saw in them her need for him. "I'm not leaving," he said in a tone that no one would dare oppose.

"Hold her hand," Ruth said with a smile. "Clyde did the same for your mum, refused to leave her."

Slayer sat at his wife's side, taking her hand. "We'll do this together."

Sky gave him a weak smile. "We have a son."

Slayer's smile lit his whole face as he glanced at Euniss placing his son in the cradle near the hearth for warmth, then she hurried to help Ruth.

"Never saw a smile like that on him before now," Euniss said with a laugh.

Sky groaned and Slayer was quick to brace himself behind her while keeping hold of her hand.

"A little bit more and you'll be done, Sky," Ruth encouraged and a few minutes later, she cried out, "It's a lass, a beautiful lass."

***

Later when Slayer and Sky were alone, the lad tucked in his mum's arm and the lass in her da's arm, they both smiled.

"He's handsome like his da and she is beautiful like her mum," Slayer said, glancing from one to the other with pride.

"She is just like me—"

"With the same beautiful two different colored eyes," Slayer said, "and she has an older brother—"

"Five minutes," Sky said with a laugh.

"Still, he is older, and he will protect her," Slayer insisted as if it would be no other way. "Now for names." Slayer looked from his son to his daughter. "I have decided on them."

"Have I no say in the choice of their names?" she asked, surprised he was so adamant about it.

"Nay, it is settled," Slayer said and looked at his son. "He shall be named Clyde." He looked at his daughter. "She shall be named Fawn."

Tears welled in Sky's eyes. "I love the names you chose, husband."

He leaned down and kissed her gently and felt a wet nose nudging his arm.

Fane had drifted slowly over to the bed to finally sniff curiously at the bundle in Slayer's arm.

Slayer patted his daughter, then his son. "Protect always, Fane." Then he looked at Angel asleep and curled against Sky's leg, and chuckled. "We may have to get a bigger bed."

Sky smiled. "We're family, all of us, and there will always be room for more."

"Aye, wife, just like there will always be room in my heart for me to love you more and more each day," Slayer said, and as if it were a promise, he sealed it with a kiss.

THE END

Note from Donna

Get in touch!

I love hearing from readers so drop me a note and give me your thoughts on the book, say hello, introduce yourself, let me know what you enjoy reading, and any questions you have are welcome.

You can reach me at donna@donnafletcher.com

Newsletter

Consider subscribing to my newsletter. It goes out twice a month, more if there is some unexpected news to share. I keep readers updated on forthcoming books, future books, and alert them to giveaways, offer a free book now and again, share recipes, and leave you with a cute joke to put a smile on your face. So don't miss the fun… subscribe!

Reviews

Some people enjoy leaving reviews, others don't. If you like leaving a review it is immensely appreciated. If you don't like leaving a review, consider spreading the word to your reader friends about the books you've read.

Thanks for reading my book!

Highlander The Conqueror

Printed in Great Britain
by Amazon